NIGHT RAIN, TOKYO

A Novel

John W. Feist

CONTENTS

CHAPTER ONE

Monday, late afternoon, September 9, 2019; Washington, D.C.

"Hi, I'm Brad Oaks, and I'm just the man you've been looking for."

Actually, of course, it's the other way around. It's Brad Oaks who needs—profoundly—the United States trade representative.

A man with a runner's build and fierce blue eyes, forty-five years old, tanned, and whose blond hair is going prematurely white, Brad smiles earnestly as he squeezes Alden Knight's hand.

"Oh? And why is that?" says Knight with narrowed eyes. Brad almost hears the gears grind in Knight's head as if thinking, *What's this guy want, a job?*

"Because I'm the last guy in this line."

Today's event at the State Department's formal reception rooms is to introduce Knight to a long queue of lawyer-lobbyists from K Street and commercial attachés from Embassy Row. The paneled walls of the formal hall serve to officially host visiting chiefs of state, heads of government, foreign ministers, and other distinguished foreign and American guests.

Knight relaxes and grins. "Actually, I'm glad there's a big turnout. But, tell me who you are."

"Brad Oaks. I'm a California lawyer, like you, and new to Washington. I'm not here to lobby you for anything, but to offer you the biggest international trade concept you could imagine. It's right down this administration's alley."

Oaks wears a khaki summer suit off the rack of the Sacramento, California, branch of Jos. A. Bank. His shoes could use a polish. With an authentic and affecting grin, Oaks presents the disarming look of the starting collegiate pitcher that he was in 1997.

"Well, Brad Last-in-Line, tell me what I should know about trade that has eluded me my whole career."

Brad's cheeks burn from the light sarcasm. *Uh-oh, I can't blow this chance. I may not get another.*

He takes a dry swallow. He knows Knight's reputation as an international trade lawyer, with thirty years' experience winning cases against countries exporting to the US at predatory prices. He knows Knight's job is to make good on the new administration's campaign promises to redo trade agreements, and insure that any foreign trade deal has something significant in it for America.

Brad, whose six-foot frame is two inches taller than Knight's, tries to calm his voice.

"Mr. Ambassador, I respect your credentials in international trade more than I can express. I also know that your administration is absolutely flummoxed about how to make something of this Wishbone Pipeline proposal from Canada. The same thing happened in the last administration. I can tell you how to solve the thing and bring home the biggest deal since Seward bought Alaska."

While hanging back to position himself so as to actually be the last in line, Brad had taken admiring notice of the decor in the main Diplomatic Reception Room, a showcase of two

2

centuries of America's fine and decorative arts. The paneling and stately Federal period furniture make the venue special and yet warmly welcoming.

Brad has also taken notice of Knight's bespoke suit from London, made of very lightweight, smoke-gray wool with a subtle burgundy pinstripe, and with a tight rosebud in the hand-sewn lapel. He sees Knight rub his left wing tip against the back of his right leg above the cuff to refresh the sheen.

Brad holds Knight's steady gaze.

Knight says, "What are you after?"

The future of all he holds dear is at stake. Brad takes a step closer to Knight and says in a low voice,

"I'm with Elgar Steel, and the Wishbone project would mean a lot to us. Mr. Knight, I can show you a way to fix opposition to Wishbone and also solve bigger troubles in the Midwest, all in one ball of wax. Or steel."

Knight doesn't exactly shrug as he says, "I'll judge that when I've got the details. I'll give you twenty minutes in my office when you're ready. Call my calendar guy, Ichiro Nagaoka, at the number on this card." Knight starts toward the crowd at a table of limp hors d'oeuvres in the center of the room.

Brad stops Knight with a raised voice. "I can be there tomorrow morning at eleven thirty if that works."

Knight turns back and says, politely but firmly, "If it works for Ichiro, it works for me. Now, please excuse me, Mr. Oaks, I've got to work the room."

Brad finds a small space and immediately dials the number on the card. He covers an ear against the buzz of chitchat in the room. He confirms the 11:30 time slot with Ichiro Nagaoka. That makes him really grin. He has just pitched out of a jam. He is undaunted by the expensive suits and careful haircuts of his untanned counterparts living out sedentary careers on K Street. He savors a major victory on Elgar Steel's Washington agenda: he's landed a meeting with the USTR.

He passes up the wine and beer on offer in favor of a ginger ale, and selects munchies that actually grew out of the ground somewhere—carrots, celery, and nuts. The other attendees here are old hands at Washington receptions. Like Knight, they are here to work the room, to make and renew acquaintances, and to gather detailed intelligence on who is working on what deals. They carry their champagne flutes or wineglasses simply as props, deferring to dinnertime their consumption of cocktails and wine. To Brad, the security detail in the room, some of them in suits, others dressed as catering servers, just blend into the scene.

A convivial, low-key conversational hum settles over the formal decor, like the lower registers of an organ prelude in the background. Brad follows Alden Knight, who now slipstreams his broad shoulders among the men and women whose Washington professional work of government advocacy is difficult and meaningful, and a far cry from common misconceptions about fistfuls of loose money from deep pockets and shallow thinkers. As people circulate, they tend to turn away from the glare of the blazing orange setting sun that streams into the room from the tall windows facing west.

Brad stops at the center table, its white tablecloth now littered with parsley shreds and baby shrimp fallen overboard from wilted crackers, to pick up a bottle of water. Unaware of the tiny laser beam from the west windows painting a red dot on his khaki suit coat, Brad slips the bottle of water into Alden Knight's coat pocket.

Just when Brad says, "Here's the first detail," a plainclothes security guard tackles Knight to the floor.

Shouts of *"Gun! Gun!"* fill the room. The punch bowl explodes in a small tsunami of pink bubbles and ragged crystal shards. Brad feels one of them pierce the nape of his neck, and he dives to the floor, bruising his forehead.

Not far from the Kennedy Center for the Performing Arts, streets and access ramps twist and overlap, carrying traffic along the E Street Expressway to and from the Whitehurst Freeway (hyperbole for a six-block-long elevated street). A patch of muddy ground next to Twenty-Seventh Street, between K Street and I Street, holds a 1978 Chevrolet Caprice the color of saltwater taffy. Its driver studies his watch, lip twitching with tension.

When new, the car had been presented to the driver's father for official consular use in the Capital of Western Decadence. The driver clings with pride to the car, which he regards as an emblem of his own stature, there being no other outward sign of it, and as his only significant material possession. He makes an executive decision, an unaccustomed achievement in his utterly solitary life. He verbalizes the decision aloud although no one else is within the sound of his voice:

"Abort!"

The Chevy groans as its front wheels drop over a low curb to Twenty-Seventh Street and its rear wheels churn up mud and debris, trying valiantly to provide traction and forward acceleration. At first it's a futile spin. Then, after a somewhat calmer crawl, the car jostles entirely into the lane. There's a surge forward, or at least as much of a surge as a GM passenger car of that vintage can muster. The lone driver weaves northerly, makes a sharp right turn onto Virginia Avenue, and right onto

Rock Creek Parkway to Beach Drive, and then to Sixteenth Street for two miles. He turns north on Sixteenth Street and blends into the suburban traffic of Silver Spring, Maryland. As he clenches his jaws tight, he reasons that since he drives so randomly—unsure of where he is going—he cannot be detected. Such is the self-taught, ostrich logic of the black-mustached man, his expression taut except for a twitch of the lip.

Darkness begins to disguise the Caprice, which is already faded and forlorn from nearly forty Washington winters and patinas of road salt. The driver is shivering from something other than cold weather. He drives around side streets of Silver Spring and Tacoma Park, and eventually returns to more familiar Washington streets an hour and a half after leaving his muddy standing place, and his too-tardy intended passenger, now somewhere far behind.

The driver will learn on the eleven o'clock news that the intended passenger had been martyred by gunshot. He will then shrug and presume the man now enjoys one of his forty-seven new virgins, as promised.

In a less elegant interior hallway of the State Department building, a paramedic finishes bandaging Brad's neck and nods to a tall woman standing at his side in blue slacks and vest, a lighter blue blouse, and a badge tucked into her black belt. Detective Patricia Quinn, of the Washington Metropolitan Police, has been moving quietly among clusters of ashen-faced guests jammed along the hallways of the seventh floor, now more interested in making cell-phone assurances to husbands, partners, and distant parents than discussing the global economy. The reception room has been cordoned by yellow tape. The white tablecloth of crumbs now is soaked with the subsided foam of forgotten punch. Quinn tries calming words and light humor to defuse the shock and fright that struck the eighty or so people who were in the room when the punch bowl died a hero.

No one else is hurt except this man sitting on the gurney he was told to lie back on, bandage on his tanned neck. *And blue eyes*, she notes with her keen instinct for important detail. By now the crowd behaves with the vacant, controlled casualness of hotel guests milling around on a sidewalk after a false fire alarm. Her technique, unorthodox but effective, is to introduce cautious levity as she takes notes about observations, and makes her own quick measurements of subsiding panic. No one in particular is suspect to Quinn since everyone is until the picture becomes clear. On the force for fifteen years, she wears her blonde hair in a ponytail and her vintage Ruger Security-Six service revolver in a hip holster anchored by Velcro to the thigh of her blue trousers. The combined look of blondeness and brash show of lethal force tends to either unsettle those with something unsettling on their minds, or reassure those without. That's as she likes it. She's interested in Brad . . . um . . . because he was so close to the ambassador when it happened. *That must be it*, she thinks as she eyes him just over the top edge of her notepad.

"Show me some identification."

There's a twinkle in her eye, Brad notes. He likes that. He smiles back. Brad is no stranger to dry humor in a tense situation. He arches his back, fumbles into the side pocket of his trousers, and withdraws his passport. He fumbles in the other side pocket of his trousers and withdraws his wallet, and from that a brand-new business card with his Washington particulars. She brushes a sheath of his hair back over a purple forehead.

Brad winces as he hands her his passport and card.

7

Quinn says, "Tell me why I shouldn't arrest you."

"Because if you do, you'll have to fill out all those forms. I'm just another lawyer who came to meet and greet the movers and shakers." More wounding than the glass cut, though, the woman doesn't smile at his wisecrack. *Losing my touch. She's a pistol. That's some pistol. What about Knight? Can I still have my meeting?*

Brad looks at the officer and says, "How is Mr. Knight?"

"Unhurt and on his way home. You were next to him when the shots were fired. Do you know him?"

"No, I'd just met him. I'd just made an appointment to meet him again in his office tomorrow."

Brad isn't so much frightened as dazed and puzzled, and that is because he has no reason that he knows of to be frightened. He had felt no real pain in his neck until paramedics rolled him over on the gurney to clean the wound. His forehead throbs. With his heartbeat slowing to a gallop, he looks around at the others kissing their cell phones. He sees in them the same fretful confusion he feels himself. Before, from his position flat on the rug, they were all a scrum of Guccis and Ferragamos. Now, they are fellow survivors.

When she stops making notes, Quinn hands Brad her own card and says, "Your passport has you living in California; your card has you in a K Street office. Where will you be the rest of the week?"

"I'll be here unless the sky falls or the earth moves, Detective . . ." He looks at the card. "Quinn, Patricia."

The Caprice, switched off and locked, crowds the corner of Oneida Place where it intersects with Seventh Street, its driver now at home in a brick apartment building. As he warms himself with a glass of tea in a silver holder, he makes a telephone call. "Mr. Tateshima."

"I have seen the TV. My brother cannot be gone, please tell me you have him."

"Your brother failed."

"What did you do to help him?"

"I provided essential motivation and transportation, both of which he failed to fully utilize. He revels in Paradise as we speak. I need your services." There is a long pause, punctuated by erratic breathing.

"What services?"

"The car. At the corner of my street. Remove its tires, and destroy them. Install four safe used tires with slight wear. Wash the exterior and underneath, and return it before the sun rises. Park it behind my building. Lock it, and keep your set of keys secure."

"You abandon my brother while his last drops of blood sink into polluted American soil. And now you order me to salve the wounds of your inherited metal car—"

"Before I forget, I must remind you that you may not claim the body at the police morgue; is that clearly understood?" Another pause.

"You are always clear."

"The cause is just."

"The cause is filthy."

"Your mother and sister are precious." Another pause.

"It shall be as you say."

"Of course, but say it."

"My mother and sister are precious."

"The way to justice is arduous. And clean any mud from the inside of the car."

9

Quinn hands him back his passport. "Well, you were in the middle of this turkey shoot, and until we get it sorted out, I'd like to know how to get hold of you. Just a precaution. You can go, but call me before you leave Washington." Her hand brushes Brad's sleeve as she turns her attention to a forlorn woman standing next to Brad's gurney.

Outside, Brad waves to the driver of the town car Elgar Steel has provided him. Just as he settles into his seat, his phone vibrates rudely. He looks at the screen: it's his boss, Sarah Jane Elgar. Brad nearly jumps with excitement and joy.

"Hello, Sarah. You won't believe it. I chatted up the USTR just as we talked about, and scored a meeting with him tomorrow morning, which is sooner than we planned, and—"

"Brad, I hate to cut you off and rain on your victory parade, but you've got to come home."

"But Sarah!"

"Look, I know, but that's secondary now. You have to come home, Brad. You have to take the red-eye, *now*."

"Why?" says Brad, in anguish.

"Brad, I hate to have to give you the news this way. Daddy's dead. We're all at the farm. And there's trouble."

CHAPTER TWO

On the Memorial Day weekend in 2018—for the first time since 1979—drivers in America fumed about long gas lines. Air travelers paid yet another fuel surcharge on fares. Just six months into the new administration, in 2017, the price of crude oil rose relentlessly after the Saudi-led OPEC producers suddenly cut their oil production. Lloyds of London increased its War Risk premium on oil cargoes by three hundred percent after two oil tankers loading at Bahrain were crippled by suicide bomber boats.

A month later, a category four hurricane swept over warm Gulf of Mexico waters, the second such in two years. Its storm surge breached the Galveston Seawall and devastated pipeline and oil refinery infrastructure, home to 44 percent of the United States' ethylene production and over half its jet fuel.

In his next State of the Union address, the president baffled the political world when he mentioned possible price controls on petroleum in view of "the regional unrest which threatens freedom of the seas, clogs international shipping, and attacks the lifeblood of America's economy."

Back in 2015, oil prices had fallen so low that the Trans-Rocky Pipeline Consortium shelved its plans to build the Wishbone oil pipeline from the Western Canadian Sedimentary Basin to refineries on the US Gulf Coast, crossing the Dakota, Nebraska, Kansas, Oklahoma, and Texas plains. Canadian political support for the Wishbone project dwindled and fell quiet following victories by the Liberal Party, first in the Alberta legislative assembly and then national elections.

In the wake of America's 2016 election, which let slip the deck cannons on the ship of state, Trans-Rocky decided to revive its application for the Wishbone Pipeline to renewed howls of protest from environmental activists. Curiously, it hit a different snag under the president's paramount foreign trade litmus test: What's in it for America? He said that "America first" would always be the number one criterion for foreign policy, but that the Wishbone project offered little new on that front.

Ernie Elgar had been the owner and operator of a loud, smoky steel fabrication plant sprawling along the marshy banks of the river and delta system that converges at the Port of Stockton, California. The plant had been built during World War II and had been strategic during that and every war since. When it wasn't producing hull and piping replacements for the Navy's submarine yard a hundred miles away, it was making everything from subway tunnels to bridge girders.

But the mainstay product, year in and year out, is steel pipe, significantly the large-diameter pipe that other West Coast fabricators can't make.

It is a family-owned business, and now the family comprises Sarah Jane Elgar and June Elgar, fifty-five-year-old twins. Both are unmarried, for different reasons.

June is very much a part of the family but very much not a part of its steel business. June distanced herself from steel, rust, and smoke ten years ago to start the aggressive environmental group called American-Canadian Environmental Alliance. She moves easily among the upper-class, guilt-ridden, grown-up trust babies of Canada and the US, and she harvests large donations to fund her ever-shifting environmental causes. The current target of her righteous wrath is the proposed Wishbone Pipeline. With her customary take-no-prisoners mode of attack, June has allied herself with powerful opponents in Canada and America against the Wishbone project. Prickly and openly critical of everyone else, June has isolated herself from men and women alike. None has tried to get close.

Sarah Jane, on the other hand, lives and breathes the steel fabrication business. She holds a master's degree in metallurgical engineering. She worked summer jobs on the floor of the plant and at job sites as a welder. Now willowy and wiry, her salt-and-pepper hair in a bob, her welding is of sculptures commissioned for the fronts of skyscrapers around the world. It was her idea to turn an idle part of the plant into a large-sculpture studio for artists from western colleges. Her father made her executive vice president of Elgar Steel five years ago, and she has allowed herself to spend much less of her time with her sculptures, and drilled into the workings of every department of the steel company. Too driven by her devotion to her family's businesses, Sarah Jane has never taken a serious interest in anyone, despite being admired and liked by everyone. Everyone assumed she would succeed her father and the business would carry on under her strong leadership. Until now.

An era of manufacturing on the West Coast teeters at a tipping point now. Two hundred workers now face uncertainty. Once strategic in wartimes gone by, Elgar in peacetime needs vision as much as leadership.

Ernie Elgar, industrialist and internationalist, five days after taking to his bed with a racking cough deep in grit-soaked lungs, dead at eighty-five.

Tuesday morning, September 10, 2019; Napa, California

After landing at the Sacramento airport at dawn, Brad makes two phone calls. The first is to Detective Quinn. She's not congenial. "I said to call me before you leave Washington, not after you've fled the jurisdiction." *Rotten timing,* he thinks. *She sounds like I interrupted her first coffee of the day.* He relaxes his jaw into a smile and lowers his voice to quiet and calming:

"There's an emergency in the family. I'm calling as soon as I could. I'll be back in a couple of days. Did you get the shooter?"

"What's left of him. Our detail got him about the time he assassinated that punch bowl from a window scaffold. How's the neck? And how am I supposed to keep you in one piece when you slip off like this in the middle of the night?" He's touched to hear concern in her voice.

"I'll be back in a couple of days. The neck is only sore from the red-eye flight. And thanks for asking."

"You may be better off right where you are. We don't think Ambassador Knight was the target. Forensics says based on the physics—you were. I have to tell you I like that you're three time zones away from the combat zone."

Brad catches his breath. He has to strain to hear Quinn say in a lowered voice, "You got enemies, cowboy. Keep in touch and keep your head down. I'm on your side, you know."

"Yeah, I know. I'm glad."

Brad stares at the phone and nearly forgets to inhale. *Me, the target? That can't be. How the hell can that be?* Keep moving, he tells himself, and dials the next number. "Mr.

Nagaoka, it's Brad Oaks again."

"Uh-huh, with a scheme to turn oil into wine, or some such."

Brad eases into a smile and says, "Ichiro, the CEO of Elgar Steel has just died. That meeting with your boss is in three hours, and I'm actually in California. It would sure be great if you could help reschedule that meeting for a day or so. Can you help me with that?"

"From what the police are telling us, I don't want you within a city block of the ambassador. But call me when you can meet some place where we can return small-arms fire."

The Caprice pulls into the driver's customary space, near a Dumpster behind the building where he occupies a cramped office. The driver has inspected and approved its appearance and change of tires. He now dials a number from his office to make a report in flat tones . . . disguised in flourishes of poetic metaphors about angels, Satan, anointed foot soldiers, and a game of inches played with shoddy American firearms. The driver braces for the storm of displeasure. It is never quite enough, he thinks. He has played the game of inches for decades. He will survive disapproval for another game. He will report again when he has such a game plan well thought out. Only a single question is posed, to which he responds with relief,

"Of course, all is clean. No, no trace. The way to justice is arduous."

The Elgar "farm" is actually a large winery and vineyard in the Napa Valley. Ernie Elgar's father had bought it during Prohibition to keep its owners from bankruptcy. He paid off all the creditors and gave the family make-work until there was a market for wine again. The grateful family remained in the house and winery, and helped make Elgar Pinot Noir and Cabernet Sauvignon award-winning labels in France, Japan, and the US. Although opposed to the family's involvement in the Wishbone Pipeline, June approves of the vineyards, less so the pricey wines they produce. She'd prefer something from lesser grapes in the ten-dollar range—a third of the starting price of the farm's labels.

Brad, stiff from his flight and pressure-drive in a rental car, enters the spacious living room, its adobe walls filled with the works of contemporary California artists. He is still in yesterday's khaki suit, considerably rumpled by now.

Sarah Jane and her sister, June, glare at each other sullenly. June Elgar twists her auburn hair and smirks in silence. She is perched on a high Shaker stool, legs wrapped around it like a pretzel, in super-skinny, pre-distressed designer jeans and red-and-black plaid Hudson Bay shirt, cuffs rolled past her slender wrists. Sarah Jane faces her atop another Shaker stool in a sunflower-colored cotton crochet Mexican maxi dress and huaraches.

Neither woman greets Brad. Sarah Jane pushes a document with blue backing into his hands and mutters, "Read this piece of dog shit."

"I'm well, thank you. I am sorry for your loss," says Brad, trying to scan what is entitled "Last Will and Testament of Ernest N. Elgar."

"Amaya Mori?" asks Brad of no one and everyone, looking up in puzzlement.

"Our sister!" shrieks June from the top of her stool, nearly tipping herself over. "Unknown to anyone in this family before now except Daddy. Randy Daddy. Seems he used to go to Tokyo every year to spawn. He drops this on us at his final curtain."

"She's ten years younger," says Sarah Jane as she slides off her stool, crosses in front of June's perch, and stands facing

Brad, some ten feet in front of him. She shrugs and throws both arms outward and lets them fall with thuds at her thighs.

"And now, she's owner of one-third of the common stock of Elgar Steel, same as each of you," Brad states calmly. At least, his voice is calm, although this development has gripped him on the inside, the way it felt years ago when he watched one of his best pitches explode off a bat and into the seats.

Sarah Jane, right fist jammed against her narrow hip, points the index finger of her outstretched left hand at Brad and demands, with a scowl, "Did you know about this?"

Brad returns her unblinking gaze and says, "No. Absolutely not. Ernie went to his San Francisco attorney for everything personal. I've never heard about this person. Does anyone know where she lives?"

June squirms on her stool and looks out the window through a strand of frizzed hair at the vineyards. With a studied attempt at coolness, she says,

"Daddy kept a whole box of stuff about her in the upstairs study. There are some of her letters in there. And there's a long letter from Daddy to Sarah and me about the whole thing. He knew this would shake us up. He was pretty contrite about it.

"She's in Tokyo. Her mother was a survivor of Hiroshima. She fostered this Amaya off to a Tokyo family who owned part of a big trading company there. The mother had been a foster child of the same family. Daddy used to do business with that company in the 1960s, when . . ."

"When he and Ms. Foster Child found mutual comfort," growls Sarah Jane as she swirls on tan huaraches and marches to pick up one of the glasses of mineral water she has prepared and abandoned on various furniture surfaces. "Brad, you have to go to court and blow this so-called will to hell."

Brad shakes his head slowly as he says, "Watch it, Sarah. There's a clause in here that says if either of you contests the will, your inheritance is reduced to five thousand dollars and two cases of wine."

Sarah Jane blinks and lets her accusatory left hand slowly fall to her side. June sits up straight and twists to stare at Brad as she tries to digest what he just said.

Brad brightens a little and says, "There is, however, a buyout provision in the will, so we could negotiate to get her third back into your hands. Let me read the papers upstairs and try to think of something.

"In other news, I came too close to a bullet yesterday, plus I'm dog tired from traveling."

The twins look at each other. Sarah Jane looks back at Brad and says, "Were you mugged or what?"

Brad says, "More along the lines of 'or what.' I'll tell you about it over wine."

Brad Oaks, born in 1970, grew up in Sacramento. His father was a lobbyist for the California mining industry. His mother was an assistant principal in a Sacramento elementary school, and had earned a master's in music education. She saw to it that he take violin lessons through high school. His father encouraged him to play baseball through college at UC Davis. His father also urged him to go to law school and specialize in water law, which he did, again at Davis. During summers, he worked at the Elgar plant in Stockton. Although Brad excelled in the law school's moot court competition, it was Ernie who steered him away from litigation—"Lawsuits are always about yesterday's business"— and into international transactions.

Brad's parents died in a foggy car crash the night of his law school graduation. With them in the car was his fiancée, who also died. That summer, Ernie brought him to the farm, where they talked about the future of the winery and the steel pipe business. Brad was devastated, but Ernie's dreams gave him purpose. After that, he didn't date at all. His interests were channeled into the Elgar businesses. The Elgar family tried unsuccessfully to introduce him to Napa Valley society. Despite the best intentions of the Elgar sisters, he did not mingle well or gladly with the Napa crowd, most of whom were celebrity transplants from elsewhere, making hobby wines from grapes bought from real growers like the Elgars. On weekends, he became a lone canoeist in the estuaries of the San Francisco Bay region and a birder. He took up astronomy. He named a star for his fiancée.

Brad lifts the lid of the shiny black lacquered box resting in the center of Ernie's desk. The lacquer inside is orange. The box is about thirteen by fifteen inches, and a good eight inches deep. He picks up the top item, a handwritten letter on Elgar Steel letterhead to his daughters. Ernie was always thorough in his memos, and this letter is no different. As he reads through the letter, Brad begins to gain an admiration for Amaya Mori, her disrupted childhood, school achievements, and artistic flair. And Brad gains reinforced admiration for his mentor, Ernie Elgar, for his devotion to the Japanese child and her mother, while keeping the secret from Deidre and their twins. The letter ends with Ernie's wish that June and Sarah Jane forgive him and find it in their hearts to acknowledge Amaya Mori as their half sister. The letter mentions his desire for the three daughters to share ownership of the steel business but does not give any details about the provisions of the will. Brad wonders why there are no snapshots of Amaya or her mother. Then it occurs to him that, knowing Ernie, if he had kept any photos he would have destroyed them just before he died. It probably broke his heart, but he wouldn't want them to be pawed over and speculated about.

Brad rejoins the sisters at noon on the farm's stone patio, the size of a small county. Sarah Jane offers a toast to Ernie with the hope that he is dancing with Deidre, their mother, dead for six years now. Brad lets the first swallow of buttery red wine settle. He puts the glass down on the tabletop and leans toward the sisters, who sit expectantly across from him. He says,

"According to Ernie's letter, this Ms. Mori has been looked after pretty well during her life. Ernie supported her college education in Kyoto, where she earned high honors. After that, she took a master's degree at Sotheby's in London, specializing in Asian art. She worked for a while at the family trading company and then opened her own gallery in Tokyo. There's no mention of siblings or a husband in Ernie's letter about her.

"If you ask me, I say that step one is to buy her shares back. I can be on a flight to Tokyo in three hours if I leave before finishing this wine. Or I can return to Washington tomorrow to try to move forward on the Wishbone project. Ladies, you are the controlling shareholders, so I await your instructions." With that, Brad leans back in his chair with his arms extended to each side.

"Washington," says June quickly through tight lips and a frown.

"Washington," says Sarah Jane calmly, after a pause.

Brad takes a slow sip of wine. He levels his gaze at June Elgar. "June, you bitterly oppose Wishbone. Don't you want our new opportunity to fail, since you hate Wishbone so much? I'm surprised at your answer. Sarah Jane's instinct on Washington is understandable. I'm not so sure I understand yours."

June stands up and starts to walk out into the sun, blazing on the open deck. She stops, turns back, and says,

"You need to do your damn job, Brad. We both said go to Washington. And that's where Daddy sent you. You can't do the company any good in Japan. So just get on a plane, go back to Washington, and talk nonsense to the senators." June's voice has risen in pitch and volume. Sarah Jane looks at her in surprise.

Brad explains, "In Washington, we have to have a unified voice, and it must come from the top. If the ownership is divided or in question, Sarah Jane's position as well as mine lacks the credibility we absolutely must have in that town. Otherwise, no one will listen to us."

"Dammit, NO!" shouts June, glaring at Brad, chin trembling.

Brad shakes his head, thinking, *Somewhere along the line, I really broke my pick with this woman. She doesn't like me, she doesn't trust me, and she can barely stand to be in the same room with me. What the hell is wrong with her this time? Is it just June being contrary? Oh no, it's more than that. She's worked up about something. Gotta keep my eye on what that's about.*

The first to break the awkward silence is Sarah Jane: "How much do we offer?"

Brad releases the eye-lock with June and relaxes his shoulders a bit. He turns to Sarah Jane and says, "That's a great question. If we can't agree on a price, the will specifies a Russian roulette clause. It's meant to be so draconian, you'd rather make any deal than resort to the clause. It works like this: You put a price on the table. Then, Ms. Mori can either buy or sell at that price, her option. Either she offers to sell her inheritance to you, or offers to buy one-sixth of your inheritance of stock, always at that price. That forces us to put out a reasonable price. Based on last year's numbers, it looks like Elgar Steel has a book value of close to seventy-five million dollars for the whole shebang."

June gasps and covers her mouth with her right palm. She gathers herself, lowers her hand, and says, "Hell, none of us has that kind of cash, least of all her. What's she going to pay us in, rice? I say we go about our business without this so-called sister in Japan!"

Brad tilts his head and shrugs. "Under the buyout clause, half the payment has to be in cash. She could probably borrow that with the help of her family's trading company. The other half can come out of future earnings or the sale of the whole business," he explains. "Do I have your authority to start the offer at twenty million and work up to, say, twenty-five million?"

"Oh. Bad. Word!" June spits out each word with the same venomous tone as her father used with that expression.

Sarah Jane reaches her right hand to grip June's forearm and says, "June, I'm the executive vice president, and I'll make this decision. I'm OK with buying her out before Brad goes back to Washington. What he says makes perfect sense. But I'm not comfortable with starting that high. Start at ten million and only go up to fifteen million for her third."

June pulls her arm from her sister's grip. She says, "Brad, you're the lawyer, you've always got a pen. Let me borrow it a minute."

Brad hands June his favorite matte-black Cross ballpoint and watches as she walks to another table on the deck. She scribbles on a paper napkin, and looks away, her shoulders slumped. He thinks, *She'll be adding up her own resources and fund-raising possibilities. Those possibilities are vast.*

She returns to her chair next to Sarah Jane and says levelly, "That number is absolutely ridiculous. How could Daddy . . . Well, I might be able to make it work for me." She stands again, turns, and starts for the French doors.

Brad says, "Can I have my ballpoint back?" His palm stings from the force of the pen hitting it. Just as she reaches the doors, Brad asks,

"When did Ernie die?"

"June found him about seven o'clock yesterday morning," says Sarah Jane. "He had died sometime earlier."

June stops at the doors to the kitchen and says without turning, "Early morning. Too early for us. Too soon in his life."

Brad says to no one in particular, "When is death ever on time?"

June glances at Brad, and then goes into the house.

Brad frowns as he watches June stalk away from the family conference. He says, "Sarah Jane, your sister must want me out of the company and out of your lives. I've never felt so despised."

Sarah says simply, "It's important to see some good in everyone. It's harder to find in June."

"I thought she was in Toronto. Were you here too?"

"No, I was still in Stockton at the plant. June's been at the farm all week because Daddy was so sick.

"Brad, walk with me in the stable. This will only take a minute."

Once on the shaded, redwood-planked stable floor, Sarah Jane and Brad walk arm in arm as they had that summer after Brad lost everything he loved. It's been their shrine for private conversations ever since. They pause briefly in front of an empty

23

stall where once, on a summer's day, Sarah Jane had planted a kiss on Brad's lips. He had blushed then but said nothing. Today, they also say nothing. Sarah Jane's mind is working, though. *I just don't know what it is about men. Well, I mean, I know about it but not really. June called Daddy randy. Is Brad randy? I'm pretty sure not. Who knows? He should be; he deserves it. We . . . well, just a kiss that nothing came of. That's what I always say, but I wonder. I think about it. Does he?*

From his cramped office, the driver of the Caprice dials another number on the secure line. He musters patience as it rings and rings. When it is eventually answered, he says,

"Nephew, you have been chosen again for glory."

"But there is still much to learn here."

"And what you learn will bring you slowly along the arduous path to justice. Can you leave for the gulf?"

"It would be awkward right now. I now have access to vital information I should fully capture. What do you need from the gulf?"

"The alcoholic girl."

"I do not need to leave this position to acquire her."

"Develop a secure plan and e-mail me when you are ready. I will phone you for your plan. It must be without flaw."

"Trust me."

"I will trust a flawless plan when I recognize it."

"You shall always be great. Myths shall be sung about you."

There is always something in the earthy smell and random soft mutters and thuds of twelve-hundred-pound horses that inspire profound trust between Brad and Sarah Jane. Reality smells better in a well-ventilated barn.

"Brad, I want to know our chances on Wishbone. In your heart, I mean. If I'm betting the ranch on a wishbone, I want to know my odds." Sarah Jane looks at Brad through a worried frown, her face tilted upward in the shadows of the horse stalls. Brad sees more than worry there—it's a fright he has not seen before on any Elgar.

Brad takes both her hands in his. He takes his time gathering his thoughts. She says nothing.

"Sarah, I believe in this plan more than I have believed in anything since the accident. Without Wishbone, we're looking at gradual decline: fewer big jobs in the market—and fewer of those coming our way. Just look at the San Francisco-Oakland Bay Bridge job: rebuilt using steel sections made in China! That hurts the people who depend on us. Ernie taught us to manage to growth, not decline. But it's not only good for us; Wishbone could fight the biggest economic threat the Western United States has ever faced. I have a good take on Alden Knight. He'll like what we're doing. He can get it approved in Washington. I think you can take that to the bank. I also think you should pay a premium for Mori's stock, if it comes to that. Losing Ernie is a blow, and this Mori person is a surprise no one needs, least of all me when all this is coming together in Washington on Wishbone.

"But I'll get her stock back into the family. I'll work with Shin Steel in Tokyo to source the steel we need for the Wishbone job. And I'll get the project approved. Bing, bam, boom."

Sarah Jane takes his elbow and starts them in a slow stroll. "Daddy always thought we'd sell to Shin Steel one day. I'm beginning to think maybe it's time."

"No. Not until Wishbone has built up our market value. Not until you're ready to retire. We need them, and they need us.

They'll serve us well as our long-term supplier. Maybe bring them into the picture in a joint venture. Buy their steel from strength. Sell them your stock from greater strength."

She squeezes his arm and presses the side of her head against his shoulder. "You are driven. Your drive is affecting. Is that enough to stake everything on?"

"If I were in your huaraches, I'd stake everything on the *plan.*"

"You're out on a limb on this one, Brad."

Brad says, "I know. And right now, I'm out of time. I just put together powers of attorney that make me official. They're on the desk upstairs. You and June sign them in front of a notary and overnight them to me at the Palace Hotel, Tokyo."

The owner of the Caprice deletes the short e-mail from his nephew and sets the reminder clock on his computer to place a call to him at the suggested date and time. He closes his computer for the day, locks his small office, and exits the building through the front doors. A small crowd has begun to gather in the lobby, an hour before the public event will start. There will be gatherers at such events who treat the meager, anemic appetizers and toasted pita wedges as an evening meal. Some will also listen to the public program, which will also be meager—just sentimental folk songs without dancing and without sentimental costumes—compared to the grand programs at the diplomatic quarters of larger nations. Those ones would be held at well-known Embassy Row addresses. *But who knows or cares about the address of this place?* the man wonders. He turns at the corner of the building and walks toward the Dumpster at the rear. He then unlocks the door of the Caprice and gives its vintage engine a few minutes to regain its still-modest best. *Patience is the best engine on the arduous road,* he tells himself.

Wednesday morning, September 11, 2019; Napa

At seven a.m., in the kitchen of the Elgar homestead, June and Sarah Jane sit across from each other at the table, watching coffee drip. Friday afternoon, they will bury their father. They are all they have left as family.

These sisters, fraternal twins, took divergent professions but always managed to retain their fondness for one another. Even so, in recent months, they have gone round and round over the Wishbone project. June didn't just oppose it because of potential oil leaks and explosions. It would go through Indian tribal lands whose leaders opposed it. It would be built over America's most ancient water resource, the Ogallala Aquifer underlying farmlands from North Dakota to Oklahoma. She would thump the table and say, "Contaminate that aquifer with an oil spill, and you contaminate water supplies forever. And for what? What does America get out of this pipeline? Nothing. Nada. Zilch."

Her father argued it would create jobs. She would have none of that. Construction jobs would go away as soon as the pipeline was finished. She played the patriotic card with Ernie, and with Brad whenever he joined the discussion. The men had little to offer against her arguments: the pipeline wouldn't carry American oil; the oil would be exported on foreign-flagged vessels. America would just be the sidewalk for Canada's export business.

So Ernie and Brad got to thinking. Ernie was an

internationalist and had mentored Brad to think that way. Ernie would say to him, "Brad, it's not enough to think outside the box; we've got to think outside the borders. Silicon Valley didn't invent the global economy. That was developed along the Silk Road connecting the Mediterranean with Japan and everything in between. Transportation invented the global economy. The pipes we manufacture go into modern transportation systems—pipelines."

Eventually, they figured out how Wishbone could be more than an oil-pipeline-export-sidewalk through America.

The idea worried Sarah Jane. She had implored them not to discuss any of their thinking with June. It was too good, too simple, and too important for the family to risk June's skilled meddling. But this morning, with the family down to just the two of them, Sarah Jane decides to open that door a crack. She stands and circles around behind June, resting her hands on her sister's shoulders.

"June, on this Wishbone project: you know how important it is to our business. What if there was also something important in it for the United States? Brad and Daddy thought of a way."

June sighs and presses her cheek against Sarah Jane's hand. Then she rises slowly, allowing Sarah Jane to ease her hands off her shoulders. June gathers and clears the plates to the edge of the sink and returns with the coffeepot. After refilling their mugs, she says, "I'm listening."

Sarah Jane hesitates, weighing her next move. *No, don't do it.*

"I won't tell you the details. Not until it's the right time. Just give me a little longer, and time for Brad to finish what Daddy sent him to Washington to do. I'm just saying that this whole problem might well come into balance in a way you could accept. Look, I know I'm equivocating on these details now, but I have to. Don't give me that disapproving look, June. You know I have a responsibility to the steel company and its employees. And you've got an ax to grind. You are committed to blocking our future and all the jobs *we* provide. June, don't be like every other environmentalist who thinks destroying progress always makes the sky bluer and the trees taller. Wait on this, and see how there's a better way."

June stands and enunciates tersely: "Do not give me that superior-air, confidentiality crap. And do not give me that 'what's best for the business' crap that Daddy always fell for. Always! Since the first time you turned serious about life, which made me look pretty foolish ever after. He always saw it in you, the serious part, and never saw it in me. I swear you had to be putting mushroom powder or something in his wine when you were with him. Me? Well, I never found your stash of mushrooms. I found Canada, though. And I found hundreds of things to fight for. The more things I fought for, the more Daddy just saw me as just an angry woman.

"Never mind all that now. We're adults here. And two can play at the secret-mission, cloak and dagger-in-the-back game. OK, so we'll both just have to wait and see what kind of new surprises drop from the sky. I'm going back to Toronto as soon as Daddy is buried. And then I am going to bury Wishbone. I think it's about time I took hold of Elgar Steel's role in the grand scheme of things."

Sarah Jane stands and takes a deep breath to calm down a bit. "Listen to yourself, June. You *are* an angry woman. It will turn you into a prune if you're not careful.

"I don't know what you mean about taking hold of Elgar Steel, but that's just the sort of sentiment that keeps me from spelling it all out to you now. You don't get to use our inside information to sink us, no matter how devoted you are to the environment.

"I'm running the place, and you wouldn't be caught dead there. The people there listen to me, and most of them have never even met you. And never, ever forget that I've got the votes to at least wrestle you to a tie if you try to muck things up.

"Keep your serious side, your angry side, and your cloak-and-dagger side *outside of the steel plant*. Fair warning, twin: I'm the one protecting the nest, so don't go acting like a predator. If the only place you can do that is Canada, then so be it. If it weren't for that, I'd never be sorry to have you closer to home or the business."

CHAPTER THREE

Wednesday night, September 11, 2019; Narita, Japan

It's an eleven-hour flight from San Francisco to Tokyo's Narita airport, and it's another hour and a half to downtown Tokyo. Unlike most of the passengers from America who tack that time to the end of their flights, in a train, limo, or taxi (their only options), Brad takes a shuttle bus to a new hotel near the airport where he's booked a room. He has a light supper and falls into bed.

After breakfast at the hotel's buffet, Brad's on his way by train to Tokyo, arriving before ten o'clock Thursday morning. He steps off the clean, uncrowded Narita Express train into Tokyo Station at a below-ground platform. His escalator gathers masses of riders as it rises four stories to the ground level, which is teeming in a controlled bedlam of morning commuters moving at quick-march. He is one of nearly half a million people to come and go between three thousand trains today at this station. Buttoned-down men in ubiquitous black suits and dark-gray ties, and women in dark-skirted suits and round-toed pumps, swarm out of the station to overcrowd the sidewalks of the Marunouchi district of Tokyo.

Many wear white surgical masks over their faces to fend off or contain airborne sicknesses. The 1918 Spanish flu pandemic affected at least twenty-three million people in Japan, with nearly four hundred thousand fatalities. The mask culture instituted in Japan as a by-product of that epidemic attached itself to a broader, do-the-right-thing etiquette that had permeated the culture for a millennium before, and the practice continued. Some even choose to wear the mask at times to hide emotions.

The fifteen-minute walk to the Palace Hotel, along the most expensive real estate on the globe, is a pleasure for Brad's cramped legs. He picks his way through more pedestrians heading in the opposite direction to gleaming, modern office buildings and deluxe Ginza *depatu* (department stores). He pulls his roller bag westward, toward the still-functioning, feudal Imperial Palace, its buildings now restored after the devastating bombing raids of World War II.

On the palace grounds, ahead of him, rises Edo Castle above wide modern streets filled with gridlocked cars. The compound holds a cluster of smooth, white-walled buildings originally built in the feudal era of the Tokugawa Shogunate. The Tokugawa military aristocracy kept foreigners out of Japan, and feudal society intact within, from 1603 to 1868, when the emperor displaced the military shogun rule. Emperor Meiji moved the imperial residence from Kyoto to this castle, repurposing it as a palace, and restored his full influence over the nation. Edo, the largest city in the world, was renamed by the emperor to Tokyo ("Capital of the East"), and Japan began to look outside itself.

The palace's buildings have sweeping roofs of black, semicircular tiles rising from the white walls in curves to meet rooflines with elaborate ornamentation at each corner of the buildings. The bases of the buildings are partially obscured by pine trees, azalea bushes, and cherry trees. The palace compound is enclosed by a stone wall, which is surrounded by a moat some sixty feet wide at this point. "Stone wall" means an awesomely large mass of the squarish stone blocks, about five feet on each side where the wall meets the water of the moat. In gradually smaller blocks, the walls rise some fifteen feet in the air. The blocks rest on one another at an angle of about fifteen degrees. The granite and basalt blocks had been transported by thousands of boats from quarries some seventy miles south, then dragged on sleds pulled by oxen. Construction of the daunting project stretched over forty years in the first half of the seventeenth century.

The combination of the angular placement and the sheer mass of the blocks give an impression of repose, a stately island of foot-traveled seclusion and quiet amid the largest city in the world. This aura of tranquility fills the forested compound, which is about three miles in asymmetrical circumference, and still guarded by three of twenty original guard towers.

Brad's shoes and roller-bag wheels scrunch hardpan fine-gravel paths in Hibiya Park, leading to an arched bridge over the moat. His hotel faces the palace across a wide, traffic-clogged eight-lane thoroughfare. Experienced though he is, Brad feels the palpable density of the city as keenly as any first-time American traveler. Tokyo's total metropolitan area population equals that of California, and exceeds that of Canada. This urban agglomeration of greater Tokyo has the largest total gross domestic product of any other such agglomeration in the world, topping $1.5 trillion.

In another fifteen minutes, he's in his room overlooking the Imperial Palace grounds and moat. He sits on the corner of his bed and opens the envelope handed to him at the desk. It's from the Mori Gallery of Asian Arts, with a Ginza district address.

The note reads, in exquisite script: "Mr. Brad Oaks. Thank

you for your glad invitation by fax machine. Yes, it is convenient to take dinner in your hotel Crowne dining room from 20:00. I am tall for Japanese and look for blue dress with coral belt please. Amaya Mori."

Brad's phone buzzes with a text: *Call your favorite cop.* He does.

"Detective Quinn-comma-Patricia, it's Brad Oaks . . . Yeah, Japan, look, I couldn't . . . What? Could you say that again?"

"I said you may have gone from the frying pan into the fire. The shooter's nearest and dearest friends are in the Japanese mafia . . . the yakuza or something like that. What are you up to in Japan, Oaks?"

"I'm just cleaning up some corporate fallout from our CEO's death. I should be finished in a couple of days. It must be ten at night there."

"I'm going to fax you how to get in touch with a detective at Tokyo Metropolitan. Tanaka. I'm liaising with him on all this. Call him if you need to. And what I do at night is my business, cowboy. Just don't go native over there. 'Bye."

Quinn's news about the yakuza is upsetting. Although Japan's overall crime scene is relatively small, the yakuza clans dominate gambling and dodgy trading, with tentacles reaching into drugs, real estate, and banking. And yet in the earthquake-tsunami-cum-nuclear-meltdown of 2011, they were among the first who mobilized relief supplies in the region. Unique. Just like everything else in Japan. Still, Brad decides not to go for his usual run in Hibiya Park.

Seated at his desk in the cramped office, the Caprice's owner watches the analog clock graphic on his computer screen approach the moment when it will chime its reminder. The man's finger hovers over the key that will silence the chime nearly at the instant the graphic reaches that moment. He has long practice at this and treasures the sensation of stopping the chime exactly when the moment arrives, or as close as humanly possible to do so. His pride traces to his boyhood days, when he and his father would scan the evening sky for the first possible glimpse of the slip of moon at the earliest appearance of its first quarter. The significance of that would, of course, vastly outweigh the significance of the chime game, but the concentration would be similar, as would the sense of satisfaction. Later generations of young men, even from his homeland, would admonish him to "get a life" over such a fetish. He is very aware they would, but he is not daunted. Even this nephew could say such a thing, but it would be imprudent for him to do so. *Ting-STOP*. He dials.

"Heroic Uncle."

"Satan spices his tea with flattery."

"Uncle, you sound like a folk song. What's up?"

"Your time nearly is. Tell me your plan."

"You cannot get intelligence as solid as that which I can gather here. If I leave here at this time, it will cost us further intelligence about the devil's workshop that can never be regained. I cannot imagine what lies at the Gulf Coast that has comparable value. Besides, the friend you mentioned is no longer there but in California. If there is secondary value in reconnecting with the friend, let it be somewhere in California and at a better time."

"I ask for a plan and you provide me opinion from your immature, tainted young mind."

"Uncle, take a moment to listen and reflect instead of preaching to me. I am inside the walls of the fortress. Why would you reposition me?"

"Tell me your *plan*, yearling camel!"

"My best plan is to remain exactly where I am, continue to steal the knowledge needed for the endeavor, and stay for as long as possible to wring the last drop of that knowledge. The friend you refer to can be reacquired whenever necessary, although you have not seen fit to tell me the value in that."

"Then 'nothing' is the plan: no movement; no change; no risk-taking. Your plan has the value of zero. Ancients of our lineage invented the zero. The world now turns on the uses of zero. It will do for now. I am pleased."

"Jayzuss."

"What?"

"Uncle, just go pound the sand of the ancient tribes. You'll be amazed and delighted with the intelligence I bring from behind the walls of the fortress."

"If I find out that you are merely there to pursue hedonist outrage in this secret, distant time you create for yourself . . ."

"If you find that out, I can count on you to ruin it. Just trust my good judgment and loyalty . . . heroic Uncle."

Click . . . dial tone.

CHAPTER FOUR

Alden Knight hangs up his phone, presses his temples with his fingers, takes a deep breath, and barks, "Ichiro, get in here." His aide appears, notebook in hand. "Ichiro, the White House wants a last-look, final powwow on the Wishbone Pipeline. On Monday, so we have some time. I want to be up to date. Find that Brad Oaks guy and get him in here so we can find out what he's being so coy about. Have the right people from our shop, State, and EPA in here at the same time. Where is he now?"

"He was in California, but the police tell me he went to Tokyo. Through the magic of heavy jets and the international date line, he can be here on the same day he leaves there. There are a couple of nonstops that put him in Dulles at four p.m. any day you say. Or do you want him on a military plane?"

"This is his pitch. Let him pay it himself, commercial. Put it together for this Friday. Get everyone in our conference room at six thirty. Shouldn't take more'n an hour. But just in case, have a working supper lined up from downstairs."

Brad fishes for the phone number of his friend Hiwasaki at Shin Steel, vice president for North American sales. Brad and Hiwasaki have done business over the years when Elgar imported Shin's high-specification steel for certain fabricating jobs. Hiwasaki and Brad developed a strong friendship while they were developing workable and trustworthy contracts between equally conservative senior executives on both sides of the Pacific.

"Hey, Sake-cup, I know it's short notice, but can you have a bite of lunch with me today? You're sure? Great. I'm at the Palace; come to the sushi bar about one o'clock."

Jerimiah Hiwasaki, Hawaiian-born, comparative literature major at UCLA, and NCAA swimming medalist, easily locates Brad in the near-empty sushi bar. Hiwasaki has a full head of short, thick, dry hair. He stands five feet ten inches in his black shoes and black slacks. He wears a light-blue oxford cloth button-down shirt, a black tie with horizontal white stripes, and a glen plaid light sports coat the color of buckwheat.

Hiwasaki shakes Brad's hand and settles himself next to him. "Good thing you're the host, Brad-san. Us salarymen can't afford street food this pricey," he says.

"Sake-cup, you're the salesman here. Treat me like a customer."

"Show me a signed purchase order, and I'll feed you the raw fish myself. What brings you to Tokyo on the cusp of typhoon season?"

Brad fills in Hiwasaki on the nascent plan to get the Wishbone project going again, the death of Ernie Elgar, and his wild-oats, wild-card heir.

"This whole Wishbone job would take X-70 steel throughout. Highest strength, highest price. Two thousand miles of thirty-six-inch-diameter pipe. Not many plate mills can even make that order, let alone be competitive. Could you handle that?"

Hiwasaki sips his Kirin beer and nods slowly. "More sushi, Brad-san?"

"Could you do it?"

Again, Hiwasaki nods, expressionless. "It would be difficult, Brad-san, but I think so. But the price . . ." He shakes his head. "Very difficult to be competitive."

"Your steel is more than competitive these days, after the US slapped those dumping duties on Chinese steel. But for a kicker, what if Shin had some equity in the job, Sake-cup? What if Shin had like a third of the profits on the fabrication of the whole thing? Shin makes the X-70 steel plates and ships them to Stockton, and our pipe mill bends the plates into pipe sections."

Hiwasaki cocks his head and says, "Interesting."

Then Brad says, "And what if we can double that?"

"You mean two-thirds?"

"No. I mean four thousand miles."

Hiwasaki lifts his eyebrows and turns to his friend. "You mean a loop?"

"Yes, I mean *loop*. Twin pipelines, side-by-side. Maybe. Just my pipe dream now, but I think there's a shot at it. Look, suppose Shin Steel joint-ventures with Elgar to supply the Wishbone project's pipe? With profits from the finished product, Shin could reduce its transfer price on the plates. Make it very competitive. And Shin would gain a presence in North America, which has long been your pipe dream."

Hiwasaki takes a slow sip of his beer. He smiles and says, "Brad-san, you never did think small. Look, I may like your dream, but I've got a conservative CEO, and he has a conservative board of directors, and this would have to clear Ministry of Finance, and—"

"Sake-cup, I've got problems too. But the Wishbone I envision could be a proving ground for similar, long-haul dual pipelines in the West, way into the future. And if Elgar grows, Shin can't help but grow along with it. As Ernie Elgar used to say, problems are opportunities in work clothes. Why don't you kick this around with your CEO? And this is all confidential, right?"

"Of course, Brad-san. Here, let me get this."

Thursday evening, September 12, 2019; Tokyo

Despite a nap in the afternoon, or maybe because of it, Brad feels a heavy dose of jet-lag fatigue as he sits at a window table in the corner of the Crowne restaurant, looking out over the Tokyo skyline. He glances at the entrance, and then around the restaurant. She's not here yet, and the place is empty. *There she is. Here she comes. Oh dear!* His phone vibrates.

"I can't talk right now, Ichiro . . ."

"Please finish your phone call, Mr. Oaks. I can wait at the front," says the tall Japanese woman. Her long, gleaming black hair is swept back to a tight bun just to the left of the nape of her smooth neck. Half a dozen flyaway strands have escaped (intentionally) to fall across the right side of her face, which she presents with a beaming smile, her dark eyes sparkling with interest. One shoulder is covered in the sky-blue silk of her straight-line dress, the other shoulder bare. Sure enough, a thin, coral-colored leather belt on her narrow waist completes the description she gave. He stands, thinking, *Her left shoulder, the one on my right, that's the bare one.* "Mr. Oaks? Shall I leave you to your thoughts?" Her voice twinkles with the same warmth as her eyes.

"Oh no. Sorry. I'm Brad Oaks. Yes, you know that. Won't you be seated?" Brad pushes the "power off" button of his phone and puts it away in his coat pocket. Although flustered, he's now very wide awake.

Amaya Mori talks easily with Brad through cocktails (she takes Tio Pepe). Brad relaxes a bit, enjoying her conversation, which easily shifts from the coming typhoon to her collection of contemporary Japanese ceramics. Brad brightens when they talk animatedly about something he has studied: early porcelains from the Arita region of Kyushu, known simply as Imari. He is charmed by her ready smile and especially her way of looking directly in his eyes one moment and then shifting her gaze away and down, sometimes with color rising in her cheeks.

They discover they both grew up with violin lessons, and had reached similar levels before college studies intervened. Brad notices she blushes slightly every time she laughs at something he says. She is careful to follow his lead, whether in conversation or taking bites of the smoked salmon appetizer. During a comfortable lull, she leans against the back of her chair and looks at him with an expectant smile. He blinks; reality crowds into his consciousness. He thinks, *All right, Oaks, this is not a date, date. Now's the time to talk about the business you came for.*

"Ms. Mori, it must seem very strange to get a faxed invitation to dinner from a stranger, and all the invitation refers to is a potential inheritance of substantial size. And actually, it is very strange."

Amaya looks intently at Brad for a flickering moment before looking down and away. She says, "You are not at all strange, Mr. Oaks."

Brad laughs. "Right. Glad you said. But it's at least uncommon to hear you've been left a big inheritance. And you have. Ms. Mori, your father died leaving you what amounts to one-third of his steel business in America. I don't know how much you know about him or about that business . . ."

Amaya lifts her hand, palm upward, and frowns briefly. "I have met my father. I received many letters and gifts from him. He has provided for my education and other support. I have very warm feelings for him. I know that I am a stranger to his family, and I have no intent to disturb them."

"Well, that is a sophisticated attitude, Ms. Mori, and very commendable. I am here to arrange for you to sell your inheritance to your half sisters for a fair price. I hope we can reach an understanding. The will provides for a means of breaking a stalemate in the negotiations, but I hope we never reach a stalemate. In this file, there is a copy of his will, a flash drive with audited financial statements and federal tax filings for five years, the articles and bylaws, and an outline of the company's sales plans for the upcoming year. The sales plans do not describe the pipeline opportunity I'm currently working on, which is too uncertain to be included. I would be happy to describe that to you after you and your advisors have considered these materials and my offer."

Brad sits back in his chair, his hands resting on the tablecloth, and says,

"I am offering you ten million US dollars for the one-third position in Elgar Steel you have inherited. Please consider these documents and my offer very carefully. Consult anyone you wish to. I would never put pressure on you, but there are external events that are putting pressure on your sisters and me to conclude an arrangement with you."

Amaya Mori exhales and looks out the window as night settles over Tokyo and black clouds cover the southern sky. Tokyo's buildings transform into garish screens of moving advertisements in electric white, sapphire, and every shade of red. The streets are forever covered with the lights of ceaseless traffic. Occasionally, the additional electricity of sheet lightning competes with the city's neon skin.

She picks the file off the table and slides it into a large, shiny white shopping bag bearing the logo of Mori Asian Arts and Antiques.

She places her hands on the tablecloth in an exact imitation of Brad, lowers her chin, and states,

"You have been very frank with me, Mr. Oaks. Now, I shall be frank with you. This offer of ten million dollars is considerably higher than the offer Ms. June Elgar made."

Brad gulps. He leans back so far his chair nearly tips over. He cannot make his mouth work. Eventually, he manages to start, "How . . ."

"She contacted me two days ago and told me Father had died. She also said that the will gives me one-third of the steel business. But she told me that the steel business is failing, and is sure to collapse very soon. She said that the business is involved in a wicked project that her environmental organization will destroy. She said I should sell my shares for two million dollars cash and be well out of a messy situation."

Amaya frowns, leans forward, and lowers her voice to say, "She said that you want to use the company to make the wicked project succeed. Her story is different from your story. I do not wish to take sides in this family fight, but I also do not want to be treated unfairly. You have spoken fairly to me. Tomorrow morning, I meet with people I trust. Then, I want to hear your side of the story of the project. If she does destroy it, perhaps her offer was fair. But, if the project is not as wicked as she describes, and if it has some chance for success, then her offer was not fair. I try to surround myself in beauty and tranquility, not controversy. But I am not a fool."

A long, wordless pause follows. Amaya's eyes range between the tall windows and Brad's eyes. She then fixes her gaze on Brad, and says brightly,

"I have enjoyed meeting you and thank you very much for a delightful dinner. Especially, I thank you for being transparent with me about this business. I think I should go now. It will soon rain. Enjoy your evening. Please meet with me tomorrow morning at eleven thirty at my solicitors' offices."

She stands and hands Brad a slip of paper with the address and phone number of Wright and Haseo. She picks up the shopping bag, shakes Brad's hand, turns, and walks out of the restaurant.

As Ms. Mori leaves, Brad's lingering gaze is broken abruptly by another tempest, this one outside his mind. He watches lightning scorch the sky before it strikes Tokyo Tower, two and a half miles away. From the lofty, full-length windows of the Crowne dining room, he can see pedestrians lean and sidestep against the wind on sidewalks reflecting the incessant light show from overhead screens, and umbrellas bend and collide as the homeward commute becomes clogged in spray and blown leaves.

Brad enters his room just as the first curtain of driving rain slams and shakes the windows. The sounds of sirens rise from the street to be heard in the room. His room phone rings. He picks it up. "Yes, Ichiro? Look, I'm sorry I couldn't take your call earlier. You have my full attention now."

"Mr. Oaks, the ambassador will be briefing the White House on Monday on Wishbone. He wants to hear what you have been dancing around about. If you have anything substantive to say on the Wishbone Pipeline, he wants to hear it at six thirty in our conference room this Friday afternoon. If you catch one of the two flights departing Narita at three fifty-five, you'll get here just barely in time to make the meeting. We'll have people from State and EPA there. So, shall I tell him the meeting is on? This is your first and last shot at this, Mr. Oaks."

"I'll be there, Ichiro. I'll have a solid presentation that will knock everyone's socks off. It's sooner than I'd prefer, given the private business going on here, but you will hear the full proposal. And thank you. Please extend my warmest appreciation to the ambassador for this opportunity. By the way, do you know anything more about that shooting incident?"

"The working theory is that it was a lone gunman and that the ambassador was not the target. That's what the police say. The shooter was Asian and had yakuza tattoos on his back. You do lead a colorful life. Which flight will you be taking?"

Brad thinks a moment. "You know, Ichiro, I'm not telling anyone which of those two flights I'll be on."

"Good idea."

He thinks: *If I call Sarah Jane now, she'll be arranging the funeral service. Anyway, I can't be sure how secure any of the phones are.*

Instead, Brad calls the front desk. "Could you please connect me with the telex operator?" There is the sound of stifled giggles at the other end. "Mr. Oaks, you are wercome to use business center to send e-mail . . ."

"No, thank you. I mean an old-fashioned telex. Does the hotel have one, or did you throw it out when you tore down the old building ten years ago?" More giggles and "Juss moment prease." After several minutes, "Mr. Oaks-san, sorry for your waiting so long. Yes, we have. Prease come to front desk for assistance. Or operator can come to room if you want." He asks

45

that the assistant manager on duty come instead.

He pulls on his sweatpants and shirt, and he scrolls through his address book for the telex number he needs. Ernie Elgar had insisted on keeping the company's old telex operational. It is in the Security office, and someone is on duty there twenty-four seven. Next, he takes out a yellow pad and painstakingly hand-prints a message:

"To: Elgar Steel, Main Security. Urgent and Confidential. Immediate Action required. (AAA) Imperative ASAP you contact Exec VP S. J. Elgar and deliver this in person or by secure phone. (BBB) rattlesnake in vineyard. (CCC) Call me soonest and DISCREET. Regards, Oaks."

The night manager studies the message, makes chicken-track notes on it with a mechanical pencil, and nods. Brad looks directly in his eyes and says, "After it is sent, please call this room number, let it ring once, and hang up. Then, destroy this paper. Do not put a copy of the telex in my box at the front desk, or send one to my room, and do not keep any copies except what you absolutely have to keep for records, and keep that one completely confidential." The manager bows, gives Brad a solemn look of obedience, and says, "Yes, sir."

Brad fumbles for his phone. Four in the morning. It's Sarah Jane. "Hello?"

"Telex, Brad? Are you in a time warp there?"

Brad brings her up to date on Shin Steel, Amaya Mori's bombshell about June, and the yakuza identification of the shooter. He explains about the meeting with Ambassador Knight for Friday.

"Now we know why June was so adamant that I go to Washington instead of Tokyo. Sarah Jane, I knew your sister

46

was devious, but this is downright sabotage. My instinct is to do as much as I can here tomorrow with the Shin people and Ms. Mori. Then I'll go to Washington for that meeting. Unless you decide you want me to do something else."

After a long pause, Sarah Jane grunts, "Oh. Bad. Word." She sounds so much like her father, it's creepy. "No, you stay right with what you're doing and the way you're doing it. June told me she's going back to Toronto, and she's on the warpath to stop Wishbone. What do you think I should do?"

Brad thinks a moment. "For right now, go limp. Let her think you're exhausted or grief-stricken, and not functioning. Let her go to Toronto. Then, get with engineering and put together a knockout PowerPoint show for me to use at the USTR meeting. Make it look simple and safe and delicious. Who else is trying to make this pipe, do you think?"

Sarah Jane says, "The Canadians are for sure. I don't know who else. The Russians can make the steel plate, but they'd have to get it to a deep-draft port. There's a pipe mill in Iran, you know. Elgar designed and sold it to them forty years ago. Just before the revolution. Exact copy of one of ours. But the costs will kill them."

"OK, you think about that, and make me proud of that PowerPoint show. In fact, why don't you just plan to come to the meeting and present it yourself? I won't call you because I'll never know when you're private. So touch base every now and again."

"Thanks, Brad. What can you tell me about my new half sister?"

Brad stares toward the white wave crests in the windblown palace moat, eyes on an unfocused middle distance. "She is poised. She is sophisticated. Tastefully dressed. She had a surprisingly quick take on a complicated picture. I detected nothing about her to suggest she would gouge on pricing. In fact, I thought she behaved as though she were an actual part of the Elgar family, not just distantly related. I liked her."

"OK, a brainiac. Always better when you're negotiating with smart people. But is she pretty?"

Brad smiles. "Aren't all of Ernie's daughters pretty?"

"Come on, Brad. Did you take a picture of her?"

"Uh, no, Sarah, I did not ask her to pose for a photograph in the Crowne dining room as I walked her through our corporate finances."

"See if you can sometime. Catch her when she's not looking."

"Sarah? You're joking."

"No. Maybe. I'm just itching to know more."

"Sarah, I think you would like Amaya. I can't say I see a resemblance to Ernie or anything uncanny along those lines, but you and she have similar interests. Art, for example. By the way, she says she has seen the weathered steel sculpture of yours in the courtyard of the new Yamato Electronics building. Ernie had written to her about it. She goes there occasionally just to try to get some idea about you."

"What do you think of her? I read the stuff in Daddy's lacquered box. She sounds like she was a sweet kid. But now?"

Brad stares at the phone in front of him . . . *Keep it plain, simple, true.* "Sarah, I don't mind telling you that she is a very engaging woman. She is beautiful. At one point during dinner, I had to tell myself to focus on business. You know me well enough to know that I never need reminding of that. Ernie must have been proud of Amaya in every way. I think that you two would genuinely like each other. I'm glad to know Amaya Mori, but right now, I'm here to settle the ownership situation with her solely in your best interests. I want to wrap this up tomorrow—today—with her and her lawyers. Help me stay on track, please."

After a silence, Sarah Jane says, "OK, no more questions. Good luck. And . . . thanks, Brad. Keep doing what you do, and we'll survive all this. By the way, Brad, at least this sabotage, as you called it, tells us that what June said to you on the patio wasn't personal, just part of her plot."

"Could be, Sarah, but maybe both. I no longer feel I know your twin."

Friday morning, September 13, 2019; Tokyo

At nine forty-five Friday morning, two young men in black suits meet Brad at the security desk of Shin Steel's headquarters in the heart of downtown Tokyo, a block from Tokyo Station. They escort him to the ninth floor and into a huge, open room of pillars without walls, but only two enclosed offices. This is a typical Tokyo bull pen, a time-honored, life-size, three-dimensional organization chart in which clusters of departmental formations are laid out in communal desks. In each cluster, two rows of desks face each other in parallel rows, topped at one end by a desk at right angles to the two rows. There, a section chief sits. On each side sit, in descending order of rank, the entire staff of that department, down to the summer intern. Every document, purchase order, and memo put to the section chief first passes through the hands of everyone on staff. As it is passed up the line, each person stamps the document with a fingernail-sized chop in ink the color of Mercurochrome.

At the far wall of the bull pen, which holds some twenty of these clusters, Kichiro Saito, the CEO, and Hiwasaki sit in offices separated by a common conference room.

Nothing has changed in the bull pen or the conference room since the first time Brad sat there in 1990 with Ernie Elgar, his mentor in Japanese deals. By then, Shin Steel and Elgar had been working together for twenty-five years. It began when Elgar sold scrap steel from California as raw material for Shin's melting ovens. It continued during the bubble years of both countries, when Elgar was importing steel plate from Shin Steel as raw material for Elgar's fabricating and construction jobs. Over the years, Ernie and Saito had developed what would prove to be a lifelong friendship.

Saito makes a short bow to Brad and expresses condolences about the death of his old friend, Ernie Elgar. Brad tells Saito how much Elgar had admired him, and tells him that he hopes business relationships may continue. He slowly recounts for Saito the Wishbone opportunity and his offer that Shin Steel joint-venture with Elgar to manufacture pipe using steel plate from Shin.

Saito and Hiwasaki speak for several minutes in Japanese. Hiwasaki says, "Brad-san, you are very thorough, very candid. You always are. Because of that, you have credibility with Mr. Saito. We will need to confer with our colleagues. Mr. Saito would like to meet with you again on Monday morning with more of his team."

"Sake-cup, what I didn't say is that I am going from here straight to a meeting in Washington at the highest level, and I would like some kind of assurance on steel sourcing."

Hiwasaki blows out his cheeks, making a long exhale. He confers in Japanese with Saito. "Brad-san, it is impossible to give you such assurances on the spur of the moment. Meet again with us on Monday. You may say only that you are in preliminary discussions with us."

Brad stands and shakes hands with Saito. Hiwasaki walks with Brad through the bull pen. At the elevator, Hiwasaki says, "What about this new owner? The half sister you told me about?"

Brad says, "I think I can trust her. I meet with her and her people in twenty minutes. I need to ask another favor. Ask your travel department to make a reservation in first class for me to Washington on the flight I've jotted down here, leaving this afternoon. Here's a photocopy of my passport and credit card. I have to be circumspect about my movements."

Hiwasaki hurries back into the bull pen. When he returns, he says, "I will have my driver take you to your next meeting. Then he will return for me. I'll have your boarding pass, and I will drive with you to Narita."

In the black sedan with Shin Steel emblems on its rear doors, Brad's phone vibrates. He picks it up. "Sarah Jane, good timing. I've got a few minutes."

"I don't. June leaves for Toronto in the morning. I'm just about to join her in the living room. Where do we stand?"

Brad gives a succinct report. Sarah Jane says, "So far, very good. At least no one's kicked you out or ambushed you. I'm dying to know what's been going on between June and Ms. Mori, but right now, I gotta go."

CHAPTER FIVE

Thursday night, September 12, 2019; Napa

"Why don't we call Brad and see how it's going?" says June. June speaks slowly, as if consciously controlling a sense of urgency mingled with apprehension. She pours herself another glass of wine. It's been a hot day; June is barefoot in denim shorts and a Toronto Blue Jays jersey.

The tension is high in the room. These women are going to bury their father the very next day. Their mother is gone. Their family is smaller by half. They don't even count that it's up by a half sister. Their home seems hollow and empty.

Sarah Jane busily distributes bottles of cold mineral water and glasses to various tables, bookcases, and trays, not because she expects guests but because it is a pervasive habit of hers. Scattering mineral water around her surroundings is something she developed as a preteen. It is something she reverts to usually when she feels a certain level of tension building within her, unconsciously. The bubbles enliven her palate. The sensation helps her keep her thoughts a step ahead of the moment. It is now ingrained in her persona. With a glass in hand, she says,

"I just spoke to him. There's a typhoon there, and he's in his room with a bug of some kind. He still hasn't been able to see this Mori woman. Actually, he said that she acted very unfriendly on the phone, and he thinks she's stalling."

Sarah Jane puts down her paring knife and stares at her sister. "Why on earth would she be that way, do you suppose?"

June smirks with a mixture of relief and self-satisfaction.

Sarah Jane says, insistently, "Hard to figure, isn't it, June?"

June looks away and pushes her fingers through her hair in exaggerated annoyance. "The whole place is hard to figure. I don't see how Daddy could stand it there." She looks back with a broad smile. "Thanks for the update." June seems absolutely radiant.

Sarah Jane clenches her fist, immediately relaxes it, and reaches for another glass of mineral water. She says,

"But this also means that Brad can't get started in Washington on Wishbone anytime soon. I don't see why you need to go charging off to Toronto just now. I have to tell you, this whole thing is catching up with me, and I could use some support."

June natters as she sets the table, almost purring. "You'll be on your feet in a day or so and back to your steel business. That's more your family now than I am. And, to be perfectly frank, Canadian environmentalists are now my main family. No offense intended, but let's both be honest. Enjoy a couple more days of doing nothing, and then ease back into bending steel. Me, I prefer to lose myself in the work of saving the planet."

Sarah Jane shakes her head. She picks another from the inventory of mineral water glasses within reach. "June, I think you have already lost your compass in that work."

June puts her hands on her hips and leans over the kitchen island. "Why don't you just tell me what all the hush-hush is about? What does Brad have about the Wishbone Pipeline that no one else has thought of? What makes you think you can beat the odds? Or beat me?"

Sarah Jane pauses and shrugs. "You'll have to find your own way without a compass. If I tell you now, you'll find a way to use it against me. Show me we can work together, and I'll show you all the cards."

The twin sisters glare at each other in silence. Sarah Jane thinks, *June's on edge because she's living a lie, just standing here, chitchatting over a stock deal she has tried to kibosh and afraid Brad will find her out.*

Sarah Jane, furious and deeply hurt, stares at her very own sister, who is well on her way to dismantling her business and the jobs of Elgar's people. Only the knowledge that Brad is on the scene where it counts, and has uncovered June's deceit before it succeeded, keeps Sarah Jane from launching a two-fisted brawl with her twin. The unspoken, wrathful energy between them, if harnessed, could melt rock.

June tires of holding her scowl and says, "I'll give up my water rights in hell before I ever give in to this foul pipeline."

Sarah Jane utters a tired sigh. She says, "I need to say this, June, and you need to listen. The family is just you and me now. The troubles with the business and the world we're in are getting bigger. You and I can't afford to fight. We're twins, and we need more than ever before to be in the same skin."

"The world is bigger, Sarah Jane, but your world is shrinking along with the steel business. Without a husband and family, you'd have no way out if it weren't for your sculpture. Since you at least have sculpture, you do have a way to break out of it.

"I've broken out of the small world you're in with my environmental alliance. Don't ask me to shrivel in the pod that Elgar Steel will become when the Wishbone pipe dream is over. At least, don't expect me to do it. Yes, in a matter of hours, we say goodbye to Daddy. After that, you and I simply say goodbye, and we go our separate ways."

Sarah Jane finishes a glass of mineral water and says,

"No, we won't. You don't really believe that. Elgar Steel won't live or die on Wishbone alone. We'll survive without Wishbone. And you'll be a good do-gooder whether or not you bury Wishbone. We need each other more than ever now. We're never really alone, June, because we have each other."

"Sarah Jane, you're not alone because you have a steel business and a winery, and you get along with everyone who works in both. You'll never be alone whether you have real family or not. Well, maybe when it counts the most, in the night stillness. All those friends and no intimacy. You are some kind of special case. You know what you need, don't you?"

Sarah Jane carefully puts her empty water glass on a glass-topped table. She stands and places her hand on June's shoulder. She says,

"Twin, I can figure out what I need in the night stillness pretty well for myself. Can you? Do you know what you need?"

June blinks her eyes away and shrugs. Sarah says,

"You need a young buck Canadian to bang you wiggy, June."

"As in senseless?"

"Mmm, well, sure, per each. Spacey. I'm thinking prolonged, incessant, as in the gateway to madness."

After deliberation, "Wiggy works."

June shifts in her seat. Without turning, she says, "I'll always come back for the harvest and the crush at least. Speaking of which, why the hell can't this winery make a wine that real people can afford?"

"Like what real people?"

"Well, hell, I dunno. Like that young buck Canadian, I guess.

Don't you think?"

"Think about what, the wine or the buck?"

"Priorities, Sarah Jane. I have them; you don't. How young, would you say?"

"You, I figure for someone thirty years your junior."

"I can make that work. So, all right, since you have figured out my future, tell me about the one for you, twin."

"Not a young buck. Older and wiser for me. I like stability, intelligence, authenticity. That takes a while to steep."

"I can see that for you, S. J. Glad you didn't say Brad, at least. You have someone in mind?"

Sarah Jane picks up a nearby glass of mineral water, sips, and says,

"I'll admit you touched a nerve when you talked about the night . . . what is it? The night whatchamacallit."

"The night stillness," says June. "So, who do you have in mind?"

Sarah looks at her nails needing repair and says, "No one I know of right now. My mind is always on the horizon, is all I'll say. Nothing there that I can see. Yet. And you? Your eyes went distant just now; do you have someone in mind?"

"As you say, S. J., too soon to talk about. The mind is always at work, wiggywise. Anyway, we have other business tomorrow. How about hoisting a glass of bold red to Daddy?

"And another glass for the young buck in my future, and another for the old one in yours!"

Friday noon, September 13; Tokyo, the Law Offices of Wright and Haseo near Tokyo's Parliament building

The entry reception space of the suite of law offices is covered in wallpaper of pale green fiber, made from, but not immediately recognizable as, bamboo. There are no framed portraits of prominent lawyers, or cartoon etchings of British barristers by Spy, or French ones by Daumier, as in so many global law offices. Instead, the walls are adorned by pottery and porcelains from various eras of Japanese history. They rest on clear plastic shelves attached to the walls at random heights. Behind the receptionist is a divider wall holding a plastic case, in which hangs a kimono of striking light-blue-and-white asymmetric streaks throughout, like falling rain. Handmade by a Kyoto artist, Amaya Mori purchased it in 2014 to hang in this place.

Brad follows the receptionist down a carpeted hallway past offices curated by Ms. Mori to suit the individual tastes of each occupant. In this special way, she is almost a member of the firm.

Amaya Mori sits between Parker Wright and Kenji Haseo in a modest conference room when Brad is brought in. Amaya smiles at Brad as he sits down.

Parker Wright is the first to speak, in the BBC-announcer tones of a London solicitor, which he is.

"Mr. Oaks. Let me first say how much we appreciate the extensive corporate information you provided Ms. Mori to prepare for our meeting. Our client has asked us to proceed without antagonistic drama. I must say I am happy to do so. Actually, that's why I prefer the Tokyo office to our London and Los Angeles offices. We do have fangs, of course, but then so do you, so it serves neither of us to do a war dance."

Amaya beams. Haseo sits expressionless with his eyes closed.

Brad says, "That certainly suits me, but we all know that an absent party to this negotiation, June Elgar, is governed by her own agenda, which is in serious conflict with Elgar Steel. Let me be frank. If your client intends to ally with June Elgar, this negotiation will not be congenial. If your client intends to act in her own best interest without destroying Elgar Steel, our negotiation will be fair and amicable."

Wright says, "That is well said. Let me also disclose to you that we are solicitors for Sunrise Trading, and that company sometimes takes commercial positions in exporting steel products."

"Thank you for that disclosure. Does your firm, or does Sunrise, have ties to Russian steel interests?"

"No."

"Does your firm, or does Sunrise, have dealings with Shin Steel?"

Mr. Haseo's eyes open. He clears his throat and says, "No. But Sunrise Trading has wanted to do business with Shin Steel for decades. Why do you mention them, Mr. Oaks?"

"Elgar Steel has a very solid relationship with Shin Steel. Does Ms. Mori have a financial interest in Sunrise Trading?"

Wright steeples his fingers, frowns, and says, "That is not really germane—"

Amaya puts up her hand and says, "Yes, I do. And I assume you know that already if you have looked into my background. My mother was a foster child in the family that was part owner of Sunrise Trading. Ancestors of her foster parents helped found the company. In 2011, they were both tragically killed in the Tohoku earthquake. I have inherited their stock in Sunrise.

Although it is a minority interest, last year, I was invited to join their board of directors. It is an honor to serve in that capacity. Few women in Japan do so. Now, if that is germane to our discussions, please explain how. Otherwise let's move on."

Brad lowers his head slightly as he says, "Ms. Mori, I knew only of the family ties, but not of any financial stake. That is why I asked the question. And the reason it is germane is that Elgar Steel and Shin Steel are considering a joint venture to supply pipe to the project that June Elgar is so opposed to. I believe that the joint venture would benefit greatly from an association with Sunrise Trading. If our discussions here go well, I believe I can help make that happen."

Haseo nods. Amaya says, "Then tell us about this joint venture."

Brad carefully reviews the past dealings between Elgar and Shin. He explains the Wishbone Pipeline project and its current status. He tells them his idea on how to revive the project. Then, he explains the plan he and Hiwasaki are talking about for Shin Steel and Elgar Steel to join forces in manufacturing the pipe.

Amaya Mori finishes writing in her notebook and looks up. "Mr. Oaks, is there no way to reconcile my sisters?"

Brad exhales and pauses. Then he says, with a slight shrug and a smile,

"They are at opposite poles on Wishbone. My idea should overcome the main environmental objections, but that doesn't mean it will overcome her efforts to defeat it. It may be enough to satisfy the US government, but not enough to satisfy June Elgar."

"Well, Mr. Oaks, how can your joint venture possibly succeed if they are not reconciled?"

Brad glances quickly at Parker Wright and says, "June is not a director." Wright gives an acknowledging nod. Brad's eyes return to Ms. Mori, and he says,

"She owns one-third of the company, the same as you. As a minority shareholder, she can do nothing to alter Elgar's regular business plans."

"Mr. Oaks, with such animosity between my sisters, Elgar Steel could never be a happy ship. Allow me a word with my solicitors."

When they reseat themselves, Parker Wright stands, arches his brows, and says, "Our client has made her decision. She accepts the price put forward by Ms. June Elgar, but she shall not sell her shares." He pauses. Amaya's face is impassive.

"Instead, she shall purchase one-third of the company from the Elgar sisters, one-sixth from each, as the will stipulates. For the price of two million dollars, as nominated by Ms. June Elgar, Amaya Mori shall become the sixty-seven percent controlling shareholder of Elgar Steel."

"Don't look so crestfallen, Mr. Oaks," Amaya Mori says after a long silence.

Brad is thinking through the options. Litigation over whether June's oral offer was meant to be under the will or as June's private deal would take years. Besides, she must have some evidence on that, or else they're bluffing. Could I get an injunction? I've got the grounds—it would cause us irreparable harm. But that gives us only a temporary stay while they fight the she-said-she-said battle. That would send a signal of weakness to Washington and to Shin Steel. Time favors their bluff, even if it is only that.

He looks at his watch. He must leave for Narita in ten minutes. He has come away from Shin Steel nearly empty-handed. It seems he will come away from Ms. Mori having lost control of the company for a fraction of its value. He considers changing his flight plans to Timbuktu. Instead he says, "I came here in good faith . . ."

"As did I, Mr. Oaks," says Ms. Mori. Her face softens slightly as she releases tightness in her jaw. She looks down and away and brushes the nape of her neck with the fingers of her left hand. She says,

"There's more, so hear me out. I do not wish to destroy Elgar Steel. It is not in my nature, and it does not serve my interests. I owe my birth father my loyalty and devotion. He nurtured this business, and he nurtured me in the only way he could, through financial support. But my Elgar sisters will destroy his company. So I will take over control, at least until it gains the Wishbone business. How long would that be?"

"No time very soon. There is so much red tape. But with the price of oil inflating at the current rate, I think the owners of the project will start within a couple of years—three or four at the outside."

Ms. Mori lifts her eyebrows. "The business you conduct has such timelines? How do you possibly foresee its direction? That must explain your earnestness, Mr. Oaks. So, in that case, we'll call it five years. If there is no Wishbone after five years, I shall sell all my stock back to my sisters. How do you call it, Parker?"

Wright says, "A 'put'; a firm option on your part to require them to buy the stock."

"Yes, that's it—'put.' A droll expression. And they will pay me twelve million dollars. That's the two-million price June put on it, and the ten-million price you put on it.

"But if in those five years, Elgar does start making Wishbone pipe, then things will be different. After that, the sisters may buy me out entirely for a fair price." She sits quietly, assessing his reaction. She smiles and says, "Color has returned to your cheeks, Mr. Oaks."

"I need assurances."

Ms. Mori lets a breath escape her now-tightening lips. "I expect to be believed at times like this, Mr. Oaks. Nevertheless, here is a written summary of my position, which I have signed. In this envelope is a duplicate tape of my telephone conversation with Ms. June Elgar. I know that you might use that against me as well as against her. I believe those should be sufficient gestures of good faith. In addition to my words at this meeting."

Brad says, "I want a written proxy giving Sarah Jane power to vote Ms. Mori's shares."

Ms. Mori says evenly, "After I have received my stock, I shall give her my proxy."

Brad sees the risk but has no leverage to insist on more assurance than she has already provided. More to the point, though, he has no heart to display lack of trust in her words. The lawyer in him might insist, but something else in him—something about her he's beginning to feel—guides his decision to take her at her word. He does not break the hold of their gaze. She exhales and finally looks down and away. The strength of her negotiating position gives way to a look of acquiescence. Between them, it is not a draw, as a casual observer might conclude. It is a win for each.

She extends her hand and says, "Have a fruitful meeting in Washington. I hope we may dine again soon."

Brad holds her hand in his for a momentary eternity, smiles, and says, "I assure you I will look forward to that as well."

On the drive to Narita, Hiwasaki shakes his head and says, "Brad-san, this is getting too complicated and too risky. Saito-san is already worried about the situation with Mr. Elgar gone. And now . . . well, I just don't know. What shall I tell him?"

Brad drums his fingers on the car's armrest a moment. Then he says, "Well, if we remove the uncertainty from it, and have a unified ownership, would Saito be onboard?"

"I think so. The Sunrise Trading angle is interesting to him. We have been locked into Ginko Trading for so many years, they are getting complacent. It would be good to shake things up. But I don't want to discuss with Saito-san until you clear up ownership and can report good progress in Washington."

Brad nods and says, "Sake-cup, I'm keeping my room at the hotel. I'll be back in a couple of days. Here's a key. I want it to look like it's been used every night. Do you think you could go over there and muss up the bed? And please send a telex—yes, the old noisy telex—to Sarah Jane Elgar at the plant. I know Shin Steel has the telex number. Tell her in the telex: 'Will meet at hitching post when I get off my horse.'" Hiwasaki rolls his eyes and laughs. Brad is not laughing.

Friday morning, September 13, 2019; Washington, D.C.

"Thank you for taking the time to see me, Ambassador Knight." Alden Knight reseats himself after shaking hands with the uniformed police officer who sits across from his desk.

"You're welcome, Detective Quinn. I'm happy to help if I can. But I think I told you everything that night right after it happened."

"Yes, sir, but now we're looking more into a possible motive. We're sure that you were not the target and that Brad Oaks was. He's an executive with Elgar Steel. I know you two talked briefly in the reception line. Could you please tell me more of what you know about him or his company?"

Knight shrugs and purses his lips. "Sure. Well, he didn't say much except he had a plan connected with the Wishbone Pipeline. He wanted to meet the next day to go over details, but I still don't know what they are. His company would, of course, benefit greatly from that project. They are one of only a very few who can manufacture the right kind of pipe."

"The man who shot at him was heavily tattooed, and one of those tattoos indicates ties to the Japanese mafia. Any idea why they might have it in for Mr. Oaks?"

Knight shakes his head and turns to his assistant. "Ichiro, any ideas on that?"

"May I have a look at the tattoos?" says Ichiro. He studies the glossy photographs produced by Quinn. Then he points to one, different from the one Quinn had pointed to.

"This one is very bad news. They are in Tokyo, small and despised by all. They aren't one of the historic Japanese yakuza clans. They are the outcasts of the outcasts. They deal in contraband and arms. I think they have ties in the Middle East."

"Bad news, indeed," says Knight. "But what's it got to do with steel pipe?"

Quinn says, "That will take some looking into. I'll pass this on to my contact in Tokyo. The attempt on Brad Oaks has to be something business related, I think. Oaks has a clean record. Nothing in the way of bad-blood personal relationships as far as we know. What part of the Middle East?"

Ichiro says, "I'm not sure. I'll have to look into that, too. Part of me wants to say Iran."

Knight grunts and says, "More bad news. Ichiro, find out if Iran has any pipe-making capacity. Elgar Steel is looking better and better here—get on to Oaks and have him bring his CEO to our meeting tomorrow. Oh, and Detective Quinn, I'm told there's been no work using those State Department scaffolds for three years now. Why are they still there?"

Patricia Quinn gives him a wry smile as she leaves. "They're still getting back to me on that."

Knight says, "Ichiro, Rod Graham's the head Fred at Wishbone. Houston. Raise him on the phone for me, would you?"

Rod Graham, the sixty-year-old chairman of Trans-Rocky Pipeline, owner of the Wishbone project, leans back in his cowhide chair the color of caramel and stares at the Houston cityscape outside his suite at the top of the JP Morgan Chase Tower.

"Well, Alden, it is good to talk to you. I hear you've taken up residence inside the Beltway. You-all won the election, and you need money again so soon? . . . Not about money this time? It's never not about money, Alden . . .

"Oh, they're fine, thanks. Well, not including Rita. You don't have kids, do you, Alden?"

"No kids, Rod. Widower for ten years now."

"Right. I'm real sorry for your loss. Well, there's only one thing worse than being the parent of a teenager, and that's being the parent of a twenty-five-year-old who thinks she's an adult but acts on the impulses of a sixteen-year-old. Rita got herself in with a bad crowd, and—"

Knight breaks in, "Look, Rod, you don't have to bring out dirty laundry on my account . . ."

"Not a problem for me, Alden. Anyway, that's about all there is to it. Had to get her out of a jam with a bunch of hotheads in town. One of them even worked here in the mail room. Was seeing Rita. Bailed her *and* him out of jail on possession charges. Now *that* was about money. Anyway, he's long gone now, and Rita's at the Betty Ford Center . . . Well, thanks, I know you are. So what's on your mind . . . ? Wishbone? Near and dear to my heart. What's up?"

Rod Graham listens carefully to Knight's report on the State Department incident and the vague links to Elgar Steel and possibly Iran. He says,

"OK, thanks for the update. I wish I could be at that meeting, or at least be a fly on the wall. You'll like the Elgar folks; they're straight shooters. They're known for consistently high-quality pipe delivered on time. But just remember, it's no sure thing how much they would supply to Wishbone. In the first place, they'd be competing with a blue-ribbon pipe maker in Canada. Of course, we'd welcome strong competition between them. With Elgar in the game, we'd have two solid sources. And there'd be business for both of them, plus we wouldn't have to go to an offshore mill . . . No, I don't have any particular offshore mill in mind. I'm just saying . . . Yes, I think it's fair to say the Canadian mill is probably the top contender, with Elgar a close second . . . Yes, he died a couple of days ago. Well, his daughter, Sarah Jane, has been head of operations, but his other daughter is trying to stop Wishbone . . . June Elgar . . . Yes, *that* June Elgar. Go figure . . . Yes, it's a hell of a messy situation . . . Right, if there's no Elgar Steel in the picture, we'd be buying from the Canadian mill and a bunch of foreign suppliers from all over the place . . . Well, you've got me curious about what this new thing is they've cooked up . . . OK, I'd appreciate a call. Next week sometime? Good."

A taffy-colored, '78 Chevrolet Caprice rolls to a stop at a dark space along the curb of the K Street corridor in Washington, D.C. The street is empty at this hour, four o'clock on a Thursday morning. Its driver wears black pants, a starched white work shirt with a pocket logo reading Manly Maids, a blue linen full-length apron, and blue latex gloves.

He walks to the rear of a building along an alley that is too cluttered and narrow to admit passage of a Chevy Caprice. He punches a keyboard at the rear door, his head turned away from a fixed security camera, admits himself, and closes the door. He uses an interior keypad to clear the building's alarm system and proceeds to a supply room where he collects a rolling cart with a trash receptacle and cleaning supplies. He takes the service elevator to the fifth floor and rolls the cart past a series of locked office doors until he reaches the one with a slip-in frame holding the business card of "Elgar Steel, Brad Oaks, General Counsel." A service key allows him entry into the office. A penlight in one hand, with the other he carefully turns over each envelope of mail and each pink "While You Were Out" telephone message form. Although there is little change from the day before, as anticipated, the man is methodical in his examination and the photographing. There is no envelope this morning he deems necessary to invade with stealth. He dusts the flat surfaces of the desk, the bookcase, and the tops of the picture frames holding images of the water's edge along the Napa River, California. The man is aware that the occupant is erratic in his use of the office, but the ritual examination will continue on a daily basis just because the path to justice brooks no deviation from ritual. He reverses his movements, his keypad attentions, and his slow walk to the Caprice, which finally comes to life after three painfully impotent cranks of the starter.

CHAPTER SIX

Friday afternoon, September 13, 2019; Washington, D.C.

Brad and Sarah Jane meet at the Washington Flier taxi dispatcher's desk at Dulles airport after Brad clears customs. It will take the taxi forty-five minutes to arrive at the USTR offices, across the street from the Old Executive Office Building, a block from the White House. Bushed from his endless day (dawn on Saturday is breaking in Tokyo), Brad dozes, his head slumped against the shoulder of his chief executive officer.

A yellowish 1978 Chevrolet Caprice pulls behind the Washington Flier taxi as it rolls past the short-term parking lot. The same Caprice parks illegally near the Farragut West Metro Station escalator as the taxi stops in front of the building where the US trade representative's office is located. The driver of the Caprice allows the car to idle, black exhaust smoke sputtering as moisture continues to attack the rim of the car's exhaust pipes. The driver is proud that his own nephew has provided the flight number for Ms. Elgar and the information that an airport rendezvous would take place. Perhaps the otherwise puerile nephew proves useful.

Ichiro meets Brad and Sarah Jane at the front desk of the USTR office suite and ushers them into the conference room. Brad introduces Sarah Jane to Alden Knight, who introduces them to officials from the Department of Commerce, the EPA, and the State Department.

Knight says to her, "Rod Graham sends his regards to you. He told me you're good people, and I like that."

Sarah Jane connects her flash drive to the laptop set up to run her PowerPoint slides and begins her presentation on Elgar Steel's long history of pipe making. Next, she shows photographs of a construction site where large-diameter pipe is stacked neatly in small pyramids by the rail spur.

Knight says, "Ms. Elgar, I hear you're a welder. Have you gone down in one of those trenches?"

Sarah Jane's eyes twinkle, and she says, "Mr. Ambassador, my pipe-welding days are behind me. I've welded on the plant floor, and, yes, my father insisted I work for a summer on a job site, in the trench, connecting up those pipe sections. These days, I weld outdoor sculptures. But the techniques are pretty much the same."

Knight fills a pause in the conversation with, "What did you learn on that job, Ms. Elgar?"

Sarah Jane looks into Knight's eyes for a long, thoughtful moment. Finally she says, slowly, in a level voice:

"That welders vote."

The room is quiet. The woman from the White House breaks the silence with rapid taps on her laptop's keyboard.

Knight replies, "I never thought I'd give a damn about how you make a pipeline. Now, I have to tell you I'm real interested in finding out more."

He turns to Brad. "All right, Oaks, it's your show now. What is it you have to tell us? And tell us what I've been trying to figure out since I first met you."

"What the hell is it you *want*?"

Brad says, "Water."

Ichiro starts to hand him a bottle of water.

Brad puts up his hand and says, "Not a bottle of water. A whole aquifer of water." Ichiro sits down quickly.

Sarah Jane switches to a second set of slides. On the wall screen appears a map of Western America and Western Canada, superimposed with a graphic of the Wishbone Pipeline route.

Brad says, "Every conversation about Wishbone comes to a screeching halt at the question, 'What's in it for America?' Everyone in this room knows that the construction jobs will go away after the pipeline is put in service. The best estimate of permanent American jobs is fifty. The environmental objections have been studied to death, and, on balance, well answered in favor of Wishbone. But, then it comes back to, 'What's in it for us?'

"Well, the answer is water. Water gathered from glacial and snowpack sources in Western Canada. That water is unused there and is needed here, in the grain fields and ranges of Nebraska, Kansas, and Oklahoma.

"Every year, the Ogallala Aquifer that underlies those states is mined for irrigation, and every year, that ancient water resource is further depleted—over the years, by enough to fill Lake Erie, as our former CEO once calculated. That depletion is irreversible. That is the real environmental disaster, not some pipeline spill."

Sarah Jane clicks to the next slide that shows the same map, but with a second pipeline running parallel to the Wishbone line.

Brad continues, "This is a 'loop,' a second pipeline running along the same right of way, indeed in the same construction trench, and installed with the same equipment and crew as the first one. The incremental cost of the second line is a fraction of what it would cost by itself. The second line usually carries the same oil or gas as the first one."

Brad moves in front of the screen so that the beam of light with shadowing pictures covers his body. He says,

"Except, the second pipeline in Wishbone won't carry oil. It'll carry . . . *water*."

He steps to one side again and points to the screen. "The first pipeline carries Canadian oil to Gulf Coast ports to be exported—with nothing in it but risk for America. The second pipeline carries Canadian water to our nation's breadbasket for agricultural and other uses. And it relieves some of the strain on the Ogallala Aquifer by reducing the rate of its depletion. Now, there's something in it for America." He pauses, and this time, he does take a sip of water.

A hand goes up. "Sanderson, EPA. Tell me the answer to the potential pollution of the Ogallala Aquifer you claim to protect?"

Brad says, "Let me answer that. The first and most important point is that the Ogallala Aquifer is not some underground lake of water. It is more like a porous sponge made of sand and gravel, with water saturating its cells. One author says the 'aquifer is wet dirt.' Moreover, most of that sponge lies to the west of the Wishbone route, and it tilts uphill to the west, *away* from the pipeline route. That means that an oil spill would be isolated and contained naturally by geology."

Sanderson continues, "Then by that same logic, the Canadian water can't be injected back into the ground and be expected to flow uphill into the aquifer, right?"

Brad nods. "You're right, but that's not how it would work. The Wishbone water line would bring water for current and future *use*, not storage in the aquifer."

Another hand goes up; a woman in a sleeveless red dress

71

and black patent pumps. She says,

"Le Claire, State Department. What about the politics? Canada has its own grain belt, and that makes up a substantial chunk of its trade balance. This would be helping their competitors."

Brad responds, "That's why I brought this to Ambassador Knight in the first place. It is a huge international deal. The potential benefits to the US are staggering in terms of the desperate water deficit in the Midwest. It would even serve as a precedent for future deals to bring water to the far west."

Knight says, "Your confidence in my deal-making ability is humbling. But I take your point. Normally, this Wishbone project is not my table. This is intriguing. Wishbone suddenly is a larger transaction. The pipeline is just an implementing detail."

Knight stands and says, "All right, I want to have a private meeting with the Elgar folks. I want everyone to understand that the information we've discussed here today is embargoed until I take it to the president. If it's leaked, I'll be relentless. But for the moment, Wishbone is theoretically in play."

After the room clears, Knight says, "Ms. Elgar, Mr. Oaks, you've given us a lot to chew on. This puts a whole new light on the subject. I can't speak for the president, but I like the ingenuity and potential. Brad, you weren't far off when you compared it to the purchase of Alaska—forever known as Seward's Folly. Is this one folly? That's what the White House will need to figure out. But first, I've got a few questions about Elgar Steel."

Sarah Jane says, "That's entirely understandable. I am the senior officer of Elgar. I'm in negotiations with a minority shareholder for proxies to make me the controlling shareholder.

When I finish, we will be united. We'll be competitive if given the chance to bid on Wishbone pipe, and committed to fulfillment of any orders we receive."

Knight says, "OK, that's critical. But there's something else I want to talk about. The man who shot at Brad the other day may have had Iranian connections. I'm unclear how they might fit in an American pipeline project. What can you tell me about that?"

Sarah Jane says, "Well, we haven't seen them in the market at all. They have capacity to build their own pipe. In fact, back in the mid-seventies, before the revolution, Elgar sold them a complete pipe mill. If it's been maintained, those things last forever. We're still using the one that the Iranian mill was based on. But even assuming all that, the costs for them to manufacture and deliver the pipe to the job site would be brutal."

Knight grunts. "Could they be competitive with you and the Canadians?"

"No way in hell," says Sarah Jane.

Knight says, "There's something here we're missing. OK, my next question is this: Do you think your sister could have anything to do with the attempt on Brad's life?"

Sarah Jane thinks for a moment. "No. Putting aside that I don't think June is capable of harming Brad or me, she's after the defeat of Wishbone altogether, not just one supplier. Working with Iran does nothing for her objectives, and collateral losses to Elgar hurt her just as much as me. But I'm wondering if I should warn her. She doesn't know the specifics of our business plan on Wishbone or joint-venturing with Shin Steel. I hate to give her all that information, but I think I have to warn her."

Brad says, "I'll talk to Detective Quinn and get her to put the fear of God into June without getting into any of that."

Ichiro steps halfway through the door and asks, "Sorry to interrupt, but should I order up dinners for three?"

Knight rises and says, "Um . . . no, thanks." He glances at Sarah Jane. "Will you excuse me for a moment? I need something from the other room."

When Knight leaves the room, Sarah Jane tugs on Brad's arm and leans to whisper in his ear, "Is he . . . ?" "Widower," he whispers back.

"Live around here?"

"He has a condo out on Connecticut Avenue. His home has always been in Los Angeles. That's where he practiced law." Brad straightens up.

Knight returns with a raincoat over his elbow. "Let's do this. Ichiro, call over to the University Club for a table for three."

Brad shakes his head and says, "You know, I haven't been in a bed for two days. Tomorrow, I turn around and go back to Tokyo to follow up with Shin Steel. If it's all the same to you, just make it a table for two. I'd like to go to the hotel and crash."

Sarah Jane says quickly, "Sure, Brad, you're out of gas. We'll pick this up at breakfast. And yes, I'm happy to join you for dinner at your club, Mr. Ambassador."

Knight puts on his coat, nods quickly to Ichiro, and motions everyone to the door before anyone changes her mind.

The driver of the idling Caprice captures in a single glance that the movements at the building's entrance present him with the horns of a dilemma. Oaks, carrying luggage for two, stands at the curb, arm extended, simultaneously hailing a cab and waving goodbye to a man and a woman who turn to walk north on Seventeenth Street. The driver, who had nodded off briefly in the idling Caprice, fights indecision and then pulls away to pursue his impulsive last-minute choice. Within seconds, he realizes his mistake as the couple on foot turn right on I Street (or Eye Street as it is sometimes written), which is one-way in the opposite direction for the Caprice. The cars behind the Caprice begin to honk relentlessly, as they are now blocked from moving ahead through the green light. The cab carrying Oaks, however, moves out of sight briskly in the opposite direction on Seventeenth. The Caprice, hopelessly ensnared in downtown gridlock, has no possibility of following in either direction.

The path to justice is often gridlocked and potholed, the driver tells himself, looking away from rude gestures unbecoming of Washington office commuters.

Sunday night, September 15, 2019; Tokyo

This time, Brad does not end his flight in a Narita hotel bed on Sunday evening, but instead pushes on to Tokyo Station, and walks in thick, humid air to the Palace Hotel. His room is fresh and inviting. Someone—Hiwasaki, no doubt—has placed a graceful orchid on the desk, next to today's *Japan Times*. He glances at the domestic headlines, the international market indexes, and studies the concert listings on the back page. Gil Shaham plays tomorrow, the Bach solo violin sonatas—all of them. What a treat. When he phones to the concierge for two tickets, he's told, "There's an envelope for you at the front desk. Shall I send it to your room? Very well. You're welcome."

Brad blinks at June Elgar's handwritten note on Okura Hotel stationery, today's date, and reads it again.

"It's been damn near a week that you've been over here, and from what I can tell, you've made no progress. I'm here to fix that. I can't get this Mori woman to return calls. I want you to set up a meeting with her. Me and her, I don't need you. You can then go back to bed or whatever you do in Tokyo. Call me at the Okura."

Brad thinks, *Did Quinn ever talk to her?* Probably not. So, rather than the comfort-food room service supper he had longed for, Brad dresses and takes the elevator to the arcade level, below the ground floor. He walks past the stores to the subway entrance. There, he picks up a public phone, calls the Okura, and asks for June Elgar.

"Quick response, Brad, thanks for that. Look, I was about to go to bed. I'm exhausted. Let's meet tomorrow."

"June, I have to see you tonight. It can't wait. You could be in danger . . . I mean it, June. Meet me in the Chinese restaurant in your hotel in half an hour. The Toh-Ka-Lin . . . Yes, dammit, I'm tired too . . . really, really tired . . . I'll tell you when I see you." He then climbs the stairs to street level and hails a cab.

June fumes as she changes for dinner. *I need this lawyer away from me. It's all I can do to stay on course in the middle of all this . . . I need to be alone now. I need him away. Anywhere else but here. Anywhere else but Tokyo. Lawyers!*

Saturday, September 14, 2019; aloft

Sarah Jane is in the air, bound for a meeting at the plant in Stockton she has called for this afternoon. She jots down thoughts in her notebook. *No specs yet. Water pipe diameter? Maybe sixty inches. Production estimates. Production schedule. Guesswork. Long shots.*

She looks out her window at the quilt-patterned mile

sections of western wheat lands. Rich green fields in perfect circles fill most of the dirt-brown squares. *Irrigation from those deep wells into the aquifer,* she thinks. *I've been seeing those circles from airplanes with Daddy since I was a little girl.*

Daddy, I get it now. There in the center of each of those circles is a well pipe and pump into wet dirt from the Rocky Mountains in some ice age before California was a landmass. You told us about this stuff, and it went over me or past me or somewhere except in my brain. I get it now. I get how farmers have mined ancient glacial waters. I don't get how you became involved. You were in your teens when you worked summer jobs testing well water. You and your buddy whose name I've forgotten.

You wanted to bring Canadian water to Southern California, cockeyed but something that I could understand. But now, it's to be western Kansas. OK, Daddy, we'll do our best. Maybe we can make some pipe, make some money, and do some good.

Daddy, to June you were randy. I know you just as my daddy and mentor and hero. I've met a man like you. He's also an internationalist, and smart. He draws out my best thinking. Very genuine. I wonder if Ambassador Alden Knight is randy? What the hell is that about, Sarah Jane? What do you care if he is? What's on your mind? You shouldn't take wine at this altitude.

"Could I have a glass of Chardonnay, please, miss?"

Sunday night, September 15, 2019; Tokyo

Toh-Ka-Lin opened when the Okura was the new showcase hotel at the 1964 Summer Olympics, just a few blocks from the American embassy. Throughout the hotel's later renovations and building of a new annex, the restaurant remained the preeminent Chinese restaurant in Tokyo, and, in Brad's experience, anywhere. Ernie Elgar had introduced him to it, thus spoiling forever his tolerance for Chinese eateries or takeouts in the US.

June joins him, looking ridiculous in a blood-orange kimono built for Western tastes and sold at an arcade shop below the main floor of the Okura. Against her neck hangs a jade teardrop pendant in a gold setting.

The first thing Brad tells her is about the attack on him at the State Department, the connection with Iran and the Japanese underworld, and their possible motive for harming Elgar Steel people. Her stubborn resistance forces Brad to go through several reiterations before June begins to acknowledge that she could be in danger. Brad gives her the phone numbers of Detective Quinn and her contact at the Tokyo Metropolitan Police. She stuffs them in her bag with a shrug of disbelief. "You just want me out of Tokyo so I can't finish what I started with my new Japanese sister. It won't work. I'm here to do what you haven't been able to even start," she says with a smirk.

Brad decides not to explain to her where the bidding stands on Amaya Mori's stock, or about the meeting with the USTR. It's clear to him that Amaya Mori has succeeded in avoiding June, and that has to be good enough for now. He prefers leaving June in the dark to telling her what would only incite greater animus toward him or Sarah Jane.

He shrugs and says, "You've wasted a trip to Tokyo, June. Why don't you go home, or maybe go see the sights in Kyoto? Or, even better, you and I could join forces and approach her on a unified basis." June laughs at that suggestion and twists her pendant.

"You think small, Brad. Always have. I'll have to do this myself, as usual. I'll see you around the Ginza. Thanks for the Peking duck."

Brad pays the bill in cash, and asks the maître d' if he can make a call from the desk phone.

"Mushi-mushi?"

"Amaya, this is Brad Oaks. Sorry to disturb you at home on a Sunday night . . ."

Amaya runs her fingers through her hair as if expecting him to appear at her door. "Brad! Oh, how good of you to call. I am glad to hear your voice. When—"

"Great to hear yours—"

"—did you get in? No, go ahead. Sorry. How—"

"Just today, actually, I called as soon—"

"—did it go? I've been hoping—"

"It went very well . . . hoping? That's good. For what?"

"Your call. Your return to Tokyo."

"For the business?"

"Whose?"

"Well, Elgar's, I suppose—"

"There is mine, of course—"

"Which has always been wonderful."

"How do you . . . ?"

"Look . . ."

". . . Know it has?"

"No?"

"It *has*, you know."

"We should catch up . . ."

"On the meeting, yes."

"Well, look, I have to catch you up on the meeting. I have a couple of tickets to Gil Shaham . . ."

"At the Suntory? The Bach? I saw in the paper and was thinking . . ."

"Yes, the Bach sonatas. Tomorrow night. Where—"

"I want to hear you. And him. The Bach. The meetings. *Anything.*"

"—should I pick you up?"

"There. I mean I'll meet you there. I'm not a pickup, Brad."

"I didn't mean . . ."

Amaya smiles at herself in a wall mirror with sparkling eyes. "It starts at seven thirty, Brad, so shall we say . . ."

"Five. Let's say five."

"It will not be open at five, Brad. Meet me by will call at six fifty-five."

"All right. At six thirty."

Amaya reaches her left arm out, palm up. "Yes, six thirty. Best idea."

CHAPTER SEVEN

Monday morning, September 16, 2019; Washington, D.C.

Ichiro pushes open the door to Ambassador Knight's office. He enters carrying a stained, tan file folder and says, "Do you have time to talk about pipe making in Iran?"

"I head over to the White House in ten minutes. What's the bottom line?"

"The export license file is very complete up to the time of shipment in 1976. CIA takes it from there. They've determined that the mill is undamaged and has been producing sporadically again since about 1983. I'm guessing they didn't have the right personnel in place until then. The purges, you remember. There's been no export of pipes up until late this summer. Then, they made twelve pipes to the same specs as Wishbone would be, and shipped them on a chartered vessel to New Orleans.

"The pipe cleared customs there and headed upriver by barge to Dubuque. It's due there any day now. That routing would serve the southern parts of Wishbone. We're thinking it's a test run. The freight and customs paperwork were all handled by Iron Dragon Trading, Tokyo. They're connected to the same yakuza clan as that tattoo. I'd say that they're definitely gearing up to tender bids on Wishbone if it goes. And I'd say they're stacking the deck."

Monday morning, September 16, 2019; Tokyo

Once again, Brad is escorted to the conference room at the far end of the ninth-floor bull pen of Shin Steel. Lying between two, ten-by-ten-foot walled executive offices, the conference room is as wide as four such offices and could be subdivided accordingly. The room doubles as a smoking room for the bull pen, so the oversized air-handling units exert extra effort, and noise. Long conferences among smoking and nonsmoking businessmen, who are usually Americans, give Shin Steel a decided home-field advantage. At the far end of the room, to the right of its doorway, stands a six-foot-high mahogany case with asymmetrical shelves along the left-hand side and a large open space beside it. A scroll hangs in the open space, with calligraphy and a maple tree freely drawn in thick brushstrokes of black ink and decorated in crimson leaves veined in brownish gold. At the base of the scroll, on the adjacent shelf, stands a pristine white porcelain vase holding a spray of freshly gathered maple branches with leaves that seem to flow from the scroll to the vase and back again. The case and its display echo the home decor of a classic Japanese interior feature, the tokonoma, which is meant to greet and honor distinguished visitors.

Had the meeting occurred in the conference room at Shin's main steel mill, located near Osaka, the visitor would have seen a much larger tokonoma, at the base of which would have been a reflecting pool containing very large koi swimming in clear water recycled from the steelmaking plant, always the pride of the works manager explaining environmental controls to his visitors.

The conference table has been pushed against the window wall to allow space (but not much) for foot traffic.

At ten o'clock, Saito, Hiwasaki, and a dozen Shin Steel executives from finance, production, transportation, and sales file into the room. All but Brad quickly go through an elaborate exchange of bows. Each bow is carefully calibrated according to rank, age, and gender in a protocol taught and nurtured from childhood. It is incomprehensible to a foreign businessman. Savvy foreigners concede their ignorance and simply don't attempt the ritual. The other ones try but display only their ignorance. Business cards, or *meishi,* are exchanged between the Shin executives and Brad. Importantly, each *meishi* is presented and received with both hands. Brad follows this etiquette. They then sit at the conference table. An interpreter translates into English Mr. Saito's long and occasionally emotional eulogy of Ernie Elgar and recounting of the business history of the two companies. Then, she translates into Japanese Brad's response,

"What I am about to tell you is business-confidential. I am here to lay the groundwork for a major purchase of Shin steel plates by Elgar Steel to fabricate into pipe for two thousand miles of the proposed Wishbone oil pipeline in America. This order might, just *might,* be doubled by a second pipeline for water, and that line could be up to sixty inches in diameter. There are other steelmakers interested in this project, maybe the Russians."

At this, the room goes into a buzz immediately, and dies down. The interpreter restates it in Japanese, and again there is a buzz. Brad says, "So you can understand the need for confidentiality." Heads nod. The interpreter restates in Japanese. Heads nod again, and Mr. Saito says, in English, "Absolutely, Mr. Oaks." The interpreter restates it; everyone nods.

Brad goes on to lay out the general basics of the business

plan. He speaks slowly and in just a few short sentences at a time to permit the interpreter to restate in Japanese. This necessarily takes a painfully long time. Brad long ago became accustomed to this conference-room process in Japan. To him, the key is to use the interpreter's intervals to read body language. Occasionally it helps, and always it keeps him alert. Finally, Saito pronounces that the proposal is "very interesting" and "will require much study." Hiwasaki beams.

"Yes, hello?"

"Mr. Tateshima, I wonder if you could tune up my car. It idles roughly and is hard to start."

"I could sell your car to certain buyers willing to pay a premium for cars as roadworthy as yours, enough for you to buy a newer, better used car."

"Mr. Tateshima, the pending question was a polite request for you to tune up the car awarded to my father, the car I already own and respect. I am now ready to put politeness aside and bring up the well-being of certain of your family members."

"Yes, sir. Are you expecting to take a long trip?"

"Yes, Mr. Tateshima, I will be driving to the Midwest for a couple of days and then driving back."

"About how far?"

"Probably around two thousand miles, round-trip."

"In that case, I recommend new belts and brakes."

"Very prudent. I cannot afford to break down in the valley of the Mississippi River."

"A newer car would be even more prudent."

"Are your mother and sister precious to you?"

"My mother and sister are precious to me. And so are you. And your venerable car."

Monday night, September 16, 2019; Tokyo

Suntory Hall is part of the executive office complex built in the 1980s by Japan's premier maker of bourbon. Built into the hillside of Akasaka, the district where stand the embassies of the US, Canada, Spain, and others, the hall's main entrance opens to a granite plaza on a street in front, and is also accessed by a long stairway down the hillside from the vicinity of the Okura Hotel.

Inside the doors of the main entrance is a carpeted lobby. Amaya Mori walks quickly to take Brad's extended hand. The handshake flows into a spontaneous hug coupled with beaming smiles. They surrender their coats to the cloakroom, his a travel-pac rayon raincoat still creased from cramped luggage, hers a complexly woven, silk-lined, wool-and-silk-blend ankle-length coat with a high Chinese collar, fashioned from vintage winter kimonos in earth colors. Her simple A-line winter dress is muted persimmon with occasional highlights of sky blue.

The concert hall's side walls of gleaming dun-colored granite rise to an upper structure in unstained panels of cryptomeria, Japan's prodigious cedar, used for centuries in auspicious structures. Above the stage, on the rear wall, rests the symmetrical diamond-shaped frame of massive organ pipes, which will, of course, be silent in tonight's solo violin performance.

Brad's and Amaya's seats are close to the stage, just to the right of center, perfect for viewing Gil Shaham. Amaya has not relinquished Brad's hand, so he comments on the music from his memory rather than program notes. Oh well, the program is in Japanese anyway, except for a few ads. The house lights dim, then go dark, and Gil Shaham walks to center stage in a circle of light.

Twenty minutes into the program, Brad frowns and thinks to himself, *He hears it fast. Way fast.* These six works for unaccompanied violin, three sonatas and three partitas, are a Matterhorn for any violinist to climb. Shaham, though flawless, practically sprints through the first half of the program.

At the interval, Brad and Amaya agree they both prefer a more pensive tempo. Amaya says, "I must say I wondered whether you would want to see me again after our last meeting. I see you have recovered from the initial shock. There was no way to warn you. Ohhhh, look over there, Brad."

Amaya tugs him in quickstep to a display enclosed in a glass case. In it are seven specimen pieces of Japanese pottery and porcelain bowls, each bearing thin but obvious veins of silver or gold. Amaya explains, "Brad, these are examples of the Japanese way of repairing broken dishes or bowls. See? The pieces are rejoined, but there is no attempt to hide the breaks. The technique is called *kintsugi* because of the shining gold in the finished work. It is made by brushing layer by layer, on completely dried surfaces, a mixture of lacquer and gold powder, then smoothed and polished. The craft is a work of conservation and admired in this country."

The final, five-minute chime startles Amaya. She straightens up, touches Brad's cheek, and says, "Perhaps we should take our seats."

Settled back in their seats, as the house lights dim to half, Amaya leans to Brad and says, "Are you married, Brad?"

"No."

Immediately, the audience breaks into enthusiastic applause. Brad looks around, startled. Gil Shaham acknowledges the applause with nods, adjusts the violin under his chin, and raises the bow.

During the second half of the program, Amaya allows her mind to drift, as it often does in concerts. *I shouldn't mind a man interrupting the tranquility I have made for myself. No, and I don't—certainly don't—mind this man. This American is so unlike what we think they are. To him, I could explain the ways of our country's art. He I could take a risk for. He I could sing to in the shower. Could disclose to him my fears. I wish it were so. I must be careful. I cannot show too much. But I cannot be seen to be distant or withholding. I think he likes me for being an individual. I cannot let him see me as being alone.*

In my life, I can never disguise that I am half-foreign—thus all foreign to Japanese people. I see it in every face that looks away. More shame when it becomes known my parents were unmarried. I live my life in a natural way but cannot escape the muted undertones of my country, my culture, viewing me as slightly less than the rest. Might that shadow in my life be contagious so as to infect him? Must I wear a mask in that case?

No, that path leads to defeat. I don't live my life as a damaged tea bowl. What is a life made of shards—of broken pieces rejoined without disguise for all to see? Like the kintsugi?

After the concert, standing in autumn air, waiting for a taxi, Brad says, "Amaya, please do not take this question the wrong way: Is your building safe?" She looks at him quickly and suppresses the instinct to treat the question lightly.

"I have never thought of that specifically before. Of course, when I moved in, I was interested in the locks and that sort of thing. There is a front desk with someone on duty in the day. I think there is a night guard and cameras, but I'm pretty vague in my mind. What in the world prompts that question?"

Brad lowers his voice and leans closer to her. He says,

"Right now, there are competitors of Elgar who seem intent on disrupting us at the top. I had a scare in Washington before my previous trip there." He lowers his voice to nearly a whisper, "Now that you hold . . . well, what you hold . . . I'm concerned."

Amaya lowers her voice and musters an earnest tone, "Well, Brad Oaks, is the Palace Hotel a safe place?"

He blushes and stammers, "Look, I'm not trying to suggest . . . I don't mean . . ."

"Nor am I," Amaya says seriously. "There are many rooms in the new Palace Hotel. With everything that's going on, I will enjoy a short stay there immensely."

Brad looks at her with increased respect for her resourcefulness. He says, "Elgar . . . Elgar Steel will pay for . . ."

"Yes, of course, Brad, I understand." They enter a taxi.

In the taxi, he says, "But you have no . . . uh . . . bag."

"There is an arcade, Brad. I have simple needs."

When she steps away from the front desk and rejoins Brad, she says, "They had a junior suite. It will do. I loved the concert, Brad, truly. I am going to the arcade for a few things. Shall we meet for breakfast?"

"Yes. There's a full buffet included . . ."

"Leave that detail to me, Brad Oaks. I appreciate your concern about me tonight, more than I can say at the moment. Rest easy and well."

She touches her fingertips to the top of his hand. "As this is an Elgar Steel accommodation, do you wish to take the extra key?"

Uh-oh, he thinks, *ambush. There is no good answer to her question. He would wish it, of course. What does she mean? I can't just take the key, can I? She looks like she might mean it. Or is that me wanting her to?* He makes what he thinks is the least-bad choice, which is to say nothing.

"Brad, the cat has taken your tongue." After a pause, she smiles and takes a step toward the escalator leading to the arcade on the lower floor.

"Um . . . not . . . now."

She nods and says, "I shall think about what you are thinking."

Which she does.

Brad lets himself into his room feeling pretty good about things. He switches on the television and settles into the desk chair, a cold beer bottle in hand, and clicks the remote until the sumo tournament matches come on screen. *It isn't Bach, but it's relaxing.* He looks at his watch. *Well, the White House meeting has started.* It will be a restless night.

The room phone wakens Brad at six fifteen. "It is time for breakfast, Brad Oaks. My room, please." On the ground floor, Brad checks the front desk before going to Amaya's suite. The attendant says, "Mr. Oaks, prease wait a moment." The assistant manager appears from behind the screen at the rear of the front desk area, bows, and hands Brad a telex in a sealed envelope. Brad's heart pounds as he opens the envelope and reads:

"Cautious optimism from AK. We are responding to technical questions. Nothing public. Light at end of tunnel appears green. Buy yourself a drink. Regards SJE."

CHAPTER EIGHT

Brad pushes the doorbell button to Amaya's suite. She greets him with a sparkling smile and bows as he enters. She wears a *yukata* furnished to guests of the Palace Hotel—an after-bath, thin cotton kimono, white with indigo-colored bamboo leaves. She pours him coffee from the room service cart and offers him a bowl of warm rice with an egg broken over the top. Her eyes shine when he describes the news in Sarah Jane's telex. Amaya says,

"After great thought, I have decided that it is time for both of us to meet with my half sister, June. We should go to her hotel together; she is alone. We have superior information now. I believe she is most vulnerable in her present circumstances. Please call her and ask her to meet with us in her room in an hour."

Brad considers the statement, and nods. "You're right. The people we're up against seem to want to eliminate Elgar as a pipe supplier so they can bid on it. June and her group want to eliminate the whole job. But I have to warn you, Amaya: she is headstrong and may not listen to reason. We must try."

"We must succeed, Brad."

June picks up her room phone immediately. Brad says, "June, it's Brad. Ms. Mori and I need to meet with you. I know you said you wanted to meet with her alone, but—"

"Yes, yes, fine, Brad." June's voice is breathless and trembling. "I'm so scared. The Toronto office of ACEA was bombed an hour ago. Hurry. I don't know what to do."

June is dressed in a pearl-colored raw-silk suit with a black-and-tan scarf when she lets Brad and Amaya into her room. Her face reveals distress and is streaked with tears. Amaya stands near the closed door, her hands folded in front of her, as she waits for Brad to introduce her. Then she steps forward and lowers her head slightly to shake hands with her half sister. June mumbles a perfunctory greeting and turns to Brad. She says, "Our summer intern . . . bright . . . working late . . . in hospital with burns. The place ransacked. No other injuries. Brad, I probably would have been there."

Brad says, "June, you were likely the target, just as I was in Washington. Let me fill you in." Brad lays out the water pipeline plan, and the theory about the Iranians.

"Those two aren't connected, are they?" June asks.

"Well, no one else knows about the water line plan. We think the threat on me was part of a plot to eliminate Elgar and improve their bidding position. But the threat on you and the ACEA is to eliminate your opposition to Wishbone."

"I won't give in to threats. And I can end this threat against Elgar at once," says June. She turns to Amaya and says, "I assume you're here to deliver the shares I want to buy?"

Amaya glances at Brad, who says, "June, you came here on a

fool's errand. Ms. Mori has simply flipped your ridiculous offer and bought a third of the business from you and Sarah Jane for two million dollars. The will gives her that right."

June sputters and stands, hands on hips. "How the hell can that be? I'm not buying her out under the will; I'm buying her out for me alone. If it's under the will, Sarah Jane and I would still have equal power. That doesn't help me. No, I made that offer to gain control."

Brad shakes his head slowly and says, "Whatever you had in mind, that's not what you said to her on the phone. No, you puffed yourself up as all-important, as 'speaking for the Elgar family who are the real owners of Elgar Steel,' when you put two million dollars on the table. You played this hand badly, June. Now she's taken the trick."

"I only said that to . . ."

"You said that to sound intimidating and to cloak yourself in Elgar authority. To sound official."

"I'LL SUE!" shouts June.

"Yet another lawsuit. What fun. You wouldn't sound so good, June, talking out of both sides of your mouth that way. I can hear it now: 'See, Your Honor, I lied about acting for Elgar when I really wanted to squash its best business opportunity for my personal environmental values.' Save your breath, June. And this thing is moving at light speed, not at glacial-lawsuit speed."

Amaya touches Brad's forearm with a gentle pressure. He turns to her and calms himself. Amaya quickly glances at him, and then down and away. Looking up, she says,

"Ms. Elgar, please sit down. It is my intent to give my proxy to your sister so that Elgar Steel can compete for this business. If her plans fail, you and she will buy my stock at the two prices offered for it, a total of twelve million dollars, and your environmental goals will not be impacted at all. But if the Iranians succeed, then everyone else fails. Don't you see? You are in serious danger, Ms. Elgar. You should think about your own safety."

June paces, stopping occasionally, counting on her fingertips. Her shoulders slump. She turns and glares at Amaya. "So you intend to oppose ACEA and me from getting my own inheritance?"

Amaya stiffens and says, "I intend to prevent you from using my inheritance to ruin Elgar Steel. You and Elgar can argue about environmental matters all you want, but on equal footing. Frankly speaking, I detest antagonism and family fights. I do not have the luxury of family, or did not until now.

"If you think about the merits of the environmental issues, as I have, you'll come to see, as I do, that on balance the water pipeline would be an environmental win, and you would have more financial resources to win other environmental victories."

"Ms. Mori, I appreciate your scientific insights. Perhaps, when I have more time, I'll give you notes on modern Japanese art."

Brad says, "June, settle down. How well do you know the new provincial government in Alberta?" June smirks and shrugs.

"That's as I thought. You're pretty tight with the new premier. Well, her progressive programs are burning cash that Alberta doesn't have. Part of her agenda is to increase Alberta's power generation. Alberta makes less than six percent of its power from hydro plants; the rest of Canada is at about sixty percent. This water plan would create jobs, and the water gathering and transmission would generate revenues from hydro power. That's a lot of potential improvement to Alberta's bottom line."

"Dammit, Brad, the tar sands oil extraction operations are an environmental disaster. They strip-mine for that stuff, Brad! It's not some simple extraction, like oil-country pumps. That's the real devil here."

"Well then, June, go after the real devil, if that's it. That's not the pipeline. It's not the steel or the pipes. It's not Elgar. Alberta has a chance here to gather water and harvest the force of it to generate electricity before it flows to the US. Maybe they would even store some of the water in those mined-out tar sand pits. Those are damn good offsets to environmental harm that the tar sand operations have already caused. You can't expect to shut down those operations, but you can expect to get something good out of the water plan."

Amaya stands and gathers her purse. "Ms. Elgar, we have delivered a great deal for you to think about. The main reason we are here is to help you to a safe place. Tokyo may not be it."

Brad nods and says, "Why not go to the farm? We can beef up security for you there."

June juts her chin and says, "I'm going to Toronto. I have an injured intern to see. I have a confused and frightened staff to talk to. I have morale to restore. I'm going to get things back to normal there as soon as possible. After that, who knows? I might take some time off and visit friends in Edmonton."

June turns sharply to face Amaya. In a raised voice, she

says, "One more thing before I leave you, Ms. Mori. Who are your heirs? What happens to the stock and the proxies if you get hit by a bullet train?"

Amaya's face colors at June's rudeness. "I shall make my arrangements immediately with my lawyers."

"And with the help of Brad Oaks?" June says with a sneer.

"No. I shall not need Mr. Oaks's assistance with this," says Amaya, looking down. "Thank you for your thoughtfulness in reminding me of my duties. Please be safe, Sister June."

In the taxi back to the Palace Hotel, Brad turns to Amaya and says, "I apologize for her reprehensible behavior, Amaya. And I'm grateful that you had the foresight to speak to her immediately about her danger. You must think Americans to be singularly boorish."

Amaya looks at the masses of people on the sidewalks outside the taxi's window and says calmly, "No, of course not; not all. I have observed boorishness in Americans and Japanese alike. As an unmarried woman living in Japan, whose mother was Japanese and father was American, and they unmarried, I have become a very accurate observer of Japanese bluntness and rudeness. You should not take on an obligation to rectify hers. On a different subject, do you know anyone in management at the Palace Hotel?"

Brad explains his brief acquaintance with the manager at the front desk. Once inside the hotel, they walk to the front desk, where Brad asks for Mr. Oki. He and Amaya exchange *meishi* and bows, and she launches into an animated conversation. After a brief exchange, Amaya turns to Brad and says, "I am going with Mr. Oki to look at an empty space in the arcade at the foot of the main escalator. I may wish to rent that location as an annex for my Ginza shop."

Brad brightens and says, "If I can be of any help . . .?"

She smiles and says, "This is my other business. I shall not need your assistance with it. Do you have dinner plans?"

Brad does. He had planned to meet with Hiwasaki. He mentally cancels that plan and says, "I would like very much to join you if I may."

Amaya nods her head, her eyes never leaving his, and says in a slow, quiet voice, "Then let us meet at the Wadakura Restaurant in the hotel at seven. Another storm is moving in later today. That and your concern about yakuza are reasons enough to stay inside."

Tuesday, September 17, 2019; Dubuque, Iowa

"Binoculars for you, Nephew."

The driver hands the binoculars to the passenger beside him in the front seat of the Caprice. They are parked on the downslope of a street leading to small-boat docks on the Mississippi River. Both men focus and observe the precarious off-loading of awkward cargo from a river barge. The barge and tug overwhelm the marina docks. Dockworkers seem unfamiliar with this particular cargo, and their inexperience has prolonged the process well into the afternoon.

"This could be a fatal bottleneck," the passenger states.

"What is needed?"

"Crane operators and crew with experience. Larger dock

facilities. These are tricky operations, as you can see, but it is really just a matter of deploying workers with the right skills. Whoever picked this spot and hired this crew is an idiot."

"I take great umbrage at that."

"My apologies, heroic Uncle, it is an oversight anyone could make. Truly."

"They gave me assurances."

"Of course, Uncle. They are despicable American predators of reverent businessmen. They are unfit for the upcoming endeavor."

"Again, what is needed?"

"Let me investigate and make a plan. There are labor union considerations I must learn about. Ideally, the proper skills and equipment would be available and at a more suitable locality than the marina down there. I must search elsewhere, meaning greater cost, but it is only a matter of time."

"Coming here to observe was essential, was it not, Nephew?"

"Thanks to your wisdom and foresight, wise Uncle."

"Will they fail to unload this cargo?"

"They have not given up. It is basically a matter of mental acuity in the physics of large mass. The most encouraging sign is that they have stopped rather than proceeding blindly. Shall we go talk to them?"

"Oh no. I do not want either of us involved directly and remembered later. We will extend our stay until they have either mastered or bungled the job. It is not rocket science, is it?"

"True, wise Uncle."

"But this can be done?"

"It is physically possible. It is an engineering problem, so it can be solved. The union rules may be less solvable, but I shall investigate all avenues. May I keep the binoculars?"

"Yes. For now. Until there is no longer a need."

"You radiate greatness, Uncle. May I ask a favor?"

"We have nothing else to do, of course."

"Honored Uncle, you are the hero of future epics sung throughout eternity. But I am not, as the infidel says, 'chopped chicken liver.' I request recognition that I am not a feckless child. I am not a misfit. I am gaining in education and in practical understanding. I am loyal to you and to the endeavor. At times, your words sting me."

"The sand in storms sting; would you have the wind apologize? You cannot expect to overcome that which simply is the truth of you. That you are young. That is good, of course. But maturity is better. Our lineage for over two thousand years rests on mature judgment, which grows at divine slowness from youth's fire. But I take your point."

"Meaning?"

"You show promise."

"That is faint praise."

"You shall be the favored nephew and indispensable aide-de-camp in the epic songs."

CHAPTER NINE

Tuesday, September 17, 2019; Tokyo, Palace Hotel

As he enters the sushi bar, Jerry Hiwasaki brushes off the raindrops that began to fall during his walk to the Palace Hotel.

"Thanks for the late change in plans, Sake-cup."

Hiwasaki laughs and says, "Oh, I am only too glad to make the change. I will say frankly I would much rather go straight home after work than make a night of it at the clubs in Roppongi. My wife . . . well, she complains bitterly about late after-work hours. It is a Japanese salaryman's habit that is hard to break. Anyway, you never did go in much for the club scene, did you, Brad-san?"

"No, and I can admit that candidly to you. It is so artificial, especially the hostesses. I don't understand how you put up with it."

Hiwasaki puts his raincoat on an empty chair and settles next to Brad. He clearly enjoys the chance to talk about such things with a friend. He says,

"I can appreciate that it may seem artificial to you. Of course, it is, in a way. But it is so ingrained in us—the Tokyo salarymen of the trading houses, the banks, even government agencies—that it is second nature. And the hostesses are simply expected to loosen the conversation when it stiffens, as it usually does. We and they act out well-understood roles. It may seem to

99

be ritualistic to one who goes there only to analyze it. Yet, for those of us who are simply there in the moment, with no such purpose, it seems to work very well. No attachments with hostesses . . . or only very rarely. No expectations by anyone of attachments, temporary or otherwise."

Brad says in a low voice, "Like the 'Piano Man,' 'to forget about life for a while.' My second trip to Tokyo, with Ernie Elgar, we used to go to a bar in Roppongi. It's gone now. Saito-san would take us. Club Maria or some such. The second time I went, a club hostess sat with me. She had a degree in literature from Nihon University. I asked her about her life at the club. She became very talkative, and I became her listener. Quite a reversal in roles. Every time I went, she would attach herself to me. We talked . . . well, I listened, about her boredom and unhappiness. I tried to lift her spirits. She was always morose. At the end of the evening, I would look at the bar bill and the charges for her time with me. I told Ernie I couldn't go back there, do what she purportedly was there to do, and then get charged for it. Ernie said it was unimportant to him and that we needed to follow the lead of Saito-san. Eventually, I simply stopped going there. It was so depressing."

Hiwasaki glances in recognition. He continues, "It's a story that repeats itself every night. And for most of us, it's paid for by our companies. Constant absences, night after night, until midnight or later, have poisonous effects on home life. But you don't have a home life, do you, Brad-san?"

Brad sips his beer, and says, "I'm a private person, Sake-cup. We've talked many times about our common love for good books. Because of you, I'm now hooked on Japanese novelists—modern ones. I read the whole cycle of four novels by Mishima. Dark and fantastical. Now *that* was a man who was alone. I live alone. I read alone."

"'In the wells of silence.' Will you always be alone, Brad-san?"

"I envy you your family, Jerry. You shouldn't jeopardize it for the sake of business customs. I can't answer your question. I may always be alone. That prospect doesn't disturb me."

"So you go on thinking big. And the business gets bigger as you continue to think big. I have known such men. Mr. Saito is one. Perhaps Mr. Elgar was one. How would you appear if you were in a novel?"

"A loner. Not very good company."

"Brad-san, live a full and happy life. I will always enjoy your company. But maybe you should think big about smaller things, too. It is the Japanese way. A flower stem. A bonsai. The sound of a cricket. A home with a child's laughter. I think such things are not unique to Japan. If the company of a club hostess seems artificial to you, it is because you are a man who is deep. So, find a woman who is deep."

"Jerry, you know my story."

"Yes, and I do not mean to invoke painful memories. How long . . . ?"

"Fourteen years."

"Thanks for lunch, Brad-san. And yes, we do share a common admiration for good literature, American and Japanese. Do you know the writer Lee Blessing?"

"Lee Blessing. Yes, he's an American playwright. I don't actually know his work."

"He wrote the play, 'Thief River.' I have never forgotten these lines from that play: 'We're born alone. We die alone. And every minute of our lives is a chance not to be alone anymore.' I hope you do not squander such chances, Brad-san."

"My regards to Yoko, Jerry. Make the most of tonight's found time."

Brad's message light is blinking on the room phone as he walks in. He calls for it and is told he has a telex. "Yes, please deliver it to the room."

The telex reads: "Roundup time at the farm as soon as you can. SJE."

Amaya Mori has been seated and served sparkling water before Brad arrives. It is his first time in the main Japanese dining room of the Wadakura fifth-floor suite of restaurants, next to the sushi bar where he has been meeting Hiwasaki. This one specializes in refined, traditional *kaiseki* dishes. She stands to greet him, wearing a pale-yellow silk dress patterned with pewter-colored ginkgo leaves, designed much like the blue one, this with a belt the same gray as in the pattern. *Oh my, it's off the other shoulder now.*

Amaya has already organized the dinner with the chef. Tonight, there will be no menus to clutter the table or bills to sign. Each presentation is an exquisite work of art. Amaya chatters easily with staff and explains each dish of seasonal, small servings as they are placed before them. He is charmed.

"Did you decide upon that space in the arcade?" says Brad.

"Yes, and I'm very pleased. Until very recently, there was a new ceramics shop there. It did not offer Imari ware and other traditional Japanese pottery. Before the hotel was rebuilt in 2009, there was always a shop featuring such items. They were of high quality, and much of their inventory came from Kyoto. Here, these small plates with our freshwater trout are *mukojuke*. They are also used in the tea ceremony to serve small sweets. These are reproductions. Authentic Imari porcelain should be on display in the arcade. I will provide that."

Brad thinks, *She is the porcelain.* He says, simply, "I, for one, would spend a lot of time in such a store in this hotel. I first became interested in Imari by shopping in the old Palace Hotel arcade. Now, I have a large collection of it. Congratulations. Do you own your gallery alone, or do you have a partner?"

"Brad, I own the gallery alone. I live alone. I am not in a committed relationship in business or otherwise."

"We have much in common, Amaya."

"Violin, Bach, Japanese ceramics. And now, steel pipes. What more?"

"Um, well, let's see. Do you enjoy baseball?"

Amaya covers her giggle with the back of one hand and says, "I have been to those games. In Japan, we call it *yakyuu* or *beesubarru*. Is it very different from the American version?"

"The game itself has slight differences, but mainly it's the same. The ceremonies and rituals are quite different here in Japan, though. For me, it's an odd juxtaposition."

"Have you played those games?"

"Um, yes, actually. I played as a kid in Sacramento. I had a baseball scholarship to college."

"So you became a research scholar of *yakyuu*?"

"No, Amaya. It only means my college tuition was reduced while I was on the team."

Brad notices Amaya's gaze drift into a middle distance. She says, with a faraway look, "Mr. Ernie Elgar greatly reduced the burden of my tuition for college in Kyoto. Then he paid entirely the tuition at Sotheby's in London, where I did postgraduate studies. We have him in common in a way, I suppose."

Brad feels Amaya's attention shift to his eyes. She straightens in her chair, smiles, and says, "By the way, have we completed the negotiation for the stock?"

Brad frowns and says, "Well, we've reached agreement on everything, including the proxy, so yes, in that sense. There is still the documentation . . ."

Brad looks at the bare shoulder Amaya shrugs. She says, "Yes, the documentation, of course. But now, we are on the same side?" Amaya smiles and lowers her chin slightly. "We are all Elgars now? The same baseball team?"

"The same team," Brad says with a wide smile. "I like the sound of that. Welcome to Elgar Steel, partner. A toast to the team." Brad lifts his glass. She brushes his hand with her fingertips and lifts her glass.

"My name, Amaya, do you know the meaning?"

"Please tell me."

"It means night rain."

Brad returns his glass to the table and looks in her eyes. With a lowered voice, he says, "Both are lovely sounds—Amaya and night rain."

When their elevator reaches the main floor, Amaya slips her arm inside the crook of his elbow. Together they stroll to the other elevator bank leading to her wing. Outside her door, Amaya says, "Do please come in, Brad."

Inside the door of her suite, she bows, looks away and down, and states, "I have arranged for the hotel to provide two *yukatas*."

Wednesday, early and late morning, September 18, 2019; Tokyo

A new storm collides with the sides of the twenty-three-story

Palace Hotel building, shuddering walls and windows. Sheets of typhoon-blown rain pepper the windows of the suite overlooking the walled, ancient Imperial palace and its churning moat waters, now visible as first light spills over Tokyo under black storm clouds. Brad sits looking at the elemental swirls of rain that intensify and slacken like the waves pounding Tokyo harbor. He hears movement in the bedsheets behind him, also heaped randomly by a storm.

"Don't be a stranger," Amaya says in a husky morning voice.

"Shall I order some breakfast?" asks Brad.

"No. I do not wish to confuse the appetites."

Brad slides out of his *yukata* and into Amaya's arms, assuring that prevailing appetites remain free of confusion.

Ting-stop. Dial tone. Numbers dialed. Three rings.

"Yes, I'm here, Uncle."

"What is this new intelligence?"

"The top people will hold secret meetings off-site in a few days."

"Can you go there?"

"If they need a driver, I can volunteer, but I don't think that they will take me."

"Why do you harbor negative thoughts? You want to be addressed as an adult, so take off your baby clothes and do the deeds of a man. The most critical information on the endeavor lies ahead of you. Can you buy the job of driver?"

The nephew stifles a laugh. "That is not done here. To suggest it would get me fired."

"What is your plan B?"

"Sorry, Uncle, what?"

"If not in the job of driver, then how will you pierce the

secret meetings? Off-site means where?"

"The Napa estate. I can fake a sickness for a few days maybe, since it will be short. There are means to get close but not inside."

"Then your plan B falls short of greatness. But there can be a better plan B for you if you can muster the courage to be a warrior. Oh, and this is the time to reconnect with your friend."

"Uncle, you are too vague."

"You cannot connect even closely adjacent dots, puppy. In Napa is where you must end it. Get the friend there. Off-site from the off-site of the satanic meetings. From there, you will take the friend to a more friendly sanctuary. That will be the start of my plan B, Nephew. That will be how your epic uncle will connect all the dots."

"I must end it?"

"As a warrior. Start planning."

"You are so vague my head hurts."

"A good beginning. Think of the head. Carefully. The head must be separated from the serpent."

"Uncle!"

"Be the warrior. Or be the martyr. You have time to reflect on your choice. You have time to plan."

"Now," she says, her voice urgent, shaking him awake. Sunlight fills the room. The rain has subsided. She wears her *yukata*, only, with shower-damp hair under a towel turban.

"Again?"

With a voice of authority, she says, "Is the time to order breakfast, Mr. Man of Steel. I take corned beef hash, poached eggs, corn bread muffins, strong coffee. You should shave."

"Not the usual rice and sardines?"

Amaya shrugs and begins to toy with a strand of his hair. "I am only half-Japanese, remember. Besides, it is not the usual morning for me. Appetitewise." She releases her hair from the turban and shakes it wildly over his bare chest, dispelling his drowsiness. She picks up the phone from the nightstand, leans close to the keyboard to find the room service icon, pushes that button, and hands the phone to Brad, who says,

"You could just order it, since you know what you want."

"Brad, it is in your hands now. I must make my hair and face, so please shave and turn your head."

His head turned, Brad orders exactly what she had said, for two to simplify the thinking process, hangs up the phone, and goes into the bathroom with the hair-turban draped over his face so as not to look.

They sit at the round table by the window, dappled with old raindrops lit by the mid-morning sun. They are dressed for a business day, except she has left her feet bare at his request. She is pleased he has fussed over feet she knows to be pretty. Reluctantly, he hands her Sarah Jane's telex calling for a roundup in Napa.

"Amaya, I seem to be passing between two parallel worlds. First, I'm caught in the urge to make this day with you longer, and then an even longer night, and another day, and on and on in this very room while we discover everything about each other, with no interruptions. Second, I'm caught in the reality that brought me here in the first place. That reality means success or failure for my company's future. I can't eliminate either reality, but I must, and I'm asking it of you as well, to find accommodation in our reality for the other one."

"You will leave today?" Her voice contains no sting of

rebuke, yet the question itself stings.

"This afternoon."

"For how long?"

"Until I return. Today, the reality doesn't tell me when that will be."

"Brad, you have an endearing ability to combine rational and emotional spaces without damaging either. I recognize that ability because I have tried to fashion my life in a similar way. But your rational life is bigger than I have known myself, so that part is new. I admire your attempts to synthesize yin and yang. And I understand the reality of your United States world. So, take a moment to tell me how you see the reality of you and me."

Brad applies firm pressure with his thumb to her narrow, high arch and holds it. Then he says,

"Amaya, bear with me. I don't organize thoughts like these very well because, well, I suppose because I've avoided them. I told you I was engaged . . ."

"I'm so very sorry . . ."

"I know, but this is just to help explain. It's been fourteen years. If I had met you ten or even five years ago, I'm not at all sure of what I would feel or do."

"You don't have to explain—"

"Please, I think maybe I do, out loud, so that part of me talks to another part of me. There is no need to tell you about those years. What is important is this year, and the ones that will follow. A friend of mine reminded me of the two sides of being alone. Not loneliness, but simply being alone."

"I have known alone nearly my entire life, Brad. I have learned to resist filling up on impulse the empty space of simply being alone."

"Yes, I know that, and so I think I can work it out better

because it's you I'm with. Amaya, tell me more of the empty space you resist filling up."

She pauses and watches the headlights below. In a small voice that rides on an exhale, she says,

"Brad, that space is so private, not even I easily think about it to myself. I have nothing of value to say to you about it. I would, perhaps, tell you what I think of it if I had clear thoughts. That space lives within me like a vital organ I cannot feel or describe."

"But Amaya, having a chance to not be alone anymore, my friend reminded me yesterday, is bigger than any other chance in this world. When he said it, the truth simply exploded in my mind. We have a chance, Amaya, but not a certainty. The importance of that chance, in my life anyway, is worth holding on to. We both must pay attention to this chance and recognize its worth."

"You have a knack, as I said, to say things simply and profoundly, Brad. And you have a profound friend. Male or female, this other Japanese friend?"

"A salaryman, married, a bookworm and a salesman."

"You pick good people, don't you, Brad?"

"Well, at least good people find me. Like the Elgars. You and I have Ernie Elgar in common, and it shows in many ways."

"And the Elgar sisters? Do we have them in common, too? Or does either of them have you in some uncommon way I should know about?"

"They took me in and provided me a new foster-world. I love them deeply for that and what they tried to do for me. They're good people. Even June, but you have to look harder for it. I am not *in love* with either. Sarah Jane has become . . . well, a 'best friend' is not an adequate phrase; more a confidante, or actually a mirror of my own mind. We are inseparable in some ways, but not in any romantic way. Well, once Sarah Jane kissed me, but that was only a crush, and at the worst time possible from my standpoint. That never went anywhere. Don't forget, she's my boss, so I guess that's not so common."

"A foster-world. A good way to put it. I, too, lived in one. May I have my foot back, please?" She twinkles her toes. He holds her foot in both hands for a beat before releasing it.

Amaya reunites her feet with gray pumps, looks at Brad, and continues,

"So we shall learn to be a couple while we live twelve time zones apart. That would be quite a feat, Mr. Man of Steel. Please, promise one thing only. Let me be a seed lying somewhere small in your mind. And let me occasionally grow to flower. Often, even. But any amount is enough."

"That's a promise. Promise me you'll think about your life alone—your empty space—and attach value to our chance to not be alone anymore."

"My empty space, which you call 'alone,' I shall attempt to contemplate it. Even though it is the part of me that I cannot feel or describe. Your flight is when?"

"In about three hours. From Narita."

"Then it is time." Amaya goes to where her carryall rests beside the desk and withdraws a clear plastic sleeve. She says,

"I have some things for you to read. I have been carrying them around to give you. I was hoping we could be together to read them, but I think I will just give them to you now."

She hands the folder to Brad. "These are copies of a few of the letters my father wrote to me over twenty years ago. When you first came here, you spoke of things that Mr. Elgar put in some of his letters.

"You may be interested in these. I treasure them. When you explained the idea for Wishbone, I thought I remembered something from those letters. They speak of places that you spoke of when you described Wishbone. Please take this folder with my hope the letters may be useful to you.

"No, don't look at them now. Another time. Come to the arcade with me for just a minute or two. I want your advice on the new shop."

CHAPTER TEN

Wednesday, September 18, 2019; late afternoon in Tokyo, predawn in Washington, aloft over the North Pacific

Jet engine noise becomes white noise after some length of time, a sensation which is different for every passenger. For Brad, it takes a couple of hours to fade into the background. Sometimes, he can block it out completely with headphones or earbuds feeding music to his brain. Most often, he just tells his brain he is hearing water over rapids beside him as he casts for rainbow trout, in a stream flowing down the mountainside toward Lake Shasta.

It was Ernie Elgar who first took him to Potem Falls, off Fender's Ferry Road, to fish. They would trek to a forest service camp in the foothills of Mount Shasta. Ernie would drive a battered Range Rover some twenty miles from Redding, five miles from the turnoff from Highway 299 on an unmarked, rutted, timber-truck road that could crack the axles of most cars, and another hour along a left fork in that road to Potem Falls. It never made sense to go there without intending to spend at least four days, since the slow, lurching round-trip wouldn't be worth it otherwise.

With that stream remembered in the white noise, Brad fishes into his briefcase and withdraws the slender file folder Amaya Mori had given him as they said goodbye. Ernie would invariably pack in cigars and rye whiskey on those fishing trips. Now, without the cigar, Brad sips rye on the rocks, thirty-four thousand feet above the cold waters of the north Pacific, and reads the letters.

August 1, 1991

Dear Daughter,

My grandparents would write to each other all the time before they were married. Sometimes two or three times a week. They lived in Kansas. I remember one letter that said something like "I will improve the day by writing to you . . ." Well, I will now improve my day by writing to you.

Look at Kansas on a map, Amaya. It is an important place in the history of America, but these days, not many people think of Kansas unless they already live there. I think of it all the time. I worked there in summers. I would take the train from California to eastern Kansas to visit my grandmother in the spring of nearly every summer when I was in high school and college (my grandfather had passed away). After a few days, I would take another train to western Kansas and get jobs with the wheat harvest. Sometimes I would shovel wheat brought by truck to a silo by the tracks. It was dusty, hot work. I would work sometimes for 12 hours and then walk to a boarding house and sleep like a stone until dawn and do it again.

The summer of my second year of college, the same age as you are now, I got a job working for the Kansas State Board of Health. It didn't pay as much as the harvest jobs, but it gave me a chance to use my brain. I had a wonderful foreman, Ralph O'Conner. Well, he was the senior employee over me and another kid, Danny Broun, whose dad taught music at the University of Kansas. Danny's a farmer now in the middle of wheat country. Well, Ralph taught Danny Broun and me quite a bit about western Kansas geology. Our job was to try to track down oil pollution caused by oil wells all over Kansas wheat fields. Those wells pump up the oil, but they also pump up salt water. The salt water would cause a lot of damage to fresh water. The farmers would complain to the state, and the state would send out crews like us to investigate.

Western Kansas sits on top of an aquifer of fresh water. They gave it an Indian name, the Ogallala. It's so important. I want to tell you about it because you won't learn about it in Japan. But that'll have to be another letter.

I also want to tell you that I'm proud of the way you are doing in college. It's hard for me to talk about my feelings and even harder to write about them. But I want you to know that I loved your mother. I couldn't bring her or you to the US because I have another life here. It truly pains me that I can't put everyone together, but that's a weakness in me. I can only hope you will think of me as a caring father, even though I put such a great distance between us. Now that I've said that, there's not much more to say. But to keep on writing, I'll just tell you stuff from my work life. And that'll fill up a long book because all I've ever done forever on this earth is work. I do take joy in work.

I hope to see you in a few months when I come to Japan. You can show me around Kyoto. I'll read up on it.

Good night and love,

Dad

Brad puts the letter back in the file. He remembers Ernie telling him stories of Kansas, and the Broun kid, and the polluted water wells. Funny he wrote to Amaya about that. Maybe he couldn't think of much else to write, they being separated so much. Brad wonders if he told the same stories to the twins.

He carefully puts that letter away and takes out the next one.

October 13, 1991

Dear Amaya,

Sorry I didn't write last month. It was grape harvest and crush at the vineyard, and with that and the steel business, I didn't have a moment to even breathe. You would like the crush. It's where kids gather and taste ripe grapes and happiness while families work. When I see them, I see you. And I know how you look because I look at your snapshot all the time. Same with your mother.

You're no longer a kid. You're officially an adult now, so I'm going to say things I haven't put in letters while you were growing up. My heart agonizes to be so distant. I don't expect you to imagine a man like me being homesick for you while he's got another home and family. I'm happy with as much of you and your mother as I've had, even though I have to keep you hidden. Forgive me if you can. A man has no pain so excruciating as the pain of remorse for betraying or hurting his own family.

For the entire 18 years of your life, I have been torn between which loved ones to betray and hurt to spare the others pain. You and your mother had to bear the brunt of my choices. I can't expect you to love me for that, but you have to believe that I do love you.

I've got to change the subject. So, by now you've looked up Kansas on the map. Now I'd like you to look at two other places in America. Look first at the Great Lakes and pick out Lake Erie. Make a mental picture of that and keep it in mind as I talk about another part of the country.

Now, look at the State of Colorado. The mountain range there is called the Rockies, and it goes northwest all the way into Canada. It's different from the mountains you have in Japan.

Well, after the Rocky Mountains were formed and the ice glaciers thawed, a huge amount of water was let loose with a huge amount of granite gravel and sand. All that water and dirt spread out eastward into the flat lands that are now Kansas, Nebraska, Oklahoma, and Texas. When I say it was huge, look back at Lake Erie. Over time, there was enough water sluiced eastward to fill up Lake Erie eight times. That water and muck settled and soaked and made an underground wetland we now call the Ogallala Aquifer.

When pioneers first settled the land, they had pretty good streams and springs and natural ponds just on the surface. When that dried up, they dug wells for their farm water and livestock. They also plowed the soil badly and ruined it. That's the Dust Bowl you might have read about. That was in the 1930s. The suffering endured by those who couldn't walk away cannot be imagined. Except, of course, by those who endured the fires of bombs.

Then, after the two world wars, farmers in the western states started drilling very deep wells with new technology for pumping up water. They irrigated grain fields from sprinklers connected to these wells.

The wells tapped into the Ogallala Aquifer. The pumps sucked out water that had lain undisturbed for millions of years. Over the next fifty years, they sucked out about the same volume of water as one Lake Erie. Now the farmers are hurting again because of the high costs of pumping water out of the aquifer.

In my last letter, I told you about Danny Broun. Well, he lives out in western Kansas, and he irrigates that way. He tells me that he can see the day coming when he won't be able to afford to keep his farm. But he's got a son, Dan Junior, and they worry about what Junior's going to do with the land. It's not a pretty picture. I feel bad for Danny.

Look, Amaya, I don't expect you to have much interest. I just like telling you stuff. If we lived closer, we could talk about stuff. As it is, I get out paper and ramble on and on just as it comes out of my head. You probably don't have a high opinion of Americans, including me. That hurts, but I understand why. It was the war, of course.

I was in kindergarten when the war started. Living in California, we saw neighbors displaced to internment camps. The only other things I knew about Japan were what I learned from ugly propaganda our government put out, and that also came out in radio and movies and comic books. Don't get me going about war. Well, it's me that's got me going in this letter, but I don't understand hate or war.

There's a theme all the time in movies and books and stories about how the characters don't understand love. That makes the story more mysterious and more romantic, I guess. But I understand love a lot more than I understand hate, the kind that becomes war.

I hope you have love in your life, Amaya, and beauty. I hope you look for it and value it. I know you are smart. I know you are pretty like your mother. I only hope that you feed love and beauty into your soul. You'll need it with all the hate in the world.

Bedtime for me. I'll write you again soon.

Love,

Dad

Brad puts the letters down. He realizes now that Ernie suffered a cancer of the spirit for half his life. Like King Lear, he died with that cancer still in him. But Ernie at least finally got it out in the open, and maybe even rectified, at his death with his three-way stock bequest. He must have figured that way, his twins would not only know about, but also get to actually know his third daughter. Unlike Lear, all the daughters would live, and share his wealth equally to boot.

And it was just like Ernie to write to a coed in Japan about geography and agriculture in America.

Ernie considered himself a teacher whose school was attended by anyone who knew him—employees, offspring, whatever. He remembers the drone of Ernie's voice filling Brad's otherwise empty life the summer he lost everything dear. Somehow that droning was a reassurance of caring, even though the voice never conveyed sentimentality. Ernie didn't so much try to teach Brad as simply open up his own rambling thoughts about the steel plant, the farm, birdlife, horses, droughts, and fishing. Brad hadn't forgotten about the Kansas stories, and they came rushing back as he read about Ralph O'Conner and Dan Broun and traveling the back farm roads to sample salty-tasting water wells. He picks up the third and last of the letters.

December 7, 1991

Dear Daughter,

I do not write on this historic fiftieth anniversary for any particular reason or significance. It is simply the date of this day that I've chosen to write you again. The main reason is to wish you a Merry Christmas! I expect to be in Tokyo in March, so I hope we can make time for a visit.

Still, the date is significant, of course. In your life, the most significant date of the war is August 9, 1945. It's a wonder that American and Japanese people ever did anything together after that date. No, it's a miracle. You must think differently, but if you can ever step back and reflect, you'll see it as a miracle too. I got into the business of selling steel scrap in Japan when they were rebuilding. I'd go to Tokyo and Osaka on sales trips and got lessons about Japan and bigger lessons about life. Those were raw days. There was still rubble. But always, there were flowers. And there was your beautiful mother.

Nowadays, my business takes me to Vancouver, Canada. I seem to have to go there for a few days every two or three weeks. One day, I'll tell you more about it. I don't much look at what's in Vancouver because I'm too busy looking at what surrounds it—the Pacific Ocean, the Lions Gate Bridge, and the mountains just on the other side of Burrard Inlet. The city is beautiful and elegant, but you simply can't take your eyes off the scenery.

I want to supply steel bridge girders in a highway project at the eastern border between British Columbia and Alberta. There's a mountain pass there called Crow's Nest. The main highway goes through there and an old coal-mining town called Fernie, where I stay. Most of the coal mines were played out decades ago. An American mining company came in there about the time you were born and built a modern mining operation. The coal from those mines is in a special class by itself, very high quality, that's used in steelmaking.

My company bends and shapes steel, but we don't actually make it from scratch. The big mills of Japan that do make iron and steel have to import all of this kind of coal, called metallurgical coal. They import it from the east coast of America and Australia. And now, they take it from the Canadian Rockies.

As I travel around in eastern British Columbia and over into Alberta, I see mountains, trees, and a whole lot of water. Vast amounts of surface water in Canada are stored in year-round glaciers and snowfields, along with high-mountain rivers that are renewed every year.

Where I live, in Northern California, we get by on water we take from the Sierra Nevada mountains. It is piped from mountain reservoirs and used in San Francisco, for example. Southern California is a lot worse off. They get some water from the mountains and a lot of water from the Colorado River. There are limits to how far these water resources can go.

So I've been thinking about a project. There's good freight rail service across Canada. The new coal mine uses entire trainloads that carry their coal and nothing else to a deep-water port south of Vancouver. I'm wondering if we couldn't just build some tank cars, fill them with water, and hook these up to the coal trains. Then, the tank cars of water could be put on boats to take to California.

I'm trying to find someone up there to listen to me. So far, no luck. So, maybe it's not railcars. There has to be some way to bring that water into America where it's needed.

I had the bank wire you some money for next year. I'm glad you're doing so well in school. Maybe you could take me to Kyoto. I guess I invited myself there earlier this year, but I really want to see it through your eyes. You have the eyes of an artist.

Love,
Dad

In the white noise of the jets, Brad puts the letters away. He clicks off the overhead reading light, reclines his seat, and nods off.

Wednesday, September 18-Saturday, September 21, 2019; Napa, Elgar estate

At the farm, Elgar Steel's senior engineers, the communications vice president, the chief financial officer, the chief estimator, three production managers, and the support staff of all of them meet to brainstorm the next steps for the Wishbone project.

Brad has completed the transfer of shares. Amaya Mori's proxy is in Sarah Jane's hands. Amaya's bank has wired half a million dollars to each sister's bank. She has signed and delivered another half million in promissory notes payable to each sister out of earnings of the company.

Brad maps out two broad external aspects of the business planning: a long campaign in Washington and the same advocacy in Canada requiring written and graphic presentations of technical information in greater detail than would be the case if they were dealing with American suppliers.

The formal meetings always end at noon, and Sarah Jane transforms herself from company vice president to hostess presiding at a large buffet on the stone patio, under a cobalt sky and bright sun. For each employee, she has quietly observed an item he or she had favored in filling their plates. After everyone has settled around the tables or benches, Sarah Jane brings a small blue-and-white porcelain bowl of a refill of that item to each guest. She sits to listen as they inevitably open up in private conversation with thoughts they had been unwilling to present in the earlier meetings. Sarah files each observation or suggestion in her memory. In time, each will be given serious, professional analysis, with due recognition to the person who voiced it.

The chartered bus that brought the Elgar people from the plant, and the motor pool's SUV with flip charts, large projection screen, and geological maps of the Wishbone route, return to Stockton at four o'clock on Friday, September 20.

One young man separates from the group, with prearranged permission from his supervisor, and sets off on a trail up the coastal mountain west of the farm with a backpack, for a few days of communing with nature.

Brad and Sarah Jane have an early supper and decide they're talked out. "Sufficient unto the day and the week," says Brad with a smile as he goes upstairs for a long sleep.

"Uncle, I have told you all I know. It is in the important papers, which I discovered in stealth, and just read to you. Twice I read them to you. Slowly the second time, as you wisely commanded. Is it not gold from Paradise covered in honey?"

"You are a warrior among warriors. You are a general of the elite guard. You have matured beyond your youthful bleats when you were a calf. You have found the key to the cave of jewels."

"Thank you, epic hero."

"I am giddy with this newfound oasis of information. All is explained. All is now revealed for greatness. The path to justice is now plain to see. Do you see it, Nephew?"

"Of course. That is why I snatched the key to greatness and handed it to you. The way of glory is the way of keen and opportunistic observing in the face of danger. Superior knowledge is the path of the general of the elite. The path to justice is superior knowledge."

"Don't be so vain, Nephew. Still, what you found is as you say?"

"Yes, epic Uncle."

"And you have the friend?"

"Yes, Uncle. So, remind me, what is plan A?"

"The new plan B is the new treasure you have found for us. It merges with plan A for a combined value that cannot be measured. Plan B will achieve the whole endeavor without boats or barges or Russians. The friend thus becomes plan C, which is in your hands as well. You will have your own songs for the ages.

"Therefore, plan A, cut the head. Plan B, steal the eggs and hatchlings. Plan C, though perhaps not even necessary, will capture the kingdom. So, take the friend to the place of our unlikely alliances where lives your protégé who calls you 'Father.' Execute plan A, then hasten to execute plan B and/or plan C. Oh, so giddy with such wealth within grasp."

"But Uncle, the Iron Dragon has been captured."

"But not your protégé, am I correct?"

"That's correct, but he was weakened when his clan was attacked and they dispersed into urban caves."

"It is enough for plan C."

"I can't keep in one place in my head the plans A, B, and/or C. I don't see clarity."

"Oh, Nephew. Listen to me. I'm only going to tell you this once."

Saturday morning, Brad and Sarah Jane saddle horses for a ride through the vineyards. Then, they take a trail up the ridge to look at some acreage Sarah Jane is considering buying. They ride in an easy silence under a cloudless blue sky, stopping at the ridgeline for a snack.

"You're different, Brad," says Sarah Jane with a laugh, running her fingers through her hair.

"In what respect?"

Sarah Jane shrugs and says, "You're less insular. Less jumpy. More relaxed than I've ever seen you. I don't know if it's jet lag or your life has taken a turn for the better."

Brad tries to look nonchalant but realizes that Sarah Jane has captured a definite change in his outlook on life. No way is he going to let on what's caused it.

"A little of both, perhaps. I'm relaxed mainly because we have Alden Knight on our side of the Wishbone debate. The policy questions shift to Canada now. We could sure use June's help there, but I suppose that's not in the cards."

Sarah Jane shakes her head and says, "You never know with her. So, she mentioned going to Edmonton, did she?"

Brad dips his head from side to side, saying, "Only in passing and then only a 'maybe,' but it seemed I'd gotten through to her at some level. Don't get your hopes up."

Sarah Jane laughs and nods in agreement. After a pause, she says,

"And don't get yours down, Brad. I think I know her pretty well. I think I'll be hearing from her sometime next week. We'll have to wait and see. Let me deal with June. She'll listen to me. June is vain. Her environmental aims are lofty but scatterbrained. And there's always that vanity. That makes for a bitter mixture. It stings her eyes, or at least her sight."

Brad recalls the ugly scenes on the patio about going to Washington or to Tokyo and the two encounters at the Okura Hotel. He mutters, without a smile, "She would be hard as hell to live with."

"She is. But she's left my world."

Brad looks out over the Napa Valley and the vast Elgar vineyards. Even at this distance, the Elgar residence and the additions made over the years seem larger than life. Its very size makes more conspicuous the solitude lying ahead for her. He looks at Sarah Jane and thinks, *This will be so empty for her now.*

Ting-stop. Dial tone. Number dialed. One ring.

"Uncle, all is prepared for glorious plan A. And I hold tickets for two to the land of plans B and C."

"Be resolute, Nephew. Be victorious but not a martyred angel."

"Be at peace, Uncle."

CHAPTER ELEVEN

Saturday night, September 21, 2019

Later that evening, they get together on the patio. Sarah Jane has put together a supper of fresh corn, tomato-and-cucumber salad, and fried chicken. Brad pours Pinot Noir for them. She lifts her glass to him and says, "To absent family."

How profound that sounds to him just now. Brad repeats, slowly, "To . . . absent . . . family. Thank you for that, Sarah."

She says, "The other day, when I was on the phone with Ambassador Knight, he said something about you. It's one of the nicest compliments I've ever heard about anyone. He said you have a 'synthesizing mind.' That says a lot, Brad. It suggests to me that he might try to get you onto his team there at USTR."

He turns. "You and Knight have phone calls?" She shrugs and waves off the question. "Did he say he would?"

"No, no. My conjecture only. Still, it's not a run-of-the-mill compliment, and it's something he might say if he had been thinking along those lines. I just thought I'd mention it as a heads-up if he springs something on you. The very thought of that is scary to me. But would it interest you, Brad?"

"I doubt it, Sarah." He adds with a chuckle, "Is my job here at risk?"

Sarah Jane rests her hand on top of his.

"Brad, you can do any job at Elgar Steel, including my own.

The plant people really respect you. You listen to them. You hear them. You make them want to think in terms of the importance of their work outside quarterly results, the big picture. And you can have any job at the winery, including my own. What you said on the trail today is absolutely right. We can bring in grapes from our Stockton-area neighbors to blend with ours to make a new label. June asked me once if we could have a lower-priced wine, and I couldn't see how. See? That's you again. I didn't put together in my mind a blend of Stockton fruit and Napa fruit.

"There's so much going on here I couldn't manage without you." She sighs. "I don't think I've ever felt so alone before."

She holds up the wishbone of the fried chicken.

"Brad, I'll keep this in the kitchen overnight. Tomorrow, we'll pull it, but for tonight, it'll hold our wishes. Be thinking about a wish. What is it you want, Brad?"

"The last person who asked me that was Alden Knight."

"And you said 'water.' Well, you might just get that water, but that's not what I mean. I don't mean it on a grand scale, as in 'save the arid west.' What do you thirst for personally?"

Brad looks away, then looks down. "I think I lost out on that, Sarah."

"Fourteen years. I know. But you can't really mean you've put all hope for a home life out of your mind. I know I haven't. I always expect to meet someone."

"My friend, Jerry Hiwasaki at Shin, tells me that I'm 'a deep man' and I should look for 'a deep woman.'"

"That's deep!"

They both laugh.

After a long pause, he says, "Maybe I did. Maybe you will."

The kitchen phone rings. Sarah Jane hurries through the French doors to pick up the cordless handset before the fourth ring sends the call to voice mail. Returning more slowly to the patio, she says, "This is Sarah Elgar? . . . Mr. Knight, what a surprise. Brad's right here if you want—"

"No, Sarah Jane, it's you I'm calling. Look, I'm sorry to break into your Saturday, but I wonder if I could ask you a favor."

She faces Brad, eyebrows lifted, chin tucked back, jaw dropped inside closed lips in a look of surprise. "Sure, Mr. Ambassador, what's up?"

"Um. Well, first, it's Alden, OK?"

Sarah Jane stands in shadows now as the sun drops behind the ridge where they had been riding that morning.

"Yes, of course. Alden."

"Sarah Jane . . . uh . . . could I ask . . . are you busy Thursday night?"

Sarah Jane sits quickly on a redwood bench, this time with her back to Brad. "Really? Well, no, I guess I'm not busy then."

"White House dinner. First biggie of the fall. Look, I know this is short notice. I'd like very much if you'd go with me. Gets underway at seven thirty."

Sarah Jane stands, looks straight at Brad, and says slowly, as if writing it out by hand, "You want me to go with you to a White House dinner this coming Thursday." Brad stands, mouth agape but managing to smile.

"And if it's possible, maybe come to town Wednesday. Ichiro can book you a room at the Jefferson . . . would the Jefferson be OK with you?"

Sarah Jane clamps her palm over the mouthpiece and whispers, "Is the Jefferson OK with me?" Brad nearly injures his neck nodding yes.

"Of course, Alden. I'm flattered and would be absolutely

delighted to join you. Sure, the Jefferson is just fine."

"Look, do you line dance? There's a good chance this crowd will do that."

Sarah Jane smiles warmly. "Alden, I'll be able to line dance by Thursday evening."

She smiles to hear him chuckle and then say, "I'm glad. Look, my life is chaos Thursday, but the day winds up with a squash game and a change at the club. It's just catty-corner from your hotel. I'll pick you up at seven ten, and we're only a couple of blocks from the White House. Bring photo ID, but I don't need to tell you that."

"So good of you to think of me, Alden . . . yes, me too . . . yes, bye-bye."

Sarah Jane holds her outstretched hand, palm toward Brad as a Stop sign, and speed-dials her dressmaker-friend's number.

"Sheila, I know it's a bad time, but . . . oh, bless her heart, say Happy Birthday for me . . . Sheila, I need a thingie to wear to a White House dinner, and I need it by Tuesday night . . . something, um . . ."

On his way to the kitchen, Brad stage-whispers, "Something off one shoulder."

"Um . . . yeah . . . something off one shoulder. I've got to be able to move around in it. There will probably be line dancing, which I don't know how to do, but I guess I'll need room to kick and stomp. You've got to go, I know, but be thinking about it, and call me in the morning. 'Bye for now."

Brad returns with a tray of tumblers of mineral water and lime wedges, which he distributes to various cork coasters around the patio for Sarah Jane's random, spontaneous use. She takes one with a smile bright enough to illuminate the entire coastal range.

"That's a pretty classy dating site you're using," he says.

"Oh. My. Goodness. What do I do now?"

"Well, you made a good start by calling Sheila. You'll look great, and you'll be fine."

Sarah Jane sips her water and gazes into the vineyards, barely visible in the last light of dusk.

Brad takes over clearing and scraping dishes in the kitchen, whistling a grab-bag mix of "I Could Have Danced All Night," "Shall We Dance," and "Thank God I'm a Country Girl." He even does a spin before jump-shooting the dish towel to the counter. Or nearly there.

He retrieves the missed shot and heads back out to the patio just as tires scrunch the gravel driveway and headlight beams bob from a rattling 1997 Ford pickup, driven by Sheila. In the truck bed are her sixteenth-birthday-today daughter, Allison, two younger sisters, and three best friends. The girls scramble from the truck and run to Sarah Jane, tugging her out of her chair by both hands, and giving six simultaneous, but different, line dance lessons. Allison demonstrates "jaunty" hips. Sheila pops a CD into a boom box, and the sounds of Austin break the tranquility of sunset on the Elgar estate. She spaces the girls apart on the wooden deck at the far end of the stone patio. She and Allison then lead them in a series of slow, deliberate, shallow knee-bends, heel-and-toe steps, foot-crossings, and lasso pantomimes, with Sarah Jane trying to keep up. Brad decides to go upstairs and catch the Giants game on TV. He mutes the sound to let the happiness come into his windows from the deck and lull him to sleep.

A full moon casts silvery shadow-ripples on the roof of the Elgar home from a hovering six-rotor drone. The drone emits three high-pitched electronic pulses to activate sparks that ignite accumulated natural gas, slow-hissed from the black pipe to the new stainless steel gas cooking range and double oven. Custom built for the Elgar's designer kitchen, this "iconic cooking experience, with stainless steel overhead hood and fan," is launched twelve feet into the timbered ceiling in a concussive fireball. The adobe walls contain the pressure of the explosion, but not the French doors, which blow outward into the moonlight, raining glass upon the empty patio. The drone pitches in the turbulence before veering in an upward arc and disappearing in the fog gathering on the ridgeline. In upstairs bedrooms, on the other side of the house, Sarah Jane and Brad waken to the blast and a deluge from the fire sprinklers.

Monday, September 23, 2019; Toronto, Ontario

June Elgar looks through the peephole in the door of her condominium, a loft in a refurbished flour mill overlooking Lake Ontario, although this morning, nothing but drizzle and fog fills the floor-to-ceiling windows. With the ACEA offices boarded and under repair, she has been working from her living room since returning from Tokyo. She has dressed for a luncheon appointment in brown boots, cinnamon-and-mustard-plaid skirt, and mushroom-colored silk blouse with covered buttons. She finishes attaching a pewter earring and then admits Constable Cross from the Toronto Police Service and Sergeant Major Tory of the Royal Canadian Mounted Police counterterrorism unit. Cross, who had telephoned for this meeting, she knows from previous interviews about the ACEA headquarters' bombing. She stares at the card Tory has presented, and then looks up at him.

Tory says, "Ms. Elgar, the RCMP are involved now because of evidence of interest to our service."

"Counterterrorism? Why is that? We're an environmental organization."

Tory continues, "Yes, ma'am, but the explosive device is very similar to ones built and used in Tehran. This particular device has not been used in Canada before that we know of. Do you have connections with any Iranian organizations?"

June says, "Well, I must say this is the first time I've given much thought at all to Iran. I mean, after the news died down about the UN negotiations back in 2015. I'm very surprised. No, we have no dealings with anyone in Iran. We have no donors from there. We do have supporters in Jordan. But Iran couldn't possibly care what we do."

She laughs a high, giddy laugh, slaps both palms against her knees, and stands. "Gentlemen, forgive my manners. I should have asked, may I offer you coffee? Or sparkling water? No?"

Cross says, "Look, June, I came back here because we are very concerned about your safety. Assume for discussion's sake you are right, that the Iranians don't care about ACEA. That's even more concerning since it suggests the attempt was personal. Besides your intern, you would normally be the only person in your offices at that hour. And the only reason you weren't there is that you were in Tokyo, which is not somewhere you normally go. Now, help us get to the bottom of this."

Rattled, June sits back down. "Constable, I am only too glad to cooperate. That explosion ruined everything in the office and nearly killed poor Christopher. So, here I am, sitting still, ready for your questions. Ask away."

Tory says, "Tell us about your relationship with Elgar Steel.

We are working with the police in Washington, D.C., who have a theory that Elgar executives are a target."

"I'm a minority shareholder in my family's business and wish I weren't, frankly. ACEA has succeeded in blocking the Wishbone Pipeline project, and that project is probably the last desperate hope for Elgar Steel. I wish no physical harm to anyone, least of all my own family, but I am determined to close down any chance for the Wishbone project to be built. Iran's back to exporting oil again, aren't they? I would think they would want what I want, to keep that tar sands oil off the world market. If you or your Washington contacts think differently, I would certainly like to know."

Tory says, "I'm not the one to figure out the geopolitical ins and outs, Ms. Elgar, but the forensic facts on the table point to possible Iranian involvement in the attempted murder of Mr. Brad Oaks and your sister, both Elgar senior executives, and now you, an Elgar family member and part owner of the very company your environmental organization is trying to thwart. These circumstances defy coincidence. I must say, your situation is riddled with conflict and confusion. But until we have sorted it all out, I am offering you RCMP protection. We can provide you a safe haven and anonymity for as long as you are at risk."

"I can't just disappear! What about ACEA?"

"Ms. Elgar, the RCMP can't possibly protect you unless you accept the conditions of our protection protocol."

June pouts. "Well, what would you do with me? Lock me away on some island?"

"We have several safe havens here in Canada. Perhaps in Manitoba. Or the Northwest Territories. If you have somewhere else in mind, I'm sure we could work something out."

June picks lint from her shirtsleeve and says importantly, "I have friends in Alberta. I know the premier there."

"We couldn't put you in close proximity to her, so Edmonton is out. What about Calgary? Once you are under cover there with a new identity, you could make discreet contact with your Edmonton friends. The ACEA offices are closed. It will take two or three months to remodel them. You can work from an office in Calgary as well as you can from home. In that time, I'm sure we can solve this Iranian riddle. I strongly urge you to do as we recommend."

June begins to think of creature comforts. "What's it like, this place in Calgary?"

Sergeant Major Tory lowers his voice and says, "Ms. Elgar, I do not have a specific place in mind. You are welcome to come to the station house and look over accommodations which might be available. They will not be as luxurious as this loft, however."

She stands as if to dismiss them. "I'm about to meet someone for lunch at LaVinia. Perhaps after that . . ."

Tory frowns and says, "Ms. Elgar, LaVinia would be way too prominent and visible for my comfort. I suggest you cancel your plans."

Sensing June's gathering storm, Constable Cross intervenes to suggest she invite her guest here for a catered lunch, even if it means a delay of an hour or so. He goes on to offer to have a uniformed policewoman come around later in the day with photos and particulars of available quarters in Calgary. Something in Cross's soothing manner, or perhaps the idea of the added attention of a personal showing of properties in her living room, brings June to consensus with the authorities. "May I tell my friends where I'll be?"

"No!"

"No."

Still squeezing for comforts, June says, "I generally fly first class across country."

"Ms. Elgar, RCMP protocol requires supervised transport. In this case, we will probably have you driven out of Toronto to somewhere off the beaten path where you will board the train west, accompanied by one of our female officers. I believe you will be provided a private roomette."

She pouts again, in earnest. "But there's never decent cell phone coverage on those trains."

The constable and the sergeant major both smile in unspoken satisfaction.

Napa County Undersheriff Don Hawks and Fire Captain Thad McCall stand stiffly on the Elgar estate patio, staring at the blackened, soggy interior of the kitchen. Sarah Jane and Brad sit on a lone redwood bench, the other bench and the table askew at the far end of the patio. Sarah Jane still trembles, even though it is now seven hours since the fire department had declared the premises safe from further fire and gas risk. Brad hands her a glass of lukewarm mineral water.

McCall turns and says, "Sarah Jane, if your family hadn't installed fire sprinklers, we would be looking at nothing but rubble. As it is, you are alive and still have a sturdy house. I don't like what I see here. That black pipe has been tampered with recently. I want you to try to remember who might have been doing work around the place the last few days."

Sarah Jane says, "I vaguely remember someone was here working, but I was in meetings all last week and didn't pay attention. My foreman, Will Turner, should have that information."

Hawks holds out a ten-by-fourteen-inch, clear plastic

evidence bag with a scorched metallic tip extending over the top. "Do you know what this is? No? How about you, Brad?"

Brad shakes his head, trying to get a better look at what seems to be a tapered, concave, thin metal sheet, bent over in a crumple at the broad end.

Hawks scowls and taps the object with a weathered finger. He says, "This here is a rotor blade off of a drone of some sort. FBI is coming to look things over and analyze this thing. You know of any kids around here with radio-controlled airplanes or that sort of thing?"

"No, Donny, I don't know of anything like that. I wish I could be of more help," says Sarah Jane.

Hawks draws himself to full height and declares, "This thing don't belong anywhere close to this house, ma'am. It musta fell off in the explosion, but its drone got away. Someone went to a lot of trouble to blow your kitchen up in the middle of the night. Like Thad says, you owe your lives to that sprinkler system. Who'd want to do this to you?"

Brad stands and describes the attempt made on him in Washington and on June's Toronto offices. He gives them Patricia Quinn's phone number, and briefly describes the suspicions about Iranian involvement. Hawks whistles and says this is beyond his department's resources. "If I was you people, I'd want to get somewhere else right away till the FBI gets a handle on this thing. I'm gonna sit down with your foreman and figure out who was coming and going around here."

Sarah Jane sighs and says, "I don't think for a minute anyone from the plant would do anything like this, but you can talk freely to the people who were out here for a few days last week. Set it up with the head of plant security. I'll e-mail him. They were gone by Friday afternoon around four o'clock."

Hawks says, "So how does Iran figure into this?"

Brad shakes his head from side to side as he says, "A whole lot of people are asking the same thing. So far, we have nothing but a few clues and a lot of speculation. But Patricia Quinn is about as up to date as anyone. She'll know the people investigating the Toronto explosion too. We have meetings in Washington coming up this week, and maybe something will develop out of those."

Thad McCall looks at Sarah Jane and says in reassuring tones, "You had it bad enough when Ernie died. Now this. I'm just real sorry about this. We'll do what we can. I'll personally work with the insurance adjuster. Seems there's damaged art in there. Napa Valley College does art conservation. You call them, and they'll probably lend a hand right away."

"OK, Thad, I'll do that next. Thanks. So, Brad, we're still going to Washington?"

"You bet we are! That's where we're needed the most. I'm going to call Knight and tell him what happened, and see if we can't get some heads together at his end."

Sarah Jane tugs on his sleeve and says, "Brad, hold on. I'll call Alden myself. He'd prefer that."

Monday, September 23, 2019; Napa

"Amaya, it's Brad. Seems I keep phoning you late at night."

"I'm so glad you called . . . I've missed you. When are you coming to me?"

"We've had a serious development here, Amaya. Someone tried to blow up the Elgar residence . . . no, no, she's fine, thank you. Shaken, of course. Look, I hope you're still staying at the suite in the Palace . . . ?"

"Yes, Brad, just as we had agreed. It's very comfortable, and I have been extremely busy fitting out the shop in the arcade. I feel safe. Well, I would feel safer if you were with me. Who is trying to harm you and my sisters? I feel so isolated here."

"Amaya, no one's certain, but the connection with Iran is getting clearer, if not the reason. They seem to want to interfere with our Wishbone work and at the same time with the strongest organization blocking it. Either that or they hold some personal grudge against the Elgar family, but no one understands what that might be. Look, we're going to Washington on Wednesday. Sarah Jane's going to a White House reception on Thursday, and she and I have meetings on Friday. The earliest I can leave for Tokyo is Saturday, but I have to be flexible with things moving so fast. No, I don't know what she's going to wear. Having something made. I don't know what color. I think it's off one shoulder. I suggested that, because of you."

Amaya Mori smiles and settles back against the bolsters propped at the headboard. Outside her window, the eight lanes of Uchibori Dori are filled with slow-moving headlights and taillights under a bright gibbous moon. "I am flattered you suggested that, because of me. I remember very well that mine seemed to frequently draw your eyes. Perhaps it will have a similar effect with my sister in the White House of America. Are you escorting her, Brad?"

"She's going as the date of the United States trade representative, Alden Knight. I'm not attending that affair."

"Oh my. She has friends in such places. Well, call me Thursday night if you feel lonely. There's a what? A baseball game on TV? You must, of course, attend to your priorities. What means 'playoff'? A 'wild card.' I see. That's all right, I can look it up. So you will be alone in a hotel room watching a wild game of cards and cannot call me. No, no need to explain, Brad. It makes perfect sense to me if it makes sense to you. I will be here, patiently waiting for you to call, or arrive, or something, Lieutenant Pinkerton . . . It's good to hear you laugh, Brad! Goodbye . . . thanks for your call. Please give Sarah Jane my felicitations for her date with an American Knight. Yes, pun intended."

"Goodbye for now, Amaya. I have much to talk to you about, but not over a telephone."

CHAPTER TWELVE

Tuesday afternoon, September 24, 2019; Washington, D.C.

Ichiro ushers into Ambassador Knight's office Mr. Arash Farahmani, chief of station, Interests Section, of the Islamic Republic of Iran. As there is no Iranian embassy in Washington, the Interests Section is a small office in the Pakistan embassy. Farahmani is the senior Iranian official afloat in America. Although the Iranian embassy closed in 1979, its empty building several blocks away has been maintained by the United States under an old treaty. Farahmani stands stiffly, waiting for Knight to ask him to sit.

Knight turns his chair to face Farahmani, but does not rise. "Mr. Farahmani, it's good of you to drop by on short notice. I'd like to talk hypothetically about a matter that may be of interest to you. Now, I don't know of any pipeline project going on in Dubuque, Iowa, requiring large-diameter steel pipe with the same specifications as the Wishbone Pipeline. However, I do know twelve pieces of such pipe were made in your country with Russian steel, shipped to New Orleans, and barged to Dubuque."

Farahmani raises his thick, black eyebrows, widens his eyes, and spreads his arms, elbows bent, in a human question mark. "This I do not know about and is not part of the mission of the Interests Section . . ."

"To be sure. Here is the hypothetical part. Let's suppose,

hypothetically of course, that the shipment was a test run in case Wishbone ever gets off the ground. Now, Mr. Farahmani, my people are experts on US antidumping and countervailing duties law. And I know that you are well aware that those statutes are designed to prevent injury to our domestic industries from products sold in the United States below prevailing prices in the home country, or below costs of production plus full transportation."

"Mr. Knight, I assure you—"

"I am simply reviewing the legal landscape in a hypothetical setting. Please don't leap to conclusions or take offense. You may not be aware that the pipe-making industries of the United States and Canada are diligent in pursuing legal remedies against what they characterize as unfair trade practices. Why, just a few years ago, the Canada Border Services Agency levied an antidumping duty of fifty-four percent of the export prices of steel pipe from several countries, and substantial countervailing duties against pipe originating in India. It seems Canadian pipe mills file cases like this with great regularity. Now, the American pipe industry is no less diligent, Mr. Farahmani. And the US Department of Commerce, the agency enforcing our laws, is no less rigorous than its Canadian counterpart."

"Ambassador Knight, the Islamic Republic of Iran pays all lawfully imposed duties on its commerce. You have called me in here to hector me over nothing." Farahmani's brow is beaded with perspiration.

"It is not nothing, Mr. Farahmani. Fifty-four percent of export price, Mr. Farahmani! And that doesn't include any countervailing duties. Your country would pay duties of that magnitude? Leaving net proceeds to you of only forty-six percent of bid price? Hypothetically?"

"This conjecture is absurd. Why do you intimidate me, Mr. Knight? We are not accused of any wrongdoing, and yet you talk about punitive duties, simply to disparage manufactured goods of Iranian origin. This is beneath you."

"Mr. Farahmani, on the subject of intimidation, I now move away from the realm of the hypothetical to raw reality on the streets of Washington and Toronto, and the vineyards of Napa Valley, California. I have in mind the very real and terrifying intimidation of people known to me personally, which I think is part of the puzzle over what your country's up to with its pipe mill."

"Preposterous. You race to the bottom of decency."

Knight says, "And just what might be discovered at the bottom of decency? Have you been contacted by a Detective Quinn, Mr. Farahmani? No? It seems there was a raid on a certain Iron Dragon Trading Company in Japan last weekend. Detective Quinn is working on connecting dots here, there, and everywhere . . . connecting them to a case of assault that occurred in front of my very own eyes at our very own State Department."

Knight swings his chair to present his back to Farahmani as he says, "Well, you can count on it. And Quinn does not ask hypothetical questions. Good day, Mr. Farahmani."

September 24-28, 2019; Washington, D.C.

On Tuesday, Sarah Jane and Brad collect what they need for their meetings in Washington. Brad phones Detective Quinn to report on the attack on the farm, and e-mails her the names and particulars of the Napa sheriff and fire officials. A zippered wardrobe bag, which Sheila made from sturdy navy-blue nylon, encases Sarah Jane's long gown, a tea-colored silk sheath off the left shoulder, with draped gathers in sensuous ripples across the front and back, opening out slightly at the ankle-length hem, and decorated with three lemon-colored darts at the originating points of the gathers at the right side, from shoulder to hip.

Wednesday morning at the San Francisco airport, near the Virgin America departure gate, Brad phones Quinn to arrange a meeting to review the latest developments. They settle on nine thirty Thursday morning in the lobby of the Jefferson.

Wednesday evening, they dine quietly in the Quill Lounge of the Jefferson. Sarah Jane retires to her room early to make two brief calls to the plant, and one to Alden Knight to touch base about the next evening. That call lasts over an hour.

Brad decides to call Amaya—it would be just coming on to noon in Tokyo—only to be switched to her voice mail. He leaves a brief status report and comments that he yearns for her as bees yearn for flower petals. *Sappy*, he thinks. If he could, he would retrieve the comment to edit smartly, but there it is. An hour later, he tries again, only to go to voice mail again. He tells her voice mail that the weather in Washington is clear and dry, with winds from the southeast at ten to fifteen miles an hour. After hanging up, he wonders why he told her that instead of something else. He calls back a few minutes later and compliments her voice mail's feet, adding that he yearns for the urgent touch of her foot in the night.

Thursday morning at five, Brad goes for a run along Massachusetts Avenue toward the Capitol, returning from the Union Station area by zigzagging through new construction around Ninth, and then K Street to McPherson Square where his office is—unoccupied for nearly a month.

Something catches his eye, and he slows to a jog-in-place. It's a 1978 Caprice Classic, in pretty roached-out shape. That was the first car he owned. Its biggest virtue was it was cheap at the time, and ran rough. He thinks this one probably does too. Same yellow color. *Damn, I'd like to get my hands on one of these. Maybe someday. It's always maybe someday with me.*

He signs in at the lobby desk, takes the elevator to his small office on the sixth floor, and lets himself in. He flips the switch that turns on, after a couple of reluctant blinks, the overhead fluorescent lights that illuminate the beige carpet, metal desk, and wall hangings of framed photos of migratory wildfowl taken from canoe-level at the edges of San Francisco Bay. The top of his desk is completely covered with neatly piled stacks of mail, separated by size. He sits in the unfamiliar chair and sorts through the envelopes containing a few bills, which he will take with him, and offers for magazine subscriptions, life insurance, travel, law books, law seminars, and clipping services, which he discards.

He leans back, looks out the window, and watches the sidewalk vendors setting up tables of stuff to sell, even though tourist traffic is minimal after Labor Day. It seems a futile task. He wonders if his desk and office offer a much brighter prospect. The office is part of a suite rented by the month, inclusive of a receptionist for every floor and telephone service. Ernie Elgar was convinced the company needed a personal presence in Washington at all times. Now, Brad is beginning to wonder about that, even though his enthusiasm for Wishbone remains high and on the rise. It's fine for now, and until Wishbone is settled once and for all. But after that? Unlikely the place for him. His mind wanders to Japan.

He holds one oversize card in the light to read the printed imperative to "Save the Date" of June 8, 2019, for the nuptials of Mr. Wilson de Santos and Detective Patricia Phelan Quinn. He blinks, then smiles. He saves this one, too.

He hopes this Wilson de Santos is the same who is bench coach for the Washington Nationals, and he's pretty sure it must be. *Well done, Quinn, Patricia!*

He's still smiling as he completes his run and reenters the lobby of the Jefferson, where he'll be meeting with the selfsame Quinn, Patricia in three hours. He is very glad he picked up his mail before that meeting.

"Hey, cowboy, thanks. Yeah, that's my de Santos, well, mine during the off-season anyway, and when he's not on his farm.

"Ms. Elgar, I'm glad to meet you. So you're in town for the big event down the street. Everyone draws extra duty on days and nights like these. We're posting a plainclothes unit at your hotel during your stay. It's that lot in the gray Chevy over there. Try not to run into it, cowboy."

Quinn reviews the key findings, namely that the Napa explosion had been from an Iranian-made device triggered by a remote control signal. No one had found the drone that carried the trigger. Quinn and the investigators in Napa are working on the assumption that the gas pipe was deliberately compromised by a workman. The triggering drone, as identified by the crumpled rotor blade, was similar to medium-range ones available on eBay for under $150. Washington Metropolitan police and the FBI independently confirm that the incident at the State Department was an attempt on Brad's life by an assailant with connections to the Iron Dragon splinter of the Japanese mafia, as well as connections with Iran. No one has come up with a motive, however. June's theory that Iranian oil exports would benefit from cutting Canadian oil exports doesn't explain targeting individual Elgar executives. All agree that the key to getting ahead of the Iranians is to figure out what they're doing.

Quinn wishes them well and leaves. One of the front desk attendants who sit at small, round tables with laptops instead of an imposing stand-up counter gestures to Sarah Jane, saying, "This just arrived for you, Ms. Elgar."

In her room, Sarah Jane opens the large manila envelope with the USTR return address and removes the formal, printed invitation and description of the reception, a printed menu, and a guest list with seating chart. On page one: "State Dinner. In honor of his Excellency Kenji Sonoda, Prime Minister of Japan, and Mrs. Sonoda, The White House October 3rd, 2019." On page three (page two being blank): "The President of the United States and First Family will host the Prime Minister of Japan for an Official Visit. The United States and Japan are strong allies who share vital interests and values, including stability in the Asia-Pacific region and the promotion of political and economic freedoms worldwide. Our Nations share a commitment to supporting human rights and democratic institutions, and this visit will highlight and strengthen our mutual cooperation." On page four: "The State Dinner will be held in the East Room of the White House. White House Executive Chef Alice Summers and White House Executive Pastry Chef Andre Poitiers have created a select menu featuring delicacies inspired by Japanese and American culinary traditions." Page five contains brief biographies of Summers and Poitiers.

Page six contains the Dinner Menu, from Toro Tartare, Bamboo Shoot and Hearts of Palm Consommé, Wagyu Beef

Tenderloin, to Silken Custard Cake, and wine pairings with each course, finishing with Sencha Tea and lemon cakes. There follows a page describing the Decor, ". . . mirroring the celebration of autumn in America's heartland, the windows of the White House will come alive with curtains of crystals evocative of early snow showers, while also symbolizing the brilliance of universal good will and hope."

On the last page: "Following the dinner, The White House will host a State Dinner Performance featuring cast members of the 2016 film adaptation of Stephen Sondheim's *Pacific Overtures*, set in 1853 Japan with the arrival of Commodore Perry and the opening of economic relations with America." Six performers are then listed with brief biographies and credits.

Sarah Jane carefully returns the printed materials to the manila USTR envelope, places the envelope in her suitcase, and begins to apply the hotel's steam iron to the gown created by Sheila. When Brad calls to suggest lunch, she quickly declines as she is not at all hungry. But she does thank him for his suggestion that she at least call for room service to bring a thermos of broth and six bottles of mineral water to get her through the rest of the day.

Alden Knight walks from the University Club across the street to the Jefferson Hotel, where his car and driver wait in the small circle drive. The doorman opens the lobby door for a radiant Sarah Jane Elgar to exit, but she is stopped by Knight's upraised hand. "Photo ID? That gown is stunning. You make me feel young." She sweeps ahead, brushes his cheek with a lipstick-preserving almost-kiss and says, "Lovely to see you, too, Alden. Of course I have my ID." She then gives him the beaming smile that he has been looking forward to.

The White House glistens in floodlights at the foot of Fifteenth Street, down which they drive in slow traffic. They are warmly greeted at each of the stations they must pass through, one with a metal detector, and verify their names on checklists verbally and by showing IDs. She does a slight double take as she recognizes one of the Marine sentries next to the door—he went to Napa High School and used to work the grape harvests— who, with an almost imperceptible twitch of one corner of his stony face, conveys both recognition and stern warning that he cannot say nor do more by way of greeting. Once inside, she stops to gaze at the President Kennedy posthumous portrait by Aaron Shikler hanging in the Entrance Hall. Knight stands beside her patiently; it has the same effect on him every time he sees it. She accepts the greetings of White House staff guiding guests into the Blue Room for champagne flutes and smoked salmon on wafers of pumpernickel toast.

The East Room decor imagines the interior of a barn in mid-America, with wooden pegs of harnesses and tack hanging next to tri-candle sconces on the long walls, and white spider-web clusters fill the windows at one end of the chamber, nearly eighty feet long. Bone-white cornstalks lean against the new satin wall coverings with jack-o'-lanterns clustered at the bases. Sarah Jane finds the decor distracting from the magnificent John Gilbert full-length portrait of George Washington, but keeps her opinion to herself. The room has been filled with round tables of eight, covered with pumpkin-colored felt and white, open-worked lace tablecloths over that. Each centerpiece is a cluster of autumn leaves and chrysanthemums in fall colors, the table of honor holding only white chrysanthemums, the emblem of the eighteenth-century Tokugawa Shogunate that preceded the modern era of Japan. Overhead, three crystal-faceted chandeliers, illuminated from within and encircled by twenty electric candles, hang from the long center line of the white molded plaster ceiling. Against the east wall, a fifteen-inch-high stage holds mock stable stalls and hay, which will be removed for the after-dinner performance. Sarah Jane quietly tests the slipperiness of the parquet floors just in case line dancing actually materializes.

She is seated between Ian McMillian, Canada's ambassador to the US, and his wife, Charlotte. A couple and two singles make up the rest of her table. The couple are Mr. and Mrs. Abe Ohita, he a brother-in-law of the prime minister. Brigadier General Hugh Braxton, retired, a widower and formerly stationed in Okinawa in command of the Third Marine Expeditionary Force, is paired on the seating chart with Ms. Claire Alcott, an unmarried, sixty-two-year-old Washington A-list hostess and donor who had, ten months earlier, accompanied Alden Knight at one of these affairs. She is distinctly unhappy about her seating circumstance at his table tonight, as she will inform the White House tomorrow in a strong letter on personal notepaper. Introductions are completed, although all but Braxton have already memorized the table's manifest. Sarah Jane ventures a sip of the white wine awaiting them at the table, a tart Virginia vintage, when Ms. Alcott, after three glasses of champagne in the Blue Room, says flatly,

"I hear you make plumbing."

Knight groans. Sarah Jane blanches, puts her hand on his forearm, and after two beats says, "Oh, I wish! Nothing that practical or profitable, I fear. We do make large-diameter steel pipe for large projects when they come along."

Everyone else at the table is relieved to hear Mrs. Ohita

chime in with a smile, "Oh, you are too modest. She is a well-known sculptor. I was at the dedication ceremony of the piece you made under commission for the Kyushu National Museum in 2007. You could not possibly remember me—I was at the rear of many admirers. You captured perfectly the spirit of the museum, which is to emphasize the history of the movement of the earliest peoples to Japanese islands from the mainland of Asia."

Sarah Jane beams, color filling her cheekbones. "It was an honor to be chosen for that job."

"Steel?" booms McMillian. "Iron worker here. Did bridges. Ever walk a steel girder over an untamed mountain river, Knight?"

Knight leans back and smiles. "No, even my misspent youth was considerably tamer than yours."

McMillian turns to Sarah Jane and says, "What are your projects these days, Ms. Elgar? Not sculptures but the other kind."

"Please, it's Sarah Jane. Well, our pipe sales last year were over three hundred million dollars, pretty much evenly divided between water transmission projects and energy projects."

"Oh my," says Mrs. McMillian. "And you have time to make sculptures?"

"Oh, you know, Charlotte, you make the time for the work you love."

Knight says, "Actually, Ian, I've been talking to the Elgar people about the Wishbone project. I know how dedicated you have been to pushing that through. And speaking of untamed rivers, you'll be interested in an idea Sarah Jane has talked to me about. Sarah, would you mind filling us in on your thinking? I think it's an appropriate time and place to bring it into the sunshine."

Although unrehearsed, this opening is not unexpected. Sarah Jane has thought about the "coincidence" of being seated next to the Canadian ambassador. She turns her chair slightly to speak directly to McMillian. "Since you know Wishbone, you know that the opposition argues risk of pollution versus no benefit to America. We think it would benefit both Canada and America to lay double pipelines in the same right of way. The second line would bring water to our Midwestern farmers and ranchers. We think it's win-win."

McMillian puts down his wineglass. He looks at Sarah Jane, and then he looks at Knight. "You never said anything about this, Alden."

Knight says, "Hell, it never occurred to us. Or to you. It's the brainchild of Sarah Jane here and her late father."

McMillian smiles. "Shades of NAFTA, eh? So, Alden, is water in its natural state a 'good or product' under GATT and NAFTA?"

Claire Alcott excuses herself and stands to find the ladies' room. A nearby tuxedoed waiter offers her a steadying arm and then is replaced by a woman from White House staff who leads her away.

Charlotte says, "Oh please! Ian, let it go. Enjoy dinner and the guests."

Knight says, "She's absolutely right. Let's talk shop next week. But think about it, Ian. I think this idea shows promise."

McMillian grunts. "Call me next week, Alden." He taps his temple. "The wheels are turning."

General Braxton and Mr. Ohita have been quietly considering one another. They have not spoken, except in introduction. They have not followed the conversation about pipelines. Their thoughts have separately wandered to other uses of steel in bygone days. Ohita's father was a teenaged tank driver in the Japanese Imperial Army's occupation of Manchuria. Braxton's father was a young lieutenant in the Seventeenth Airborne Division's relief of Bastogne. They could, if they were so inclined, have spoken volumes to one another. Both their fathers had survived the fighting in those theaters, and both were in the process of being redeployed in the summer of 1945 for the eventual battle in mainland Japan. Had it not been for the momentous decision of the then-occupant of the White House, who had played a waltz on a piano in this very room, their fathers might well have met as combatants. They might well have not had sons.

Following Sondheim songs from the principal singers, the Air Force string quartet, plus banjo and guitar, moves to the center of the stage. Tables and chairs have been arranged to leave a long, open space on the parquet floor. The quartet strikes up "Achy Breaky Heart." Younger White House staff scurry to make a line in the cleared space. Alden looks at Sarah Jane and mouths silently, "You don't have to." Sarah Jane pushes back her chair, takes Alden's hand, and moves to the line. The staffers open up the center for them. Alden laughs.

A young woman takes the lead, and the line begins to weave in the slow steps, taps, and clomps of a Texarkana roadside dance hall. The First Couple moves to the line when "Country Girl (Shake It for Me)" starts. That's when an emboldened Sarah Jane adds jauntiness to her hips, drawing anonymous whistles from the back of the room. "Boot Scootin' Boogie," however, exceeds the levels of preparedness of both Knight and Sarah Jane, and they scoot instead for their seats to the applause of the Ohitos, Braxton, and the Canadians.

They return to the dance space, however, when the line dancers finish and the music shifts to "Bridge Over Troubled Water." Sarah Jane leans into Alden Knight, and her fingertips touch the nape of his neck. She says,

"So where did you learn line dancing, Alden?"

"I'm kind of a jeans-and-boots guy, Sarah Jane. I was stationed in Fort Hood, Texas, and picked up a lot of bad habits I missed in school. Line dancing, for example."

"Um, other examples?"

"Did not involve dancing in lines."

She nudges him. "What schools?"

"Well, I went to Stanford Law."

"Have any fun there?"

"Oh, sure. At the football games. A pizza dinner at Cara's south of campus was kind of high society. Where did you go to school?"

"UC Davis undergrad and spent two years after that at UC Berkeley in the art department. Did you grow up in California?"

"No, the Chicago area. My dad was a lawyer there. They sent me to Chicago Latin all the way through high school."

"Really? So you are fluent in Latin?"

"Ha. Hardly. They teach you that for grammar and to do research in original sources. But they also teach French, even Chinese, and I managed to get through those."

"Impressive." She squeezes his hand, presses even closer, and whispers in his ear, "Mr. Ambassador, the music is over. People are gawking."

The return drive from the White House to the Jefferson Hotel following the event would take three or four minutes in the eleven o'clock hour on a weeknight. Sarah Jane knows at least that much about Washington's traffic patterns. But tonight,

Alden Knight instructs his driver to tack on thirty minutes by way of the George Washington Parkway and Spout Run on the Virginia side of the Potomac to see the city lights.

The ambassador turns tour guide for a few minutes before falling silent when Sarah Jane rests her head on his shoulder. In the dark loop of road in Spout Run that circles back toward the city, he says,

"I can't tell you how much I've enjoyed your company this evening. Usually, these things are all display and a relief to get away from. You make it a new experience."

"New? You talk about new? What about me, a farmer-welder from the sticks?"

"Come on. You're a global artist and maker of infrastructure. You're what Washington wonks blather about day in and day out but rarely lay eyes on. You were the center of attention of a pretty jaded crowd, to say nothing of my center of attention."

"Alden, I'm not one to go out much."

"I'm not one to enjoy going out much, but tonight was the exception. I'd like to make it more regular if that's not too direct."

"You are a negotiator! Well, when's the next White House dinner? I'll check my calendar."

"I have in mind something much less lofty. Like a pizza and rosé."

"At Cara's? I thought that was in Palo Alto, California."

"It was, years and years ago. It closed down a long time ago. No, I say pizza to mean more casual, more frequent."

"So you're thinking about dates with me?"

"I am."

"I guess temptation is the first stage of negotiation. I'll be honest, it is tempting. Let me get back to you on that."

"I couldn't have hoped for a better answer."

CHAPTER THIRTEEN

The next day, Brad and Sarah Jane walk seven blocks in bright sunlight to their one o'clock meeting at USTR. Patricia Quinn smiles when they enter the conference room. Knight introduces them to: Virginia Henderson, on the Canadian desk at State; Ralph Fergus, from the CIA; David Baker, FBI; and Meredith Holmes, White House deputy chief of staff, who smiles in admiration as she greets Sarah Jane. Knight states he wants to brainstorm about the apparent Iranian connection to the attacks on the Elgars. He asks Quinn to brief the meeting on what's been learned to date.

She acknowledges that Baker and the FBI will be taking over the investigation now, but reviews the same findings as she did on Thursday morning. She adds that she interviewed Mr. Farahmani of the Iranian mission but hit a stone wall with him. Knight asks for a roundtable discussion of what the Iranian objective could be. Since most of the people are new to the file, no one speaks up.

Quinn reviews what June Elgar had proposed to the RCMP, a move to block Canadian oil exports. Knight says that in his conversation with Farahmani, the prospect of paying high dumping duties had not seemed to faze him. Fergus from CIA asks Sarah Jane about ballpark pricing compared to costs of production and transportation. Her estimates produce shaking of heads and a low whistle. Then Fergus asks about pricing if

Elgar were eliminated as a bidder. She estimates the bids might be somewhat higher, but the price leader would still be the Canadian mill, and the Iranians would still have to bid way below delivered costs. Heads shake again.

Knight says, "OK, maybe it's not happening. Why would anyone put high-quality steel pipe in American soil at a huge loss?"

The room is quiet. Suddenly, Sarah Jane stands and paces. She says,

"No one would. But someone like Iran might want to put *faulty* pipe in American soil, and not care how much it costs. Bad pipes along the Wishbone Pipeline route, which goes near cities, rivers, and bridges, would be like bombs."

Knight slaps the palm of his hand on the table . . . *bam!*

"Alden," says Sarah Jane, "I'm a welder and a metallurgical engineer. You can make bad welds look good, and good welds act badly. Welding is inspected, of course, but it can be done. You can add tiny amounts of contaminant during the electric arc-welding process that could escape detection. And since the mill operators know where every piece of pipe is going along the route of the pipeline, they'd only have to mess up a few critical pieces to do a lot of mischief."

Sarah Jane reseats herself next to Knight. He turns and looks at her. "That's an impressive piece of intelligence analysis, on the spot and spur of the moment. It makes my skin crawl to think about pipe bombs of that size." He turns to look at Fergus. "In this town, we wring our hands over a nuclear Iran, and it blinds us to everyday threats . . . less dramatic ones. Sarah Jane, you have now given me a brand-new national perspective on Wishbone that tops even the imported-water brainstorm of Brad Oaks over there."

Brad is immobile. It occurs to him to be deeply frightened about the attempt on his life a few weeks before. Up to now, he has not thought of the gunshot as anything personal, not even after he heard Quinn say it was. Not even when he was taking precautions about using the telex or which plane to catch. That was like dodging hailstones. *But someone who aims a gun at me to take my life—that is an affront. It is no one else's business whether I live or die. That's my personal domain.* Until now, it had been a blur of a crowded room and flying glass, and who knows what was going on. He could even manage to flirt. It was like lightning striking the Tokyo Tower—distant and random. *That's it, random—because it couldn't be a deliberate act, not directed at me, without a reason. I'm all about reason. If there's no reason, then it's not really there. But now, Sarah Jane, out of her reasonable engineer's and artist's mind, has stated the reason. Now, with a reason—this reason—it really was there. It really still is there. The reason didn't go away. Will it ever go away? Will they go away? Is it now their business whether I live or die?* "We're born alone. We die alone."

Agent Baker breaks the silence. "So now, the theory is: the Iranians want the pipeline to go ahead, and that's why they targeted ACEA. They also targeted Elgar people to get Elgar Steel out of the bidding?"

Sarah Jane says, "Basically, yes, that's it in a nutshell. They want us out of the bidding so they can pick up a larger pipe order. Wishbone won't rely on the Canadian mill for the whole pipeline. But if Elgar's out of it, then the Wishbone project has to go deeper into the international market, and that's where the Iranians are."

Knight says, "That's exactly what Rod Graham at Wishbone told me."

Baker says, "With a larger order, they plant more defective pipes, and more disastrous failures along the pipeline. You're right, it wouldn't matter what the costs or duties would be. It's still a weapon, with a little bit of revenue, and a bloody bargain."

"So what's next?" asks Knight.

Brad says, "Ambassador Knight, did you say that you got hold of the twelve Iranian pipe sections?" Knight nods. "Well, the next step would be to get every one of those pipe sections tested. Especially the welded seams."

Sarah Jane says, "I'll have my chief engineer lend a hand; he literally wrote a book on weldment failures."

Everyone mutters agreement. Baker says the FBI will take on the inspections. He goes on to say he'd like Sarah Jane to go into protection, just like June, until the immediate danger is over.

Knight says, "We know the most likely motive for all of this. It's an FBI case now. Ralph, I guess you'll run this by the counterterrorism people in town for focus and assessment. Ms. Holmes, you've been keeping notes on that little laptop, so I reckon you'll keep the White House up to speed. Virginia, you'll take this to the Secretary.

"Frankly, I think State should head up negotiations with Canada. This office is more about tariffs and trade barriers, so we'll get into the NAFTA weeds for you. I've already got Ambassador McMillian thinking about this, and I'll follow up with him on Monday. Let's get to work. Baker, why don't you stick around for a minute?" Knight tugs on Sarah Jane's sleeve, and she sits again, with Brad following suit.

After the conference room empties, Knight says to Sarah Jane, "I don't like the idea of you going back to California. Dave, what are you thinking, protectionwise?"

Baker says, "Frankly, I think the best solution is for her to stay right here in D.C. I have more people here, and I'm sure Quinn's department can lend a hand too. The thing is, I don't think we can use the Jefferson."

Knight says, "How about at the University Club? Great rooms, and I can get us great member rates."

Sarah Jane says she'd prefer the Club anyway—the atmosphere is a lot less precious than the Jefferson over a long stay. That settled, Baker shakes hands all around and leaves.

Knight says, "Look, I hope you two don't think I'm abandoning this project. I can work best in the background, and we all need this to follow what we call around here 'regular order,' meaning the right channels, despite the populist tidal wave of the last election.

"This kind of negotiation is not strictly part of my brief. As I said, we're more about tariffs and such. Honestly, I don't want my part in the negotiation to look like personal favoritism. By the same token," he looks directly at Sarah Jane, "I don't want this project to dictate the pace or direction of my personal agenda." Sarah Jane turns beet red.

"Brad, Detective Quinn asked me to give this to you after the meeting." Knight hands Brad a red-white-and-blue envelope. "Two passes to tonight's playoff game against the Dodgers. But if you don't mind, I'd like to borrow Sarah Jane for the evening. I've lined up Secretary Burns and his wife for dinner with us at the club. I don't know of anyone who can make a better pitch for the second pipeline than her. She had Ian McMillian hooked on the first cast."

Brad says, "Sure, that's great. Sarah, I wouldn't be able to score a meeting with the secretary of state in six months on my own, if then. You know, I'm going to try to get Jeff Colbert to join me. It's time to get our plant's congressman up to speed before he reads about it somewhere."

Walking to the Jefferson, Brad says, "Sarah Jane, I'm going to head back to Tokyo tomorrow. You've got the helm here, and that's as it should be."

Sarah Jane, the sun glinting in her hair, smiles and says brightly, "Brad, if you think that's where you're needed, fine. But Brad—"

Sarah Jane's phone rings. They stop as she fishes it out of her leather carryall. She stares at the sidewalk as she listens—for a long time. People on the K Street sidewalk collide or jostle past her until she slowly moves closer to the curb.

"What's the driver's name?" She walks up to Brad and looks at him with the phone still at her ear. "This is Donny Hawks in Napa. He's been to the plant. He just interviewed everyone who came over to the meeting last week, except they can't find the driver of the SUV. Listen to this. His name is Masoud Farahmani. He's in this country on a student visa and goes to Rensselaer Polytechnic in New York. In metallurgical engineering!" She pauses and listens, then looks back up at Brad.

"Three years ago, he traveled to America for one month with an uncle, also named Farahmani, both on a Pakistani diplomatic passport. Wow. OK, Donny, thanks. This is probably the key to the whole thing. Get hold of Detective Quinn, and give her a full report, and find out who at the FBI she wants you to contact out there. Well, because Quinn and the FBI are interested in this other Farahmani for the potshot at Brad Oaks, among other bad things. This is spooky, but it's going to help a lot. Oh, and please coordinate with our plant security so they can reconstruct what this kid could have had access to there and at the meetings at my place. OK, Donny, thanks."

She steadies herself on Brad's arm and says, "Let's go get a glass of a bold red wine."

In the Jefferson's lounge, Sarah Jane says, "Brad, I need you at the plant. I've left Eddie Sandoval in charge, but he's going to need help if he gets in over his head on something. I want you to stay on top of the inspections of that Iranian pipe. And I want you to head up the investigation of what that Farahmani kid learned about us and figure out what we need to do about it. That's going to take at least through the end of the month. Maybe by then, this mystery will be solved."

Brad expects her to ask him if he agrees. Uncharacteristically, this time, she doesn't. He frowns as he attempts to rein in opposing internal forces.

She says, "Do you have a problem with that?"

"No, Sarah. Very sensible. My mind was elsewhere."

"Really? That's not like you."

They meet again for breakfast the next morning. Sarah Jane tells him Knight and Burns spent most of the evening reliving the 2016 nominating campaign, and the inside story of what landed Burns his job at State. Burns had listened to her with his full attention. He said he remembered a hallucinogenic scheme put out by a California engineering firm in the middle of the last century, about piping water from Alaska to Southern California, and said that at least this scheme shows greater restraint. But he said that with a twinkle in his eye, and Knight told her later that Burns likes the idea in general but would need more detail. Knight commented that with Burns, greater detail always means: How hard is the president pushing it? He told Burns that he had that covered.

Brad says, "Colbert is on board. I'm glad I got to him early. He will want to be seen as delivering something big to our workforce. The water pipeline will help him with the environmentalists. He said he would put his chief of staff on it and see where they go from there. He's on the Agriculture Committee and can work the Kansas, Oklahoma, and Nebraska delegations." Sarah Jane nods approval. Then Brad says, "So how long before you go back to Stockton?"

Sarah Jane stretches out her legs and says, "Brad, I don't know, and I'm really in no hurry to leave. I have to tell you, I enjoy the attention I'm getting. Actually, I like Alden a great deal. I haven't felt this way . . . well, maybe ever. You know me pretty well, Brad. I've never had what you'd call a significant crush on anyone. But this seems different. I could see him in my life. It's hard to explain."

"No, you explained it eloquently. You have a 'chance not to be alone anymore.' That is crystal clear."

On his way to the airport, Brad calls Amaya. She picks up on the third ring. He tells her what he must.

"I had a premonition that your message on my phone would not come about. But it is not a fateful ending. It is a last-minute business change, and so we must think of it as normality in our lives. It is a new normality that I welcome even with disappointment. I shall look on it that way."

"Good. No other way of looking at it would be true. But it's not safe yet for you to return to your place."

"I must resume the rest of my normal life, Brad. I feel safe enough at home. I shall leave this hotel room tomorrow. Call me, Brad. But do not call me all the time. I must hear from you, but too many reminders will cause my throat to ache."

163

Tuesday morning, October 1, 2019; Napa

Brad stands on the patio, looking into the blackened, sodden kitchen. With him are Donny Hawks, Thad McCall, Eddie Sandoval, and Will Turner. The vineyards surrounding the estate have begun to drop yellow and dark-red leaves. It is eight in the morning. Sheriff Hawks methodically briefs them about his findings at the Stockton plant, as follows: *Masoud Farahmani hired on at the plant in May. Although he wanted to work in the pipe mill, it was down for maintenance and upgrades. Besides, Elgar doesn't just start new hires in the mill. They put him in the motor pool as a mechanic and occasional driver. Right about then, the company's transportation department started working on ideas for reducing the cost of hauling pipe to potential job sites for the Wishbone project. Farahmani got wind of it, went to his boss, and said he wanted to work on the problem. So they let him sit in on two planning sessions.*

Sandoval says that they were brainstorming ideas for backhauls from north-central states to the West Coast. One idea was to haul pelletized hay for export to China, but they couldn't make the numbers work. The Farahmani kid figured out it would work if the pellets went to a port on the Mississippi River and out through NOLA to the Mideast. They called it "feasible case freight estimate" or FCFE. It was the basic backhaul idea they were working on, not a precise transportation plan with the precise locations. Anyway, they gave him two hours a day out of the garage and in front of a computer to figure out costs and routes. Farahmani took to it like a duck to water. It turns out the transportation department doubles as a sort of in-house travel agency, making airline and hotel reservations for anyone on business travel.

Brad brings both hands to his temples and squeezes as if to stifle the realization that Sarah Jane always uses that department to book her travel. He never does just because his trips are last minute and he likes to pick his own hotels.

Within three weeks, he had a very convincing FCFE put together, using Dubuque as point C. Under that plan, a truck tractor would leave the plant, pulling two truck beds. One would carry Wishbone pipe, and the other would carry an empty container. It would go to a delivery point on the Wishbone right of way, off-load the pipe, and go to grain elevators in Nebraska. There, they'd load the container with pellets, drive to Dubuque, drop the container, and return to the plant. When Sarah Jane called an all-hands-on-deck meeting in Napa in September, he volunteered to drive the SUV with the engineering drawings and maps. One of the drawings was a schematic of this FCFE, just marked A to B to C to A. He had slept in the SUV on Wednesday and Thursday nights. He had given the plant notice he would be quitting on the Friday of those meetings. He said he wouldn't drive the SUV back because he was going backpacking along the coastal range. Even though he had enrolled online in a welding class at his college in New York, he never showed up when the class started.

Brad says, "So Farahmani had access to the house here for a couple of days. I'm interested in knowing if there's anything missing."

Will Turner says, "Well, they've accounted for all the artwork based on the insurance inventory. Nothing is missing in the way of silverware or electronics. I haven't searched the upstairs office because I never go there."

Brad says that's where he'll start. The office still smells of acrid smoke, but the flames never reached it. Everything on the desk and tabletop had been soaked, but spread out on towels to dry. By now, he knows pretty much everything that had been in the office.

But he can't find Ernie's lacquered box with Amaya Mori's information and mementos.

He pulls apart file drawers. He looks everywhere. He looks again.

It isn't there. His knees buckle.

"Hey, Will, can you come up here?" he shouts.

Will does, but cannot help. Brad feels panic take over his body. He slumps to the floor. Hawks comes in behind Turner. Through choking tightness in his throat, Brad blurts out telegraphic phrases about the box, Amaya, her inheritance, her stockholding. Donny turns on his heel and radios his office for a name he had written down the last time he talked with Sarah Jane. He barks an order to a deputy to call that name, Inspector Tanaka of the Tokyo police, and tell him to be on the lookout for Farahmani and to check on Amaya Mori. "Where? Hold on." He returns to the office, where Brad is pale, perspiring, and keening, "Nooooo." After a few minutes, Hawks speaks into his radio again: "Try Mori art gallery. I'm right here, on hold. You try to get Tanaka on the line." Hawks boosts the volume of his radio receiver, turning it into a conference call.

After a long pause, the radio crackles from the sheriff's office. "It's midnight there. Tanaka's not there. They'll call him at home. Do you have a number for the woman?" Brad opens his smartphone, scrolls to Amaya's cell phone, and hands it weakly to Hawks. They wait as the deputy relays the number to Tokyo. An epoch passes.

The radio crackles again. "There's no answer on that phone. Should they trace it and send someone?"

Brad clutches his waist. He howls, "Yesssssss!"

At four thirty that afternoon, Eddie Sandoval sits in the Elgar living room, instructed by Sheriff Hawks not to leave Brad Oaks alone. Brad has recovered his composure. He has given Eddie an earful about Amaya Mori, the priorities in his life, and how they have changed in the last few hours. Eddie says, "I'm guessing Sarah Jane sent you to babysit me. And now, I'm supposed to keep my eye on you."

Brad's cell phone rings.

"Tanaka here," says a quiet voice. "Pardon my interrupting, Mr. Oaks-san. Mori-san has not worked in Ginza area store or Palace Hotel store in three days. Her apartment security reported to local station this morning, not seeing her that time too. I have been briefed by Detective Quinn and FBI concerning one Farahmani man in suspicion. Such a named man entered Narita airport four days ago. He is not at local address declared on entry document. Officers are searching. I am sorry no more better news. Can you tell me other contacts in Japan if not bothering?"

"Mr. Tanaka, thank you for your call and your efforts. This is a very dangerous situation. He has attempted to kill me and Ms. Mori's American sisters over business involving Elgar Steel. If he is dumb and violent, then the situation is desperate. But if he is smart, he might believe he can get what he wants through forcing her to give him her stock in Elgar Steel. He is educated and capable of smart planning."

Tanaka pauses and says, "Then we must assume smart. Otherwise very little hope. Who should I contact in Japan?"

Brad tells him about her lawyers, Parker Wright and Haseo, and her relationship with Sunrise Trading. Tanaka says that is helpful and apologizes for any distress caused by lapses in the Japanese security network.

"But, Mr. Oaks-san, there is another possibility."

"Yes?"

"That he is smart and violent."

Brad ends the call. He looks at Sandoval and gives him the gist. "I need to go to Tokyo, Eddie."

"Yes, you do. You don't really think I need a babysitter, do you?"

"No. I just know I need a taxi."

"Let's go. I'll drop you at the airport on my way back to Stockton. I'll talk to Sarah Jane."

Phoning from Sandoval's car, Brad books the last first-class seat on the next flight to Tokyo, leaving at seven p.m. His next call is to Tanaka's office with his flight information. His next call after that is to Sarah Jane's voice mail, where he brings her up to date about developments and his plans.

On the flight, Brad strains to clear his head of fear and confusion. He makes an agenda in his mind—no notes on napkins, just in his mind, the way he would prepare for a start in a crucial game. He would keep to the essentials, and try to recognize when to keep the unknowable or unacceptable out of his preparations. He must only concentrate on what he knows and can accept. Now, here he is again: top of the ninth inning in a scoreless tie. *First, I must extract Amaya from Farahmani. I assume she's alive. If she's not, game over. Unacceptable. So I must proceed, believing she's alive and thinking rationally. Next, only after I get Amaya back, will my future include her? I*

*know that yes, it does. Next, does she feel the same? I think—
I'm sure—she does.*

*But we have to spend unhurried time together to know that
with certainty. It's worth trying. It's worth spending as much
time as it takes. That's my ultimate purpose of going to Japan
this time. Nothing else takes precedence. All right, let's say we
decide we must be together. Where? Do I turn my back on
Elgar? Does she turn her back on her business? Not enough
information; that has to reveal itself when we get away
together. So put it out of mind for right now. It has to be
decided then, after she's out and we're quiet.*

*What do I do to get her out? Whatever I can. Whatever
Tanaka will let me do. What if that is nothing?*

Brad tries to grasp the concept of doing nothing. *Nothing to
do is unacceptable.* There has to be something. Brad flattens his
seat and pulls the blanket around him. He snaps off the console
light. The white noise of the jet engines behind the first cabin
begins to bleach away his thoughts. *Where is she? What is she
thinking? She's alone—she needs her chance to not be alone
anymore. What is she thinking?*

White noise. The plane is steady. He feels almost weightless.

In the white noise. Floating. Like the canoe.

Moments later, in this canoe, his eyes blink open wide with
fear and conviction.

Yes, that's it. That's better than nothing. It's everything.

CHAPTER FOURTEEN

September 29 or maybe September 30 or maybe October 1 or maybe October 2; Ikebukuro district, Tokyo, in a cramped, dark space

Running, running, running. Why? Where? Ahead is all, no stopping. Stones. Feet. I can't feel my feet. My feet are bound. Running, running, running.

Thirsty. Head hurting. Running, running, running. Is my mother running? No, I am running. Who is that, ahead? The child just ahead? My mother? Is Mother just a child? No, I am just a child.

On fire. No, no, not Mother, please! Make me on fire, not Mother. No, I'm running. Who is on fire? White air. Burning. Don't burn, Mother, please run.

Running from white sky fire. Falling. Scraping. Mother! Lift me, Mother! Take me, Mother! Stillness. Numb. Stones. Shards of cement. Why are they hot? My feet are scorched cold and scratched. White light behind my mother.

In the white light. Running.

White light spills over the sweating heap that is Amaya Mori on the cracked concrete floor. The white streak of light shatters her dream. A hand pushes a dish of sliced, salt-pickled daikon radishes and a plastic bottle of Xanax-laced green tea into the room, on the cement floor's streak of white that narrows and turns black again with a click-lock when the door closes. A door she does not remember clearly. She drinks three sips of the liquid. She has learned to count the sips between shafts of light and door-clicks. Three sips now and then dream, or count the length of a dream, and sip; a hundred sixty-three dreams will mean survival until another bottle of cold tea will slake her salt-parched thirst of fire.

No Nabeshima porcelain dishes from eighteenth-century feudal Japanese nobility. No woodblock Edo-era engravings from her shop. No Bach sonata. No light. No Brad. In her next dream, she is running.

Wednesday, nightfall, October 2, 2019; Narita and Tokyo

The official at the final desk to clear entrance to Japan at Narita airport stamps Brad's passport, but holds it against his chest and motions to a group of Japanese uniformed police in dark-blue raincoats. A woman with short black hair, wearing glasses and a dark-blue suit with a white blouse, approaches, bows quickly, and extends her small hand to Brad.

"I am Ms. Hiradi, Interpreter Branch, Tokyo Metropolitan Police. Mr. Tanaka sent us to meet you. Do you have luggage?"

"Ms. Hiradi, how do you do. Thank you for meeting me. No, I had no time to pack. I am ready to go with you."

The police car comfortably holds the four who drove it from Tokyo to Narita. With Brad in the front passenger seat, no one rides comfortably for the ninety-minute return trip, lights flashing, to the Metropolitan Police headquarters. Ms. Hiradi sits stiffly in the center of the back seat, tilting despite her efforts to stay upright as the car accelerates up and around circular ramps to an elevated highway.

She tells Brad that Mr. Tanaka is willing to discuss the case at the station now or in the morning. Brad says he wants to meet right away. Ms. Hiradi gives short instructions to the driver in Japanese. Then all settle in for the ninety-minute drive. The two men on either side of Ms. Hiradi in the back seat snooze, and then snore. She counts miles. Except for the steady sweep of windshield wipers against heavy drizzle, the occasional radio voices, and the snores, the car is silent. Finally, Brad recognizes the headquarters building. It is within sight of the Palace Hotel and across a wide thoroughfare from the Imperial Palace's moated stone walls. The car enters a cavernous underground parking lot.

Ms. Hiradi leads Brad to a windowless conference room, where a bulletin board with passport photos of Amaya, Brad, and Farahmani have been pinned among arrows and phrases in Japanese scrawled with red and black felt-tip pens. Other blank sheets with sketched generic face profiles are pinned with no connecting lines or comments. The room is about thirty feet square, holds three large tables in the center, and has smaller, single-person desks along the walls.

A man in his fifties with gray-streaked black hair combed straight back from a high forehead approaches Brad He is five nine and very slender, and stands straight, with a long, pallid face resembling a wooden mask. He has been in the Tokyo police force for twenty-three years. He holds a desktop tape recorder in his hands. He bows quickly and says:

"I am Tanaka. This call came to Sunrise Trading offices five hours ago. The quality of recording is poor. The Sunrise official recorded it by holding a cell phone to the earpiece of the office phone. We have boosted volume as much as possible. Listen hard, please." Tanaka pushes a button on a tape recorder. The voices are faint and tinny, but in English. Brad makes out Amaya's wavering voice.

". . . until Thursday, noon, and then if he does not have what he needs, he will shoot me—"

A man's voice, tight with tension, breaks in: "Send a clerk with the stock and the money, unarmed, and both women may live to breed"—breathe?—"in this country of insects. Send him to Yasukuni Shrine and the heroes' judge." The tape ends.

Tanaka says, "Yasukuni is the shrine honoring fallen soldiers from the Imperial Army. Most foreigners would not know of it or not choose to visit it. A Japanese accomplice might. A certain ideology seems indicated, maybe militaristic and anti-American. A 'country of insects' has pissed me off. That was dumb of him."

Brad has not visited the shrine. "Heroes' judge?"

"Dr. Radha Pal from India. A judge of the Tokyo Tribunal after World War II. He alone refused to cast the guilty vote on the most serious, class A war crime defendants. Because evidence rules were unfair, he said. This shrine has a monument for him. It is a strange place to hold stock exchange business. Our doctors are studying this tape.

"Mr. Oaks-san, in Tokyo, we are more police officers than New York. More than any other city in the world. We capture more than ten thousand foreign nationals per year, about twenty-five a day. This insulting Farahmani comes to our island. Another indication of dumb. He will not remain free and will not live in comfort. Still, we must assume he is smart and violent. We treasure our citizens. This is not usual situation. We have given highest priority to this case."

"Thank you, Tanaka-san. Just know that I treasure Amaya

173

Mori. She is the highest priority in my life."

"Mr. Oaks-san, here is what we know now. The man who is with Farahmani is a known yakuza crime family lieutenant. He and his group are Korean, disowned even by Japan's worst criminals. In fact, we have taken our information from other yakuza people, who are not good but less bad than this one. His name is Kim. We have tip about him. He is at a gambling place run by his clan in Ikebukuro district. He is there with Farahmani now, and Ms. Mori. There is a complication. They hold also an American woman. We are planning. We must act tomorrow morning. Two-hostage situation is more difficult."

Brad has for the entire plane ride visualized exactly what he should do to bring Amaya to safety.

"Inspector Tanaka, let me make it easier for you. Exchange me for Amaya. I hold all the cards for what Farahmani wants. He wants to get in the supply chain for a major pipeline in America. I work for an American pipe supplier, Elgar Steel. Well, I can hand over stock certificates and proxies giving Farahmani effective control of the Elgar company. He can put in his own board of directors and officers, and he can run the business any way he wants. Farahmani worked there for a few months himself. I don't know him, but I can talk to him about the project and help him get what he wants. Or at least promise to help him get the business orders his country wants. American officials know the Iranian intention and would not allow it to succeed even if they get the pipe orders. This is just to get Amaya out of there. I can give him what he wants. You can't. You can, however, give him safe passage out of Japan."

Tanaka looks away from Brad. Without a word, he stands and walks to the end of the room and stares at the wall for two long minutes. His shoulders slump. He returns to Brad and says,

"Mr. Oaks-san, I have been briefed on the Wishbone Pipeline project. This other hostage is the daughter of Mr. Graham-san who would build and own the Wishbone pipeline. So it seems the Farahmani has a great deal of leverage. He sits on the catbird, as you say." Brad does not correct him.

Brad leans back and rubs his eyes. "Inspector Tanaka, did Farahmani find the Graham woman in Japan, or did he bring her with him?"

Tanaka displays a small smile. "Yes, that is the right question. They came together. So, you are thinking that if the heiress of Graham is such good leverage, why come to Japan in the first place? That is what we are thinking as well. So, it seems that his objective is to control Elgar, the pipeline manufacturer, and not Graham, the pipeline owner. Detective Quinn told me that Iran wants to sell leaky pipes to pollute American farms. Is that correct?"

By now, Brad is irritated and frustrated as well as apprehensive. Why must he have to work so hard to put himself into the hands of his killers? He nods, and says curtly, "That's close enough. Inspector Tanaka, I am here, sitting in front of you, an official of Elgar, the pipe manufacturer. You are looking at someone he needs more than he needs the Japanese citizen he has abducted. You are looking at the key to her release. Why do you even hesitate?"

Tanaka stiffens and narrows his eyes as he says, "Allow me to make the police decisions, Mr. American steel executive. We must use the yakuza. The clan chief must help us with negotiation. He can promise Farahmani to smuggle them out of the country. Kim certainly will want to accept. Farahmani may not trust clan chief, but he has no other option. I have planning to do. It is late for you. Please go to your hotel, and sleep if you can. Tomorrow will be a stimulating experience."

Wednesday, nightfall, October 2, 2019; Washington, D.C.

"June! Where are you? We've been worried sick. Protective custody, yes, I know."

"You can't begin to know, Sarah. Train for forty hours. No cell phone signal. Now this Bleak House of a hotel. It's all Brad's fault, Sarah. Why don't you fire him and let us get back to normal? That's right: there is no proof of anything ever! That's what makes him so dangerous. Where are you now?"

"June, get a grip. I'm at the University Club in Washington. I've met a man. Why is that funny, June Elgar? No, he is not after our money. You're paranoid."

"Sarah, you have never just 'met a man.' And at this stage of the proceedings, no man just shows up and 'meets' you. Pay him, and put him away for a rainy day."

"June Elgar, do not insult me, and do not insult United States Trade Representative Alden Knight. Hello? Yes, that is exactly what I said, so zip it and listen. I'm not calling to gossip or catfight. This whole thing is connected: the thing with Brad, the bomb at your office, and the bomb in our kitchen, June! The connection is Iran, so listen.

"They think that Iran is desperate to keep us from bidding on Wishbone pipe. That's why they've harassed you, me, Brad, and now Ms. Mori. The Iranians have kidnapped her for her stock in Elgar. Brad's in Tokyo now. He's got a crush on her, June. Got it bad. So life is not all about your inconveniences, girl."

"I'm sorry, Sarah. Kidnapped? I met her, you know. She's

good people. Is there anything I can do?"

"Well, finally; I thought you'd never ask. Yes, actually. You can talk to your Mounties. With Farahmani in Tokyo, maybe they'll relax enough to let you talk to your friends in Edmonton. Find out if there's a chance for a water-export possibility to the US with the Wishbone Pipeline. This should be an opportunity for you, too. It's got to be better than the alternative, a monstrously expensive pipeline clear across British Columbia and through pristine mountains to a Pacific port. Instead of your group always opposing, you can push for something good. Good economics for Alberta, good environmentally for Canada, and good for the Ogallala Aquifer in America."

"I have to admit, Sarah, I've given that a lot of thought. It's been hard for me to get my head around supporting Wishbone after we fought it so long. But this water trade-off appeals to me. I think it'll appeal to my friends in Alberta. It would be a big infrastructure project, it would put those tar sand pits to use holding water, and it would bring in revenues. Not bad, if I do say so myself."

Sarah Jane allows herself to relax and smile—until June says,

"So this bureaucrat, he's your lover now?"

"You can't leave things alone, can you? You have to wound me? I won't be drawn into that clumsy trap, and I won't let you continue to insult my new friend."

"Ouch. All right, distinguished ambassador, then. And lover?"

"That is none of your business, June. You really know how to needle. Very fetching, I must say. Look, I'm going back to California first thing in the morning. I've got a steel business to run and the farm to fix up again. By the way, Brad's got me thinking about blending grapes from Stockton and Lodi with ours in Napa for a new ten-dollar label from Elgar. I was thinking of asking you if I could call it 'June.' I won't be asking you now."

"That's a bribe, and it's beneath you. And it's yummy. You said Brad's idea? Get that notion out of your head. I and you thunk this one up, don't you think?"

"You are vain and deceitful, June. Good to hear you're back to your old self. Good luck with the Mounties and the provincial powers that be. I almost love you."

"And you, and you. Look, I didn't mean to wound, and I didn't know you'd be sensitive to a little needle. It's good that you are. It means you're serious about someone. High time. I hope you're responding."

Tuesday, 6:30 p.m., October 1, 2019; Houston, Texas

Rod Graham closes his phone and looks at his wife. Her eyes widen. She sits on the edge of the Louis XV–style gilt sofa, eyes fixed on her husband.

"That was Chief Allen. They haven't found her exactly, but there is news. She was at a motel in Napa, California, recently, and they think she hooked up with that Farahmani again. They think now they may be in Tokyo." He sits next to Helen, takes her hand, and says quietly, "They believe the two of them are involved in a kidnapping of someone who just bought into Elgar Steel. They think maybe baby Rita is also kidnapped. This has something to do with the Wishbone project. The Tokyo police are about to make a raid of some kind."

Helen Graham utters a pained moan and slumps into a ball

on the silk-upholstered sofa. Rod Graham pats her shoulder as she sobs. Then he says, "I've got the number of the man in charge at the Tokyo police. I have to call him right away. Are you all right here for a few minutes?" Helen does not respond except in sobs.

After a minute, she nods weakly. Graham stands and walks into his study. He phones Inspector Tanaka's number. He is told that Tanaka is unavailable. He explains why he is calling. A moment later, a woman's voice answers and expresses sympathy for their pain. She gives her name as Hiradi and launches into a detailed report on what the police know about Rita's situation in Japan, and a general description of the police plan to recover her.

Thursday, 7:15 a.m., October 3, 2019; Tokyo

Brad walks from the Palace Hotel to the police station under a steady drizzle. He wears the brand-new light windbreaker he purchased in haste at the San Francisco airport. It is black and orange, emblazoned with the logo of the San Francisco Giants. The morning air refreshes him as he strides the mile from his Tokyo home to an uncertain future.

Today, the conference room is nearly filled with uniformed police officers, sitting at small tables with computer screens, or moving quickly from table to table. The air hums with low-voiced conversations. Tanaka stands near a large flat-screen TV facing into the room. He is in his blue uniform, with black boots and a black tie knotted tightly in the collar of a starched white shirt. He sees Brad enter, and moves quietly to join him. After a quick bow, he says,

"Please forgive my discourtesy to you last night. You made a brave and useful offer. I have discussed it with my team and also the American embassy people. We are in agreement with you if you still want to proceed. I spoke to you disrespectfully and in haste. I apologize." He bows again, a little lower, and holds it for three beats.

"Tanaka-san, apology accepted. I bit first; you only bit back." Tanaka looks at Brad with relief in his eyes.

"We have a plan, Mr. Oaks-san. We will divide them and attack on two fronts. We will draw one of them to the Yasukuni Shrine. Probably, it will be the one called Kim. The Farahmani will prefer that because he is total stranger to Japan. Our experts think Kim is Japanese military zealot. This shrine appeals to such kind.

"The shrine is losing popularity and does not attract foreign visitors much at all. So, a very strange choice. Advice from Police Administrative office says we should go there as demanded in the ransom call. They have no experience on the streets and spend easy days in easy chairs. Still, l will follow their guidance.

"This Korean man, Kim, was kicked out of yakuza syndicate seven years ago. He had failed to protect his clan 'father'—really, his mentor—during a sting raid on a common yakuza scam in this country: extortion through digging up shameful details in the lives of business or government officials. Then he fled to Turkey and worked in a small village in the countryside, far from the cities with Western lifestyles. He pretended to become Muslim convert, but his true beliefs were Shinto, and he idealized the ways of the samurai from before Meiji era, in Middle Ages. Thus the experts favor using Yasukuni Shrine.

"A group in Iran ran Craigslist ads for Japanese-speaking Muslims, and he took a job that put him in Iran. It is a steel pipe manufacturer. A small world, Mr. Oaks-san, is it not? Anyway, in that time, he became associated with one of the executive families, name of Farahmani. One from the family is a Masoud Farahmani, about same age as Kim. These two enjoyed survival games in the mountain regions of Iran. We think Farahmani became Kim's new mentor, or 'father.' Kim's old clan tried to keep him under observation. They wanted to punish Kim for his disloyalty. But they have not-so-good contacts in Iran and lost track of him.

"Suddenly, Masoud Farahmani and a young woman both enter Japan a few days ago. She is daughter of the president of Wishbone project. Almost immediately, the Ms. Mori you have such value for becomes the second kidnap victim of Farahmani with the help of Kim. We suspect that Farahmani had such plan all along, coming into Japan.

"You see the complexities. They bring a Western prisoner into Japan. They abduct a Japanese citizen, Ms. Mori. Our problems are bigger by two orders of magnitude. Farahmani must have great power over Kim. Or maybe Kim does not want to again disobey a 'father' and take more shame in his life. Either way, it was dumb move to enter Japan.

"The positive fact is that the Japanese yakuza clan can see no benefit from the Farahmani's crimes. They only benefit if they cooperate with us. Therefore, the clan will cooperate with us. They tell us that Ms. Mori is called 'plan B' by Farahmani and the other one 'plan C.'"

"What is plan A?"

"Mr. Oaks-san, we believe plan A was to murder you and Ms. Sarah Elgar in the night by gas explosion. Plan B is hostage for ransom of Elgar Steel, and plan C is hostage for ransom of Wishbone Pipeline."

Tanaka uses a laser presentation pointer as he says, "We make exchange in exactly three hours. That will be ten thirty. I will describe what you see on the large screen.

"You are looking at the main entrance, the torii gate and first inner garden, of the Yasukuni Shrine. On the street in front, you see a taxi rank with five waiting taxis. The shrine and gravel entryway have the same number of visitors as were there this time and day one year ago. Some carry old photographs of Japanese soldiers whose spirits are enshrined here. You will see a few young people carrying protest signs against militarism. In the background, you can see a small group of men in old World War II uniforms. They are reenacting a morning drill using the old Rising Sun wartime flag, the leader with a curved sword. The reenactment drill is very rare, but there have been such long ago at this shrine. Over there, the men wear the traditional costumes of Shinto priests at this shrine, blue tunics and wide white trousers. They are gathered in clusters of three or four. On the screen, you see the stone monument and bronze medallion with the face of Dr. Pal, the heroes' judge. A gardener sweeps the path leading to the monument."

"Mr. Tanaka, I really am not focusing on the tourist attraction of the shrine today."

"So, Mr. Oaks-san, all the people you see in these pictures, and at the shrine, even driving the taxis, are thirty-seven of the forty-five thousand members of the Tokyo Metropolitan police force." Inspector Tanaka bows quickly again and says, "I must step away for a few minutes." He walks briskly to his desk under the large screen.

Ms. Hiradi brings Brad a lacquered tray with a small ceramic pot of steaming tea, a Western-style cup and saucer, and one yellow rose. He thanks her. She stands next to his chair.

He looks up, and she says,

"Mr. Oaks, if you want, I can stay here and give you translation of everything being said. If you'd rather just be alone, then I understand."

"No, please stay. That is very thoughtful."

She sits, her hands folded on the table in front of her.

Brad nods slowly and says, "Thank you."

An hour later, Tanaka joins him, now dressed in a black suit and raincoat. He says, "We have spoken again to US embassy people. They have been extraordinarily cooperative. By the way, we have been in constant communication with your friend Hiwasaki-san of Shin Steel since before your arrival in Japan. We have also discussed the situation fully with Ms. Mori's lawyers in Tokyo. They are providing a crucial piece of the plan. You have very strong friendships, Mr. Oaks-san. That says much good about you. It is an honor to be beside you. Do you use well a handgun?"

"No, Tanaka-san. But I can point and shoot."

"Really? It would be too dangerous then. May I mention that Ms. Hiradi, who quietly serves you tea, is handgun marksman with highest score in my department." Brad swallows. Ms. Hiradi blushes and waves her hand vertically in front of her face to brush away the praise.

"Ms. Mori has brilliantly told us on the recording there is one gun. We now know the yakuza sold it. But since they are working with us, there is no firing pin in that gun." Tanaka's masklike face forms a humorless smile. "Perhaps can they sue yakuza for defective product, lawyer Oaks-san?" Brad smiles in return. "I cannot deny you a weapon if you ask me for it. My advice is that it is too much risk."

"I can handle a baseball bat pretty well."

Tanaka looks at the Giants windbreaker and then says, "Hmm. What is lifetime average?"

"I was a pitcher. I hit .147 lifetime."

"Pretty bad. Even for a pitcher. Best case is to outwit them. No need for guns or bats under best case. We will hope for that. We must be able to improvise as things develop. I have a question about American baseball, Mr. Oaks-san," says Tanaka, turning his head to observe Brad.

Brad has actually loosened up somewhat because of Tanaka's jibes, as intended, which fall on him like cold rainwater, startling some of his anxiety away. Or like shaken shampooed hair. *Oh dear God.*

After a moment, Brad settles his racing thoughts and nods his head.

"So, what means 'hum baby'?"

Brad relinquishes a small, quick smile. "It has no meaning. Yet many meanings. It is a term complimenting hustle or effort from one player or coach to another player. Someone who makes up in effort what he lacks in talent. You say it sort of softly like this, 'Hmmm baby,' which makes it personal. When Roger Craig managed the San Francisco Giants, he'd say it a lot, but I'd heard it before that. Let's say I'm up and bunt one to third. I beat it down the line just ahead of the throw. The first-base coach comes up behind me and says, 'Hmmm baby.'"

Tanaka nods and says, "It is time for us to go. You are to think like a pitcher, not slugger."

Tanaka and Brad sit side by side in the rear seat of a black car with Shin Steel logos on the rear doors parked behind the taxi rank at the shrine. A small-screen TV facing the back seat displays the same images as seen in the conference room.

Tanaka speaks in low, methodical tones. Brad listens intently, but his torso and arms shiver involuntarily in random bursts. He cannot keep a certain thought from looping in his mind: *It is no one else's business whether I live or die.*

At ten o'clock, two men walk into view. One, a tall man in a dark suit and bowler hat and carrying a large black umbrella, walks past the taxi rank. He carries a slender briefcase in one hand. The other is the Korean named Kim.

The gardener with the broom begins to sing a wavering lament as he sweeps. The men walk past the massive torii gate, toward the wooden shrine, where they stop at a crosswalk of raked gravel. The man in the bowler gestures with his umbrella tip to the right. They turn toward the two-story museum and stop again. The man in the bowler turns left and walks at an angle to the Pal monument, and puts his briefcase on the ground. Nothing seems to happen.

The military detail takes a few turns bringing the unit closer to the monument. Brad looks at his watch. He watches the second hand sweep and the minute hand slowly approach ten seventeen.

Tanaka mutters, "Batter up. You get no practice throws."

Carrying a black leather briefcase with a Sunrise Trading logo, Brad exits the car and walks unhurriedly along the graveled entryway to the shrine. He stops and looks at the signage maps of the grounds, his eyes moving over the dotted lines representing paths. He starts again, walking slowly along the graveled path. He stops, looks left and right, and then starts again. Where the small path leads away from the main gravel entranceway, he faces the museum building. To the right of that is a glass-fronted modern building holding a display of a WWII Mitsubishi Zero fighter, green with red sun emblems. To the left is the Pal monument. He hesitates, and then slowly starts toward the monument.

Tanaka barks something into his radio, and the reenactment drill team march toward the monument. With lusty shouts and waving of the sword, the drill leader orders the unit to halt. He then proceeds to berate a marcher who has stumbled. Kim and the man with the bowler and umbrella turn to watch the drill. Brad arrives at the monument and touches the elbow of the man with the bowler, causing him to jump in surprise. Brad bows very low and holds his bow. The man with the bowler and umbrella says,

"Please dispense with the formalities, Mr. Oaks. It's me, Parker Wright. I am under-pleased to be here, but you are needed at a meeting in our conference room. Did you bring the stock certificates and proxies?"

Brad looks up quickly, and some of the tension leaves his face. He says, "Parker, are you in on this? What's going on?"

"Mr. Oaks, I can only say that I have been sent onto the field at the end of the game. I don't want us to waste time chatting in the rain. Come with me. Shake hands with Mr. Kim. I fear that you and he are going to be fast . . . um . . . companions."

Brad extends his hand, looking at Kim's eyes. Kim grabs Brad's wrist and quickly inserts the end of a woven steel sleeve over Brad's index finger. He pulls back on it, and the sleeve tightens securely over Brad's finger. A thin steel wire connects the other end of the sleeve to Kim's wrist. Brad's finger is immobile, and he has become Kim's prisoner.

"This Mr. Kim here is very bad news, I'm afraid. My best advice to you is not to attempt to struggle. Follow me."

Wright steps away from the monument and strides proudly back to the wide graveled path, followed by Kim, attached to

Brad. They turn right and continue toward the street. When he reaches the street, Wright stops, takes out his cell phone, and stands with his back to Brad during a brief conversation. He does not hail a taxi. Instead, he walks quickly along the sidewalk and opens the passenger-side front and rear doors of a black sedan. Wright slides into the front seat; Kim and Brad climb into the rear. The sedan crawls away from the curb to join a clot of traffic at a gridlocked intersection.

Tanaka speaks again into his radio, "So, phase one successful. Now begins the hard part."

CHAPTER FIFTEEN

Alden Knight and Sarah Jane stroll arm in arm to the University Club after a quiet supper at the Quill Lounge in the Jefferson Hotel. As they wait for the light to cross Sixteenth Street, Sarah Jane points to the stone building adjacent to the south of the Club. "What's that building?"

"Now it's the Russian ambassador's residence. That's why there's a Russian flag on that flagpole. Back in the Cold War days, it was the Soviet embassy. Before that, it was the embassy of the old Russian empire. Sort of a case of what goes around comes around."

"Nice. Marxist neighbors for you and the plutocrats of your conservative club.

"Alden, have you ever thought of being that kind of ambassador? To Russia or somewhere?"

"No, Sarah, that's for the partisan donor elite or celebrities."

"You are elite in my eyes, Alden."

"You flatter. Another of the many reasons I'm falling in love with you."

"You need so many reasons? Mine is a short list, Alden. You're stable, intelligent, and authentic. And randy. That made the short list."

The light changes. He squeezes her hand as they cross

Sixteenth in a chilling wind and walk into the club's lobby. They take the elevator to Sarah Jane's suite.

Inside, Knight takes a call on his smartphone. When he finishes, he powers-off the phone and looks at Sarah Jane curled in the middle of the king bed. He says, "That was Ichiro. Everything's in place, just waiting for the principals to arrive. So, Sarah Jane, still on board with giving away your father's steel business?"

"It's for a good cause. But I'll be penniless."

"I'm with the government, and I'm here to help."

"I'm frightened, Alden."

He sits on the edge of the bed and takes her hand. "With reason, Sarah. But the Tokyo police are peerless when it comes to this. I know that's not a comfort, but . . ."

"Oh, but it is. You're the comfort, Alden. You are a rock for me."

"I was thinking tonight maybe I should just . . ."

Gripping his hand in both of hers, she says, "Stay, Alden. Please."

"Yes."

Ting-stop. Dial tone. Numbers dialed. One ring.

"Hail to you, honored Uncle. We are in place. Soon, you will be an American capitalist for the glory of our lineage that reaches to the Babylonians before the Hellenic age of Greece."

"Focus on today, not ancient history. Be watchful for the deceptions of the cunning Satan who pulls the strings of those around you. This day, you will become the general of the elite guard and my most trusted warrior. Are the women there?"

"They are. Any last-minute instructions?"

"Leave them with Kim afterward and proceed to Haneda

airport as planned. It is my genius that we have plans B and C."

"I failed you in plan A."

"It matters not. It could not be helped. The path to justice is twisted with surprises. Plan B is so much better, as you well know. Concentrate on the success of the moment."

"So I leave my friend? And Kim?"

"You do. There are many, many more such friends in your glorious future."

"But what about Kim? He and I go back. I can't leave him here."

"Why not?"

"Because he belongs with us. With me."

"He was useful to us, to you, but that was then. He serves no purpose after this in plan B. When that plan succeeds, as it must, there is no purpose for plan C."

"What will become of him here?"

"If he is worthy, he will survive to walk again on the path to justice. You are wasting time. Focus on the endeavor. Focus on plan B. Don't let it slip from your grasp. Plan B does not end there—it ends with me here. Is that clear?"

"This is clear. I don't like it. But it is clear."

"Then make your own mind clear. Anticipate crafty traps."

Thursday, 11:15 a.m., October 3, 2019; Tokyo

The large conference room of the Law Offices of Wright and Haseo has held many transaction closings over the years, from corporate mergers and long-term natural resources supply contracts, to modern glass-clad Tokyo skyscraper financings and large cargo vessel transfers. Against the walls around the perimeter of the room stand sleek black pedestals holding ship models encased in plastic boxes. Each display is marked with date of build, launch, length overall, deadweight tonnage, name of vessel, flag of registry, and name of the Japanese shipyard where it was built.

Parker Wright, Kim the Korean, and Brad Oaks enter the conference room. Seated along the far side of the table are, from left to right, Mr. Haseo, Amaya Mori, Rita Graham, Masoud Farahmani, and Ms. Hiradi, dressed in a black suit, a white blouse, and a red-white-and-blue scarf tied at her neck. Clipped to the lapel of her suit is a plastic badge identifying her as a notary public from the US embassy.

A leather blotter lies on the tabletop in front of each person, and three have been set on the opposite side of the table for Wright, Kim, and Brad. Two aluminum carafes of water sit on each side of the table, beads of cold condensation covering up two-thirds of their sides.

Brad sits facing Amaya. She looks exhausted, her eyes red-rimmed, her hair matted, her dress smudged. She directs a hasty, withholding smile at Brad. Next to her sits a disheveled Rita Graham, her face frozen in fear. In front of Ms. Hiradi stands a twelve-inch-high cast-iron instrument with a hand lever and stainless steel disks ajar to receive pages for being impressed with the crimping of an official seal.

Wright glares at Farahmani, who fidgets with nervousness. Farahmani attempts to assert dominance: "No one will get hurt if this goes as smoothly as—"

Wright intones, "Mr. Farahmani, please respect the formality and solemnity of the transaction about to occur. Your silence, rather than your utterances, will assure the speed and smoothness of this distasteful transfer. We shall begin now. Mr.

Oaks, do you possess a new share certificate of Elgar Steel, Incorporated, representing thirty-three percent of the company's issued and outstanding common stock, made out in the name of Masoud Farahmani?"

Brad fumbles with his untethered hand into his briefcase and draws from it an embossed share certificate, with a green filigree border and engraved lettering, and hands the certificate to Wright. Wright examines it carefully, and passes it across the table to Farahmani. Farahmani stares at it blankly and hands it back.

Wright says, "Mr. Oaks, are you the duly elected and incumbent corporate secretary of Elgar Steel?"

"I am. I hold here a certificate of election and incumbency to that effect, executed in California and witnessed by the sheriff of Napa County."

"Please execute the share certificate in your capacity as corporate secretary of Elgar Steel, and hand the document to the representative from the United States embassy in Japan for consular authentication."

Brad sits motionless for a moment. Then, he holds his right wrist to steady his right hand as he swiftly places his signature on the document. He passes the signed certificate to Ms. Hiradi, who inserts the page into the jaws of the seal and crimps a circular impression just beneath the signature. Brad then hands the certificate of election and incumbency to Ms. Hiradi, who crimps a seal just below the signature.

Wright says, "Mr. Oaks, do you possess written powers of attorney duly executed by the legal and beneficial owners of the remaining sixty-seven percent of the issued and outstanding shares of Elgar Steel?"

"Yes, I do."

"Have their signatures been notarized by a United States notary?"

"One has. The other was notarized in Canada."

"Has the Canadian power of attorney been authenticated by a Canadian consular official?"

Stillness falls on the room. Brad shakes his head.

Wright says, "Mr. Farahmani, the time-honored protocol and best legal practice is for the Canadian proxy to have consular authentication. We can suspend the closing of the transaction for the time needed in order to have the authentication performed at the Canadian embassy in Japan. I expect we should allow up to four hours, or possibly until the next business day. Alternatively, you may, if you are comfortable with the authenticity of the signature, waive the customary practice and proceed here and now."

All eyes turn to Farahmani. His forehead develops tiny beads of perspiration, and his eyebrows pinch together under fret marks. He turns and points to Ms. Hiradi and says, "Have her do it."

Wright allows an audible sigh to escape his mouth. He looks toward the ceiling, and then gives Farahmani a withering look. "Mr. Farahmani. I am not in a position to give you legal advice, and neither is my partner, Mr. Haseo. However, may I point out that the person you refer to is a representative of the Embassy of the United States, not of Canada?"

Farahmani states in a strong voice, "I want her to do it! I want all of the documents to have the same seal."

Wright then turns to Brad and says, "Mr. Oaks, who is named the proxy for the owner of shares covered by the powers of attorney?"

"It is blank at the moment."

"Please print the name of Masoud Farahmani where appropriate to appoint him proxy for such shares."

Brad reaches into his briefcase and withdraws two legal-sized documents with blue backing. Struggling to hold his right wrist steady with his left hand, he prints Farahmani's name in the blank spaces, and hands each of them to Ms. Hiradi for authentication with the seal, one at a time.

Ms. Hiradi then collates the share certificate, the certificate of election and incumbency, and the proxies, and delivers the stack of documents to Farahmani. Farahmani stares at the documents and rubs his thumb and index finger over the crisp crimping of the authentication seals on each and every document.

Brad hangs his head in shame and defeat.

Wright stands and booms, "Mr. Farahmani, the formalities of transfer and delivery of the documents passing effective control of Elgar Steel to you are now concluded except for the critical final steps, namely the release of Mr. Oaks and your immediate departure. I hand you this document, which is official safe passage all the way to your plane. Mr. Oaks will accompany you as far as the boarding ramp, where he will leave you as you board. I have authority to assure you of no interference from any officials, and that your plane will be free to depart with you safely aboard. The Sunrise Trading car and driver will take you and Mr. Oaks there now."

Wright abruptly turns in an about-face and stares at the wall, rocking up and down on the balls of his feet in agitation.

Farahmani stands and looks for a spare folder for the documents. Brad scoffs and slides his briefcase over the table. Farahmani opens it, pushes the documents into it, and closes the clasps. He turns to Rita, who starts to rise. Farahmani pushes her into her seat and shakes his head. Brad, now released from the restraint, stands and starts for the door, saying, "All aboard, Farahmani."

Parker Wright bobs on heel and toes again and declares, "Mr. Farahmani, if you are carrying firearms, you may relinquish them here and now, or wait for the airport security people to take them. The safe passage document doesn't cover that."

Farahmani hesitates and then hands Kim his recently acquired used handgun.

After the suite's outer door closes behind the two men, Amaya slumps with her head against her arm on the table and sobs. Haseo attempts to calm her, but she shrugs him away.

Ms. Hiradi removes her American embassy badge. She moves briskly around the table to the side of the Korean, Kim. She opens her suit jacket to reveal a black holster riding at her right hip. She looks Kim in the eyes and says, "Mr. Kim, the firearm you point at me is not registered as required by law, even though it has been disabled. You are under arrest. You will be taken by the uniformed officers just outside the door to a Metropolitan Police jail. You are under suspicion of committing one or more crimes in Japan, in addition to carrying that unregistered but insignificant pistol. Sometime during the next forty-eight hours, while you are in detention, the police will notify you of the crimes you are being charged with. We have no Miranda warnings you may have seen on American TV dramas."

Three uniformed policemen have entered the room. One of them places the finger-sized, woven stainless steel restraining tube in a plastic evidence bag before Kim is handcuffed and pushed out of the conference room and the building into a waiting detainee transport van.

Ms. Hiradi crosses back to the other side of the table and puts her arm around Rita Graham, now sobbing uncontrollably. A female police paramedic has entered the room and joins Ms. Hiradi, who says, "We are taking you and Ms. Mori to hospital for examination and treatment for the substances you were forced to consume. Your parents arrive in Japan tomorrow from Texas, America."

Amanda Mori stands. "Thank you, but I won't be going to hospital. Parker, please book me into the Palace Hotel, and have Dr. Neff come there in two hours, my own doctor. Tell Brad I'll see him tomorrow, perhaps, depending on how I feel. Right now, I want to go to bed and sleep off whatever they gave me."

"Ms. Mori, the hospital would be better . . ."

"Thank you, Ms. Hiradi, but this is what I know to be best for me. I want to go where I can sleep without disturbance. I know from experience that a hospital is the last place I could do that."

Wright says, "Won't you come home with me? Olivia would be overjoyed to cluck over you. She has been distraught since you went missing."

"The Palace Hotel, Parker. I don't wish to argue. See if they can give me the same room I was in last week."

"At least let me take you there."

"Yes, very well, Parker. I welcome that. You have been a prince from Camelot today. And please call Dr. Neff yourself, not your secretary. She is also Olivia's doctor; you can get the number from her."

"Of course. I'll speak to her myself."

"Ms. Mori, we will want to take a statement . . ."

"I understand. Tomorrow, I promise. I am exhausted. I can be of more help tomorrow."

"Call me at the number on this card. We can come to your hotel."

Friday, 11:50 a.m., October 4, 2019; The White House, Oval Office

"Alden, don't get comfortable. I've got five minutes, and that's more than enough time. You've been on the Wishbone deal?"

"Yes, Mr. President, but—"

"Take your but and butt out of here. I'm thinking this is over your head. I'm thinking I should give it to State and let a real deal closer finish it."

"Mr. President, I suggested that State take this over at a meeting last month. A White House staffer was there."

"That's a fake fact, Alden. This is my idea. You're a lawyer, Alden, not a closer. You'll talk this thing to death. I want the total package for Thanksgiving dinner. A turkey Wishbone. I like that. Short. Hashtag. Easy to grasp. I won't keep you, Alden. Always a pleasure."

CHAPTER SIXTEEN

Friday, October 4, 2019; Tokyo, Palace Hotel

"Brad Oaks speaking."

"Hello, this is Loretta Neff . . . yes, hello. Look, Ms. Mori wanted me to give you a ring. She's sleeping. She looks OK from my standpoint. She particularly wanted me to give you assurances that she was not violated. And that her feet are OK. That's supposed to mean something to you, but it eludes me. Anyway, I've told her it's better if she gets only medical attention for a couple of days. I'm staying in her suite. I'm having a colleague of mine drop by later today. A 'shrink,' in your parlance."

"Should I be worried?"

"Damn right you should. But she's in the best of hands. Mine. My colleague is Japanese. He's an adherent of purpose-based trauma recovery in Japan."

"All right, Dr. Neff. I believe the Tokyo police want to interview her . . ."

"So they do. That's my next call. Won't happen today. We'll see about tomorrow."

Friday, October 4, 2019; Washington, D.C.

Sarah Jane hears the phone in her University Club room ring just as she taps her card key to the magnetic sensor on the door. She manages to pick it up on the third ring.

"This is the front desk. There's a call from Japan. Hold on."

"OK, thanks . . . hello?"

"It's me, Brad."

"My God, Brad, we've been worried sick. All I got were bulletins from Detective Quinn. Are you all right?"

"Yes, fine. It was pretty hairy, but we broke up the attempt on Amaya and the Graham girl. The Tokyo police did it."

"You did your bit and more, Brad. You are one brave dude. Tell me what you can."

"Sarah Jane, it went like clockwork. That said, I have to tell you I was shaking in my boots the whole time. Amaya looked so small and scared. She's OK now, but they gave her some crud to keep her quiet, and now her doctor is trying to get it out of her system. And her brain, and that's the bigger worry."

"Look, Brad, you convinced me a long time ago she's a brainiac. Like you. Like me. We brainiacs keep it together somehow. Anyway, that's what we have to count on."

"I haven't seen her since we got her back. I'm hanging around the Palace until her doctor says it's OK. I think I'd like to stay here next week, Sarah."

"I think you should too. Not because of Amaya, but we're being expedited to tie up the whole Wishbone package. The White House took it away from Alden and gave it to a new face at the State Department."

"That's ridiculous!"

"So was the election, but there you have it. Alden's still in it, but it's a secondary role now."

"I'm pissed."

"Hold it in. We only have till Thanksgiving to produce a done thing." Brad's end of the line goes quiet. "Brad, are you there?"

"Yeah. I'm thinking. Best case is I can get some letters of intent. That should satisfy State. But even a letter of intent is like pulling teeth in Japan. They're going to want a Mount Fuji of technical details."

"Brad, we only have preliminary drawings from Trans-Rocky on the oil line, nothing on the loop."

"I know. We can do this, Sarah. Here's what I'm thinking out loud. Bear with me, I'm just improvising. How about you send Sandoval here with whoever he needs? I was told this morning that Rod Graham is coming in tomorrow. Since he's here about his daughter, I can't just pounce on him, but he's bound to have a little time on his hands sometime next week. I'll talk to him. Tell him what you told me. We've got Shin Steel here, and now Elgar and Trans-Rocky. Maybe he can get some of his people over here too. We can rough out enough blueprints for a pretty solid letter of intent."

"You think pretty fast on your feet, Brad Oaks."

"You flatter. Look, Sarah, someone has to work the Canada end of this. You once told me June would listen to you. This is the time."

Sarah Jane says, "You and the Tokyo police just broke up June's bombers. She ought to listen now. I'll go to work on her. Maybe even get her to Washington to meet the new people at State. How much of this can I tell Alden, Counselor?"

"Tell him the basics, but let us keep the commercial details to ourselves here in Tokyo. The water deal is paramount. Tell him we'll have our end of it by Thanksgiving."

"OK. I'll get on to Sandoval and June right now. You take care of your Amaya and Shin Steel."

"My Amaya. You make it sound so simple."

"It is, Brad. It's you lawyers who complicate everything."

Masoud Farahmani, cramped and exhausted after a twenty-one-hour flight with two connections, unlimbers from a taxi in front of the Embassy of Pakistan. He blanches at the fare, but pays it with his credit card. Clutching his new briefcase, he mounts the stone steps and passes through the doorway to the security desk. He is met there by an embassy official who notes the name on today's manifest of visitors. After he passes through the metal detector, Farahmani is led down a long hallway to a door with a pebbled-glass window marked Islamic Republic of Iran. He knocks. After a muffled voice says, "Enter," he lets himself in.

His uncle sits alone at a desk under a small casement window facing the street. The man rises, smiles broadly, and hugs his nephew. They sit, saying nothing, their eyes aglow with victory. Masoud reaches into his briefcase and hands the bundle of documents to his uncle, who looks them over. He looks carefully at the authentication seal, and frowns. He quickly opens his desk drawer and produces a magnifying glass mounted on a tortoise handle. He examines the crimped impression. There, he sees across the top of the circle, in English, the word "Witnesseth." He looks closer at the phrase in Latin on the lower arc of the circle. His shoulders sag. He looks up at his nephew and states,

"You are the excrement of Satan's gelded camel."

"Why? What does it say?"

"In Latin, it says, '*Vi Coactus*.'"

"What does it mean?"

"Signed under duress."

Outside, on the street, just behind the parking lot of the building bordering Pakistan territory, Detective Patricia Quinn leans against the front fender of her squad car, watching a police tow-truck mechanic attach the brackets of a wheel-lift device to the front of a 1978 Chevrolet Caprice Classic. A pale-yellow evidence tag dangles from each of an extra set of four muddy, used tires stowed inside the Caprice.

She drains the last of a Starbucks tall cup of black coffee, strolls around the hood, and says something to the driver, who blips the siren twice. Quinn dials her cell phone. After a moment, she says,

"Good afternoon, Mr. Farahmani, it's Detective Quinn. I wonder if you and your nephew would have a few minutes for me outside your office. Now is a good time for us. Come out any door. Someone in a uniform is there to greet you. Mr. Tateshima is helping us with your car."

Monday, October 14, 2019; Tokyo, Palace Hotel

Brad holds an ikebana arrangement of chrysanthemum blossoms, sprigs of pine, and maple leaves secured in shallow water in an oblong white porcelain bowl, and manages to free a finger to ring the bell to Amaya's suite. He tries to settle his heartbeat. He swallows. He breathes. She opens the door.

"Come in, Brad." She is smiling. Her face seems happy.

"Is there somewhere I can put these?"

"Brad, such a thoughtful arrangement. Are these from the

arcade?"

"Yes. Well, I helped pick things out."

"Your special touch. It shows. Put it down here, and kiss me."

He does. It feels the way it should. He kisses her again. He says, "Does your doctor condone this kind of behavior?"

"Which one? I have a doctor for the brain and a doctor for the rest of me."

"Take your pick."

"They are in complete agreement on your visit. No restrictions." She sits, kicks off her hotel slippers, holds up her feet, and twinkles her toes. "See?"

"I see. Beautiful." Brad leaves out comment on the visible black-and-blue discoloration above her ankle bones, caused by plastic binding. "This will sound lame, but how are you?"

"It sounds wonderful. It sounds loving. At least that is how I hear it."

"All of that."

"My doctors tell me that I am in normal health at this stage of recovery. It has been over a week now. I have no signs of dependency on the drugs they gave me."

"What did they give you?"

"A benzodiazepine. Brand name would be Xanax, but this was off-market counterfeit, and worrying because impure. It is meant as prescription tranquilizing drug, for panic attacks. It is not an opioid. I hate the thought of it and have no desire whatsoever to ever have it again."

"That's a relief, Amaya. I probably could have used some myself. Panic is exactly what hit me when I realized they'd found your name and address. I fought that panic all the way to the gate of Farahmani's plane at the very end."

"Everyone fusses over me like a baby. Is there no one who has tended to you, Brad?"

"There is now," he says.

"You were the brave hero I knew would rescue me."

"A drugged-induced dream hero."

"I did dream. But not of you. Of old figures from inside my mind somewhere. Of hot stones. Of my mother before I ever knew her. The mother of her childhood stories, from the time of her own panic."

"You don't need to talk about it."

"My other doctor, the one for my head, tells me to try to verbalize as much as I can. He helps me a great deal, mostly by saying things I already know and believe. He has studied Dr. Morita, who is famous in Japan. Morita lived at the same time as Sigmund Freud in Europe. His approach is to find purpose and live moments with a purpose."

"That's pretty strenuous stuff after all you've been through." Brad furrows his brow.

"No, not like that, Brad. Everyday purposes, is all. Concentrate on a small purpose and don't let yourself get distracted by the bad memories. I learned a new word, Brad: 'ruminate.' He says that people ruminate after an experience like mine. He says the word literally means to 'eat again,' the way a cow chews a cud. I will keep from ruminating mostly because I do not like the image of such a chewing cow." She shivers, and laughs.

Then she looks at him, her brows raised. "How is Rita? I think her experience must have been worse. I did not talk to her much. I think the Korean man raped her."

"Rita is very much in worse shape, although her injuries are not severe. No, her problem is that she had been addicted to alcohol and other junk before all this happened. She had just come out of a recovery center when he brought her to Japan. Then, they gave her the same stuff they gave you. It's caused some sort of relapse. She's still in the hospital. Her parents are here. You won't believe who they are."

Amaya nods quickly and says, "I already know, Brad. They are the builders of the same Wishbone of your business. The Korean and Farahmani were going to ransom her for that project if they didn't get control over Elgar Steel."

Brad's mind is elsewhere, deep in thought. After a prolonged pause, he looks back at her puzzled expression. Getting back into the moment, he says, "Did you hear them talk about their plans?"

"No. I learned this from Inspector Tanaka and Ms. Hiradi. Tanaka-san considers you to be his new son, by the way. He talks baseball stories with you as a heroic athlete."

Brad paws away the praise with outstretched arm. He tilts and dips his head in a kind of shrug and says, "We got off to a rocky start, but I like him too."

Then he stands and walks to the window overlooking the neon sheen of Tokyo. He gathers his thoughts. He has come to her room filled with a personal need to talk. Now that he's seen she is stable enough to hear his secret thoughts, he turns back and says,

"I don't want to talk baseball, or police or Wishbone right now."

She is quiet for a long moment. "You have another purpose, Brad?"

Brad gathers the strength to utter something he has only once in his life delivered before, and never thought he would again. "Yes, a very different purpose. Personal, you and me."

"I am never too tired to hear you speak of that, Brad."

Brad's face is suddenly frozen. Words refuse to obey his needs. "I have thought so much about . . ." At this point, not even breath escapes his mouth.

"Brad, come rub my feet." Her soft voice seems to revive the frozen gears. He returns to his place beside her, and she places her feet on his thigh. She says quietly, "So much about . . . ?"

"This."

"That's all?"

"It's everything."

"Start from the beginning. You 'have thought so much about . . .' what, Brad?"

Brad is unhurried. His words are measured. His face has relaxed now that he is actually looking at her and beginning to say what has crowded all other thoughts from his mind lately. He starts,

"Let me begin with a simple truth, Amaya. I have decided what my foremost desire in life is. I want to live the rest of my life with you. All the other complicated questions, like 'where,' circle in orbits around this one simple truth: we have a chance to be together. That chance was attacked violently. An attack was made on me in Napa Valley, and then one was made on you here. But the chance has survived those attacks. We can embrace the chance, or reject the chance, or ignore it—squander it, in the words of my friend Hiwasaki. We can't allow all the complicating side issues such as business or geography disguise the real question. And I want to embrace the chance to be together and never let it slip away again."

Amaya brings her hands to her eyes. Her shoulders tremble. She lowers her head. Moisture spills from her eyes, past her fingers, and along her wrists inside the sleeves of the Palace

Hotel *yukata*. Brad does not attempt to interrupt the natural responses that take Amaya's usually composed attention. He rubs her feet. He waits. He experiences a calmness of purpose unfamiliar to him.

Finally she sniffs, dabs her eyes, and says, "The flower blossomed, didn't it? From the seed I put in the back of your mind."

"It's as simple as that, I suppose."

"I have heard that lawyers complicate everything. You have simplified this."

"Put aside that I'm a lawyer and everything else about me and where I come from. I'm the man who loves you and will spend my life with you, if you will take me."

Amaya says, haltingly, "Where you come from and what you do are what define you as you are now. Your life choices have defined you. You are much more than a good foot-rubbing individual. It is the entire you that I love. I cannot put any of that aside. I want to live my life with you, in your complicated life and the complexities of what have made you Brad Oaks."

Brad wants her words to stay in the air. He wants to replay the words. He wants to put them in a picture frame for his bedroom wall to greet him every morning.

"Did you hear my answer, Brad?"

"Ohhh yes, I did. I'm saving the words. I'm putting all your words that add up to 'yes' into deep recesses of my mind, as I did the seed you planted there."

He stretches out alongside her on the sofa and kisses her. He says,

"The Japanese way is a path to simplicity. I don't wish to cope with the complicating questions in the orbit around my head."

"Nor do I. At the moment."

Brad says, "At the moment, yes."

"The simple truth is enough for now."

"It is sufficient," he says.

"There is an expression. Does it fit us now, Brad? 'Sufficient unto the day'?"

"That is complicated."

"Why, Brad?"

"It comes from Scripture. 'Sufficient unto the day is the evil thereof.' There's no evil in this day. So it's not exactly apt to say the expression applies in our situation . . ."

"You talk too much, Brad."

CHAPTER SEVENTEEN

Friday, November 1, 2019; Tokyo, Palace Hotel

Brad stops by the desk to see if Eddie Sandoval and his people have checked in yet. The desk clerk looks at her monitor and says they have not. Then she hands him a message left for him by another guest. Brad looks at the message on the elevator to his room. It's from Rod Graham. Brad calls from his room phone.

"Hello?"

"Rod, it's Brad Oaks."

"Oh, hi. Thanks for your call. Can I buy you a drink? It's the least I can do for what you did to get Rita out of a hell of a mess."

"Sure, Rod, what do you have in mind?"

"Well, Helen's at the hospital. I just came from there."

"How is your daughter?"

"She's a mess. But, less than the mess she was the last time you saw her. And again, I thank you for that. It's going to be a long pull for her. Somehow, this time, I think she'll make it. She had one hell of a scare."

"She's lucky you and Mrs. Graham came over here. She would have been in a world of hurt in this country all alone. Want to get a drink in the bar of the Crowne Room? OK, well, it's five o'clock now. Let's meet there in half an hour. If you haven't eaten, we could just have dinner too if you're free."

"That sounds great. I'll tell the desk to route my calls to me there in case Helen calls."

Brad hangs up and calls Amaya's suite. "How're you doing?" he asks.

"I have just finished my reading assignment from my Dr. Shrink. And I am checking off my accomplishments on my purpose list for the day. Can you come see me?"

"After dinner, hon. Rita's dad just called, and we're going to meet in the Crowne."

"Please give him my regards, and also to Rita. Don't make it a late night."

Brad grins as he heads for a shower. *She sounds just like a wife would,* he thinks. *How about that?*

Rod Graham is already at the bar when Brad arrives, sipping Johnnie Walker Black on the rocks, looking out the hotel's tall windows toward Tokyo Tower. He looks like he's been pulled through a knothole. He's still in the same sports coat, denim slacks, and white work shirt with a Trans-Rocky logo that he wore on the plane. He stands and pumps Brad's hand and starts in again about the rescue of Rita.

"Hey, Rod, it's OK. You go on like that, and we'll never talk business. But thank you. It was an experience I'll never forget. Just glad Rita's as good as she is under the circumstances. What's the latest on Wishbone?"

"Well, I guess you heard, the White House is in on it now, and they've handed the ball to the State Department. Not sure that's going to do any good, and there's a fair chance they'll screw it up. Alden Knight says he's still carrying what he calls 'a watching brief,' which I guess is lawyer talk for tracking pitches from the dugout."

"That's gotta be tough on him. How's he taking it?"

"Alden? Hell, he's in high cotton. He's in love!"

"Geez, don't I know. And with my boss, too."

"Speaking of Sarah Jane, you and I have work to do here this week. I've got a couple of engineers coming in from Houston, and I understand she's sending a team. We need to tell them what direction they're going in after the jet lag and booze wear off. Which I have no idea what it is. So why is it that we're having a Chautauqua convocation of my engineers and your engineers in the most expensive city in the world?"

Brad laughs and turns to face Graham. He says,

"Call it fate, I guess. Fate that brought Rita, me, and you all here at the same time. Our pet project is getting newbie treatment in the US State Department. Here's why I suggested getting us in one place this week.

"The president wants to expedite Wishbone, and he's not one to wait for a whole lot of staff time. He wants a package for approval by Thanksgiving. Nothing happens until the engineers map out the new water project and come up with some cost estimates."

Rod swirls the ice cubes in his glass. "I get all that, Brad. What I don't get is why they can't do it in Houston and Stockton, where they have desks and know where the lunchroom is."

"A lot's going on here that affects Wishbone, Rod. We're sourcing the steel plate from Shin Steel, we're going to joint-venture the pipe making with Shin, and their home office is in Tokyo. Sunset Trading is here also, and they're going to have a boatload of minutiae questions we have to answer before they sign on to the deal, even with a letter of intent. Have you ever toured a Japanese steel mill?"

"No, but I've seen all of them in America."

"A rye on the rocks, side of water, Mr. Oaks?"

Brad says, "Thank you, and bring my father here another of what he's having." He turns again to Graham and says,

"You're in for an eye-opener then. I'll set us up for a plant tour at Shin this week. Maybe the first full day our teams are in town, to sort of set the scene. Then I'll fix up spaces for them to work in a neutral corner, so to speak, which will be Sunrise Trading. Their people have to have the same detailed briefing as we give Shin people, only in advance. So we'll do it at Sunrise and then bring the show to Shin, hot off the presses. Your people will have one work room, ours will have a separate one, and in between, we'll have a conference room to start and finish each day. We'll compress this in a campaign, and everyone will have the same story to tell. I just think it's more productive this way."

"Yeah, you're right. It's a good idea. And it takes my mind off what's going to become of poor Rita. Hey, how's the steak in here?"

"As good as you'll ever get. Or we can just pop into the teppanyaki restaurant if you want to watch them grill it in front of you."

"No, let's stay here. More private. Those tables are kind of communal."

"Good idea, Rod. When do your people arrive?"

"Not till tomorrow about this time. The Elgar folks?"

"Today, any minute now. Before I forget it, Amaya wants me to give you this." Brad hands Graham a business card. "That's the psychiatrist she's been seeing. She swears by him. You probably have your own people in Houston, but as long as you, Helen, and Rita are here for a while, you might want to consult with him."

"OK, I'm grateful for that. You be sure and tell her."

The maître d' approaches them and says, "Mr. Graham, sir?"

"Yes?"

"Sorry to disturb you, sir. Mrs. Graham is on the telephone for you. You can come to my station to take it."

Rod frowns, looks at Brad, who gives him a nod of assurance, and walks slowly to the phone, a slump taking over his muscular shoulders. Brad takes a table toward the back, away from other diners, and looks out at the neon borealis starting to fill up the maze of Ginza district buildings. When Graham returns, he does not sit. He clutches the back of a chair and says, "Rita's in a bad way. I'm going over to be with Helen. Rain check on that steak, OK?"

Brad says, "Of course, Rod. I'll make the arrangements with Sunrise and Shin tomorrow. Nothing for you to do on this thing for two days anyway. It's a travel day tomorrow for your people. If you can't get away, I'll be glad to host them at dinner after they get in. And the next day, we should give them a free day to acclimate. We'll have a joint meeting with our people in this hotel at the end of the free day and bring everybody up to speed. Then the next day, everybody goes to work at Sunrise. Well, assuming you're able."

"You're a take-charge guy, Brad. No wonder Sarah Jane thinks so highly of you."

"Go be with your girl, Rod. Godspeed."

Brad goes to the maître d' station to make a call.

"Amaya? Look, I'm in the dining room. Rod had to go back to the hospital. Do you feel like coming to the Crowne Room?"

Amaya feels a small thrill along her spine. "Poor Rita. Well, I have to get back out in the world sometime, and the Crowne is as good a place to start as any. Give me twenty minutes."

She's lost weight, Brad thinks as Amaya walks to his table. She is in black slacks and heels, with an indigo-colored silk top buttoned to her chin. Brad stands, and Amaya kisses his cheek. She looks around.

"The suite is a luxury, Brad, but I have to say I'm glad to get out. It seems I've been in one confinement after another lately. Could we just get away sometime soon and walk in nature? Next weekend? Anywhere."

"Of course we can. I'll have to wait and see how this week of meetings goes. Next weekend might be a tight fit."

"And so it starts again. The business war on love. What are you having, Brad?"

"Make love, not war: that's my new anthem," says Brad. "Just as soon as the engineering teams leave, we'll go somewhere out of the city, OK? Whether that's a weekend day or just after, does it matter?"

"Of course it doesn't matter; that would be wonderful. I do not intend to be a jealous mistress of your business." She glances up and then straightens up in her chair, her face rigid. "Brad, look who's here."

Brad's eyes linger on Amaya's obvious alarm as he turns in his chair, and then he looks to where her stare was directed. He sees Tanaka standing at the front station of the restaurant. Tanaka is looking at him. He bows his head quickly as Brad turns to look at him. Tanaka stands expectantly.

Brad quickly dispels the idea of walking to meet Tanaka. Amaya's reaction keeps him from leaving her. He looks from Tanaka to Amaya, whose chin trembles despite clamped jaws. Brad says,

"Amaya, I'm going to call him over here unless you don't want to be around him."

After a long pause, Amaya breaks her stare and looks at Brad. She says, "It's better if you call him here. I said I wanted to reenter the world, and it is happening. I'll be fine if you are here."

Brad decides on a compromise. A nearby table is empty. He stands and beckons to Tanaka. As Tanaka walks toward him, Brad makes pointing motions to each table and raises his eyebrows. Tanaka nods and points to the empty one.

"No, please do not get up on my account, Ms. Mori. I am very sorry to disturb you. I did not realize you were with Mr. Oaks-san. May I say that you look remarkably well so soon after your ordeal?"

Amaya continues to rise to her feet and bows before extending her hand. "Inspector Tanaka, I am pleased to see you as well. Thank you. I am being pampered too much in these elegant surroundings. I feel much better. Will you join us?"

Tanaka bows and shakes her hand. "No, thank you. If you would excuse me just a moment, I have a matter of short discussion with Mr. Oaks-san. Please forgive my interrupting. I won't be long."

As Amaya resumes her seat, Tanaka and Brad sit at the other table. Brad says, "Need me to pitch relief again, Skipper?"

Tanaka sits looking at him. He shakes his head slowly. Finally, he says, "Give him one good outing in Japanese league, and it goes to his head." Brad throws back his head and laughs. Amaya stares at him, as does the waiter coming for drink orders. The waiter stops at Amaya's table and takes her order, juice of fresh mandarin orange on crushed ice. Then she says in a strong voice,

"No more for him, please."

Tanaka orders a Suntory All-Free nonalcoholic beer. Brad

orders rye on the rocks, but the waiter shakes his head and gestures to Amaya, who smiles. Brad laughs again.

"So what does bring you here, Tanaka-san?"

"Do you remember Iron Dragon Trading Company? We raided its offices just before the kidnapping?"

"Yes, I do. It scattered a lot of yakuza, as I remember."

"Just so. But we carefully searched the headquarters. Reviewed many files. There is something you should see." Tanaka reaches into the inside pocket of his suit and withdraws a letter-sized envelope. "You please read this, and tell me what you think."

Brad opens the unsealed envelope, withdraws photocopies of a two-page form, and studies it. He says,

"Tanaka-san, this is a request for a quote on X-70 steel plate made to the specifications of the Wishbone Pipeline, the original oil portion. The tonnage would indicate it would make about a hundred fifty miles of pipe, more or less. It calls for shipment to Iran. It is addressed to a steel mill in eastern Russia."

"Look at the date."

"I did. It went out in September."

"Brad-san, what is the significance of this to your company?"

"Well, it confirms this part of the Iranian scheme you helped us shut down."

"Yes, that was my surmise."

The waiter returns, places a coaster and a tall glass in front of Tanaka, and carefully pours the nonalcoholic beer. He then places a short tumbler of rye on the rocks in front of Brad, who says, "Thank you so very much. But didn't she . . .?" tilting his head toward Amaya.

The waiter smiles and says, "Yes, sir, she did. But that's not my table."

"Tanaka-san, this will be important evidence for the US authorities."

"Again, Brad-san, we surmised that as well and sent original papers to Detective Patricia Quinn."

"OK, that's good work." Brad turns and lifts his glass in toast to Amaya, who smiles and returns the gesture with her orange juice. Brad returns his attention to Tanaka, who says,

"There is now more. Please look at this document." He reaches into his jacket again and withdraws a two-page form with an Iron Dragon logo.

Brad examines the new document and straightens up in his chair. He says,

"It's a request for quotation on the same steel plate delivered to Iran, but this time, it's addressed to Pakistani Steel."

"The date, Brad-san?"

"It went out two days ago."

"A dragon is hard to slay, Brad-san."

"But now that we're alerted to pipe manufactured in Iran, I don't think Trans-Rocky would buy any of it from that country."

"Before I leave you to your evening with the charming Ms. Mori, please be so kind as to also read this paper," Tanaka said, handing him another envelope.

"Tanaka-san, this is like a game with Russian nesting dolls, one inside another."

"Yes. But don't take your eye off the strike zone. Read."

Brad examines the new papers. This time, he is looking at copies of several telexes from Iron Dragon Ship Brokers to brokers in Oslo, Bremen, and London. Brad looks up and says,

"Tanaka-san, they are all inquiries looking for ships to lift large-diameter pipe cargo in Iran for delivery to Cape Town, South Africa. To be off-loaded there with ship's tackle. To be then reloaded at the same port by another ship's tackle for transshipment to NOLA." He looks up and says, "That's New Orleans, Louisiana."

"Pitch, a nasty slider perhaps, Brad-san?"

"Spitball, Tanaka-san. This is vital information to Mr. Graham, to me, and to the United States."

"We now try to slay the dragon?"

"Not my call. Someone from our embassy will get in touch on that, probably. In my humble opinion, we would let them spend a great deal of money to buy steel and manufacture the pipe, and only then stop them."

"Not your call. But, a good one if it was. Thank you for the non-beer. Enjoy your evening."

Brad murmurs, "Hmmm baby."

Brad turns to the table where he left Amaya. It is now empty except for a folded note at his place. He reads, "Got an itch to see my arcade store. Let's order room service. Something simple."

Nothing's simple, Brad thinks as he walks to the front service desk to sign the chits.

Friday, November 8, 2019; Stockton, CA

Sarah Jane hears the phone in her office from about thirty steps away. She mutters, digs her foot into the linoleum hallway floor, and sprints to pick up the receiver before it goes to voice mail. Puffing, she says,

"Elgar Steel, Sarah Jane Elgar speaking."

Brad says, "You sound breathless. I can call you back if this is a bad time."

"Don't go away, Brad. Just let me sit a minute. Go ahead and talk."

"I'm telling you, Sarah, I've never been prouder of our people than this week. They were great. They got along with everybody here. By the end of the week, we'll have a pretty good first draft on the engineering. Rod Graham is pretty happy too. More importantly, it looks like Shin Steel is going to give us a letter of intent for the steel and another one for the joint venture. And the letters of intent are tied together with a famous Japanese Side Letter. That one came from Sunrise on the last day."

"When do I get Sandoval back? I'm going nuts here."

"OK, well, Eddie and his people need next week to finish this. They can leave the weekend of the seventeenth sometime, unless you have to pull them out sooner."

"Why not sooner?"

"Sarah Jane, we can't cut corners with these Sunrise people. They'll have to explain everything thoroughly to dozens of other Japanese office workers who arrange the commercial and legal details, plus financing and clearing Japan and US customs. Some of them will be involved in Shin's participation in the joint venture. When inevitable frictions arise with Shin, it will be the Sunrise Trading people who will hammer out resolutions."

"Well then, what do you think of the Sunrise people? Are they the right ones?"

"Sunrise Trading is a relative newcomer in the steel sector. They got into it after World War II through imports of metal scrap at first, then a small ship brokering operation, and then export of steel fabricated goods from the smaller steel mills of

Japan. The largest steel mills remain hooked to their traditional trading houses. Sunrise is hungry and out to please. And Shin wants them."

"OK, sure. Damn, I'll be glad to get our people back though. I never really knew how good Eddie is until the week I don't have him."

"He and the Trans-Rocky chief engineer simplified the routing and bypassed the Sandhill Crane wetlands. She's a steady influence here, that's for sure. Cindy Atherton."

"Don't get too invested in their engineering, Brad. The State Department plans to hire Booth engineering to oversee the whole project."

"Oh. Bad. Word. Sarah, the letter of intent with Shin is going to be based on the plan we develop next week."

"That's fine, Brad. Don't change a thing. Bring home the signed docs, and we'll just go from there. I think Booth just wants their logo on this thing and not to sweat the details much. And another thing, the new guy at State wants a meeting in Washington, and they've asked for you and Rod Graham to be there."

Brad looks for his calendar. "Hold on a sec, Sarah." He puts the phone down and retrieves his calendar from the briefcase he dumped on the desk in his hotel room. "OK, I'm back. When?"

"They want it on November 29. Black Friday. The day after Thanksgiving. Perverse, huh? Of course, Canada's Thanksgiving is a month earlier, if that means anything. I say perverse. This guy at State has pretty much taken charge. He's going to expect to set the schedule and momentum from now on."

"What's his name?"

"Something Dimitrikov."

"Never heard of him."

"He's new to Washington. He's part of the new exchange program the administration has with Russia. MSNBC calls it 'The New Wheel and Deal.'"

"How is Knight with all this?"

"Docile. I'll get back to you on that. You going to the meeting or not?"

"Sure, I'll be there. Graham's the customer; I'll be there if he's there. What about you?"

"Not invited. But June's going."

"No way!"

"Way. She's on cloud nine. Thinks they're going to pin a medal on her. She's scheduled a press conference at her new Toronto offices for a week from today. Try to catch it on Skype. Brad, this is a ton of fun, but I've got real work to do. When do I see you?"

"I'll get back to you on that."

"How's my half sister?"

"Delightful. I'll get back to you on that, too."

"OK. Um. I'm going to LA for a long weekend."

"You never go to LA."

"I'm meeting Alden."

"Wow! Want me to hold off calling till you get back?"

"That'd be great. Ciao."

Saturday, November 16, 2019; Downtown Los Angeles, The Jonathan Club

The private, century-old Jonathan Club, located in the heart of the Los Angeles financial district, houses a survey of impressionist and plein air paintings from renowned California masters. Sarah Jane remembers fondly her previous visits there with her father, tagging along on his business trips to the then-thriving Kaiser steel mill an hour's drive east. An art history student at the time, she had spent hours roaming the club, floor after floor, dodging the housekeeping carts, to view paintings hanging in all its hallways that she could never have seen otherwise. The sensibility of the Jonathan art collection had inspired acquisitions for the Elgar home in Napa Valley, though on a much more modest scale.

She has gone downstairs to the paneled dining room to wait for Alden to finish changing. They spent the day browsing art galleries, looking for replacements for three pieces that could not be saved after the fire sprinklers. The oil paintings had taken well to heroic restoration efforts, but not one of her favorite watercolors, a gauzy, pastel scene of a Southern California eucalyptus grove in mist.

When he arrives to join her, she dabs a cocktail napkin against shower droplets still at the nape of his neck, and kisses his cheek. She beams and says,

"I must say, for a 'jeans and boots' kind of guy, you certainly have a penchant for dark-paneled exclusive clubs. I love it. I never tire of coming here. You're a dear for suggesting it."

Alden says, "I like that it's quiet and unpretentious."

A waiter says, "Drink, sir?"

"Sure." He glances at Sarah Jane's glass of her favorite bold red wine and orders a Campari and soda and a couple of dinner menus.

"Well, Alden," Sarah Jane says, settling back, "you're very comfortable and unpretentious yourself. I look forward to every chance we have to be together. You must miss Los Angeles."

Knight grins and says, "The feeling is certainly mutual,

Sarah. As for LA, I do and I don't. Washington is just as intense as it was here for me. I still have some leftover bad vibes from living here, though."

"I'm sure. I still ache for Daddy. Brad took forever to get over the loss of his fiancée. He never did entirely."

"Right. It's always there."

It has been on her mind, too. "Is that a problem for you now? Is it a problem for us, Alden?"

"No. I'm clear-eyed about all that, including that some part of it is always going to be in me. But I wouldn't be chasing you all over the country if I had reservations. I wouldn't subject you to anything uncomfortable, and I wouldn't be able to stand that sort of inner conflict."

"I'm glad you said it like that. I've never really been in a situation like this. Hell, I've never been so smitten before, to tell the truth."

"Yeah, well, I can imagine it would cause you concern."

She starts to frown. "It's not concern . . ."

"OK, the exact word for it is not so important, but we're talking about the same thing. Look at it this way. You know that scar on my right thigh?"

Sarah Jane blushes. She sees him notice.

"That's an old, old Army training wound. I don't even see it half the time and never feel it. But I know it's there and still wince when I do think of it. You look at it, and you must think it's foremost on my mind. But it really isn't."

"It can't be that simple, Alden, but you're sweet to put it that way."

"It's not the same thing exactly, but after ten years, it's getting that way. I don't look back, Sarah. I like to look forward. And when I do, I think about you. Take Brad; how long has it been for him now?"

"Fourteen years."

"OK, and look at him. He's got it bad for Amaya Mori. It's written all over him. It can happen, his fourteen years or my ten years, or for someone else, maybe even a couple of years. The number doesn't really matter. You and I can't make the scar tissue disappear, but we both can live in the present and plan for the future."

Sarah Jane swirls the last bit of wine in the bottom of her glass. She looks at him, and nods once. After a pause, she says,

"Have you got it bad for me?"

"Yeah, I do, Sarah. Doesn't it show?"

"To my eyes, it does, Alden. But goodness, man, we're both workaholics, and this project thing has been a fluke overlap. It'll get settled one way or another, and then what?"

"I like what you're doing in your life, Sarah. A rare bird is what you are. But down to earth, without pretense. Never mind the project. I just want to be in your life."

"I like what you're doing in your life too, Alden. You're an internationalist with an instinct for fair dealing and progress. Neither of us wants to go it alone forever. The day will come soon enough when we have way too much time on our hands. And then what?"

"That's what I mean. And 'then what' will be the most that we can make of it, which is more than either of us could do with all that time on our hands."

"You are persuasive."

Alden hesitates and exhales. "Sarah, this isn't some tricky case I'm trying to argue. I'm telling you my secret self here."

She says urgently, "Oh, Alden, you are truly dear to me. I don't for a minute mean to imply that you were going litigator on me. I have never doubted your authenticity."

"Isn't authenticity one of the things you said you liked about me?"

"One of them. The other was—"

"I know, I know. But in that case, I need some oysters and a light supper."

Sarah Jane giggles and says, "Alden, I was going to say intelligent. But I like where you're going with this. Let's order."

CHAPTER EIGHTEEN

June Elgar, in jodhpurs, a faded denim shirt, boots, and a white hard hat with maple leaf insignia, steps forward to a bank of microphones in the glare of lights towering behind TV cameras. She stands at the entrance of the now fully restored headquarters of ACEA and its small staff. She taps a microphone with a fingernail, to the distress of a soundman who pulls away headphones in pain.

"One-two-three, *un, deux, trois* . . . is this thing on? *Est-ce que* this, um *chose* um . . . *marché?*"

Glancing around at nodding heads, she continues: "This is a special day for the American-Canadian Environmental Alliance. We proudly reopen our headquarters just three months after terrorists attempted to thwart our environmental and climate-saving mission. With the steadfast support of our generous donors, and from the national and provincial governments of Canada, we today reopen our doors with renewed determination, undaunted by threats or acts of terrorist opposition, and at no small risk to our personal well-being. Standing here beside me is the brave man who was here when the attack occurred, then a hardworking, unpaid student intern for ACEA, and who suffered painful injuries for his loyalty."

She turns to beam at a man in his late twenties whose six-foot-four-inch frame looms next to her. He blinks and runs his fingers through his golden hair, then fidgets with the button of his new bespoke blazer, which June helped him to acquire on a recent weeklong field trip to London. His teeth gleam in the lights when he grins and waves his hand weakly.

"Christopher was spared serious injury and has fully recovered otherwise. He is with us again, and I'm proud to announce is my chief international liaison. He brings to our work remarkable vision and energy.

"Saved for last, though, is our jewel for the health of the planet. We today announce the most significant compact ever formed between Canada and the United States, heralding a new era of mutually beneficial commerce that actually helps the environment. Beginning with an idea of mine that occurred to me nearly two years ago, I take great pride in announcing a concept I think will achieve success in the last and final link in turning the Wishbone Pipeline project from the proverbial sow's ear to a silk purse. While it is true ACEA long opposed the initial plan for the project as an environmental disaster, my modest proposal will turn that disaster into an environmental victory that is of no less than providential proportions to the Earth's future and hope for future generations of Canadian and American workers and farmers.

"My simple idea, obvious, it seems, only to me, is to lay a water pipe alongside the oil pipeline. *Ta-da!* This insight of mine will capture the imaginations of the new governments of Alberta and Canada, and in turn persuade the American authorities to overcome mountains of red tape and indecision. This brainstorm will turn into the first-ever sale of Canada's abundant western waters to the citizens of America's heartland to help replace rapacious wastage of their own precious Ogallala Aquifer. The Wishbone project will thus provide Canada a double-dip of benefits, if I may express it in that term. Oil and water, in parallel pipelines, will provide an unparalleled union of environmental and commercial blessings. Thank you for your attention. My staff will distribute copies of my remarks."

Monday, November 18, 2019; Washington, DC; 16th and M Streets

Adjacent to the south side of the University Club, a black SUV pulls up to the curb. Gregor Dimitrikov opens the rear door of the van and steps to the locked gate at the short circle drive to the stone building, with the tall flagpole displaying the flag of the Russian Federation. The gate's lock opens with a buzz, and then closes behind Dimitrikov, who is greeted at the building's front door.

Inside, Dimitrikov and the Russian ambassador shake hands and turn quickly to reviewing a document brought by Dimitrikov. After a cursory read-through, the ambassador takes out a fountain pen and makes bold-stroked marginal notes. Dimitrikov studies the notes and says,

"Russian industry can produce so much?"

The ambassador scoffs and hands the pages back to Dimitrikov with trembling hands. He says,

"And more. But we are not greedy pigs. I have no time to provide you lessons in industrial history and statistics. Good night."

Next door, in her suite at the University Club, Sarah Jane places a call to Japan.

"Brad Oaks speaking."

"Did you see it, Brad?"

"I saw it on Skype, Sarah. I can't believe it. I can't believe your beloved sister, June. I've never witnessed such theft of intellectual property, and on camera. I suppose you knew this was coming, Sarah."

"Come on, Brad. Of course I didn't. Still and all, she did it. She got the Canadian part done."

"At the expense of her own father's legacy. Her twin sister. And me, of course, but I guess that hardly counts."

"Suck it up, Brad. There's work to do. There's a job to bid on. Then, there's pipe to make, and there's new life in Elgar Steel. Come to the farm. We're having Thanksgiving on Saturday instead of Thursday, and Alden's going to be there. You have time."

"I know."

"So, you just want to go back and mope at the Palace Hotel?"

"I don't mope. I'm with Amaya . . ."

"Bring her! Time she sees the winery and sits down with me for some girl talk. Come here after your meeting at State. Time it so you meet her flight from Tokyo at SFO."

"It's only been six weeks, Sarah Jane. She's still pretty subdued. Anyway, I'll ask her. We'll see. Thanks for the invitation."

"Don't let her go into a cave. I don't know much about psychology, but I know that animals want to cave when they've been wounded."

"Yeah, that's what the doctors say too. But you don't want a trauma patient at your party."

"It's family, Brad! Don't overthink the thing."

229

*Friday, November 29, 2019; Washington, D.C., State
Department building*

Two floors below the elegant mahogany offices and the halls
where the Alden Knight reception took place, in an unadorned
small conference room holding a center table formed by four
smaller tables pushed together, with mismatching chairs hastily
assembled for a meeting, Brad Oaks and Alden Knight sit in a
small cluster of people waiting for a meeting to start. Brad tries
to avoid the eyes of June Elgar, who looks miserable and alone
at the far side of the table. The door opens, and a stocky man
about thirty-five years old, with black hair and wearing a lumpy
wool suit, strides in and takes his place at the head of the table.
He says,

"Thank you all for meeting with us at the State Department.
I'm Gregor Dimitrikov, US Department of State. I am taking the
place of Ms. Le Claire; some of you may know she resigned her
position. I intend to succeed where she failed in this delicate
proposal.

"Since these meetings have usually been held in
Ambassador Knight's shop, please go around the room and
introduce yourselves again for my benefit. Let's start with you,
Ms. Elgar."

"June Elgar, American-Canadian Environmental Alliance."
She smiles and looks to her right. She does not react to a wink
from Brad.

"Rod Graham, CEO of Trans-Rocky Pipeline."

"Brad Oaks, Elgar Steel."

"Alden Knight, USTR."

"Ian McMillian, Canadian ambassador to the United States."

"Mr. Oaks, I welcome you back to the State Department. I realize you might have some trepidation after the reception you received at your last visit."

"I'm glad to be here. But I did notice that the old scaffolding is gone."

"Yes. We informally call that area the Oaks Windows."

Brad chuckles and says, "Wow. So, it's true: 'some men have fame thrust upon them.'"

"Perhaps this day will thrust even more such fame on you, Mr. Oaks.

"OK, this meeting is to achieve something that has eluded you for too long. Today, we shall achieve agreement on combining the Wishbone Pipeline with Canadian water, on terms that will make everyone happy or no one happy.

"Ambassador McMillian, why don't you start us off."

McMillian says, "I am willing to negotiate, without prejudice to object when the final terms are tabled." Brad and Alden nod their heads again.

"That's a given. It's never over till it's over. The US side is here to make a deal. It seems to me that sometimes Canada makes agreeable sounds, particularly in the press, and yet at times like the present, straddles the fence. Ambassador McMillian, you have the floor."

"We are a nation of agreeable people, Mr. Dimitrikov, and we are no strangers to reaching agreements with the country where we spend seventy-seven percent of our foreign trade dollars. You are suddenly moving this negotiation at an artificially fast pace. Nothing in the real world, including the price of oil, justifies a panic mode for deal making. There may indeed be a historic transaction at our fingertips, but the thirty-nine million people I represent are looking for what's best for them. A deal may be in Canada's best interests. But haste is not."

"Mr. Ambassador, what do you need with more time? The previous administration dithered over your pipeline proposal until you missed the market. Well, the market is turning your way again. For the life of me, I don't see why you are dragging your feet."

"For the same reason you are in such haste, I suppose: the water. Water is the new factor in the Wishbone equation. And it's our water and always has been. There are millions of Canadians who don't ever want to sell our water no matter what they get in return. I'm not one of them, but I am responsible to them for making a bargain beneficial to my country. Even though we grew tired of the red tape that strangled the earlier Wishbone proposal, this water pipeline adds a whole new dimension, and I only just heard about it in September."

June says, in a quiet voice, "I've been in close communication with the Edmonton government for weeks now. They see it as a win-win."

McMillian says, "But even they have not done a proper economic analysis of the thing. They don't know how they will gather all this water or at what cost. They haven't taken into account the possible impacts on the Canadian economy, particularly the grain markets, or on the fragile environments of our rivers and glaciers."

Dimitrikov says, "What does it take to get you to yes?"

"We would be willing to give the green light provisionally to the double pipeline concept. The proviso would be that we must evaluate whether it will be our water that flows through that second pipe or more of our oil. And no one has proposed any sort of compensation to Canada for the water you hope to import."

Dimitrikov says, "An eloquent prologue, Ambassador, but not an offer. What terms and conditions do you have in mind?"

McMillian touches his fingertips together and says, "Ever the push, push. Like a troika on a snowy night. I propose we focus on negotiating a heads of agreement."

Dimitrikov says, "An agreement to agree, and in diplospeak, it isn't worth the powder to blow it to hell. The US side needs something more specific."

McMillian says, "Look, we are willing to give firm approval to a second pipeline, the so-called loop. But whether it carries water or something else is a different, more complicated matter. Our proviso would have to be that the Canadian side will have the right to conduct its own economic impact study before committing to exporting water to America."

Dimitrikov turns to Rod Graham. "When do you have to know whether you're transporting oil or water?"

Graham says, "Well, we have to know in at least a year, because the differences between an oil pipeline and a water aqueduct are epic. Give us a year. That sound about right to you, Brad?"

Brad says, "Well, I agree that a year is about right."

Brad then slams his palm on the table and lets the resulting reverberations die off before saying, "But what happens if Canada says no to water? We're then left with two oil pipelines and a whole lot of unhappy American farmers and environmentalists."

Dimitrikov says, "Mr. Oaks, your views on legal issues arising out of that business are germane."

"This isn't what I came away with from Edmonton," says June, with moderate force in her voice. "This isn't what the

ACEA board approved. This isn't what I announced at a press conference. This is all about even more tar sands oil, with the environmental offsets simply a maybe."

McMillian says, "The US side is forgetting a key aspect of that: the compensation to Canada for its water. The key question is, what compensation should persuade us to transport water instead of twice the oil?"

Knight puts his hand on Brad's arm as Brad is about to beat the table again, and says, "But Ian, your initial reaction to this was positive. I take it the same is true of the Alberta government." He looks at June, who nods. "So can't you say that the value to Canada is apparent on its face, unless this further study shows it to be clearly detrimental?"

"I see where you're going," says McMillian, "which is fine as far as it goes, but then what about price?"

Rod Graham says, "I'd know how I'd price it."

All turn to look at him.

Dimitrikov says, "Mr. Graham, I'm thinking we're a bit out of your league here. We are dealing with vast natural resources, so why don't you just let the experts—"

"I'd rely on public-private incentives and market forces."

"We can call you with the upshot of this if you'd like, but you can feel free to head back to Texas and to your construction planning—"

"Mr. Dimitrikov, I'm standing here with breath in my chest and a sentence I'd like to finish, if you please!"

Dimitrikov rolls his eyes, and thrusts out his hand in a quarter circle, palm up, as if ushering Graham into the room.

"You want to monetize water. Fine. Start with monetizing the carbon footprint of the tar sands. When delays killed Keystone in the last administration, one of the pipeline's executives wrote a postmortem on the whole sorry affair. He claims they should have proposed a carbon tax of fifteen to thirty dollars per ton of emitted carbon dioxide tied to oil sands production. He says that the producers would have agreed to that in principle. You could take, say, ten dollars in carbon tax, and it gives you one and a quarter billion dollars per year. That finances a lot of water.

"Then, you let the water users in the Midwest organize local associations and submit bids to buy the water. So much a year for five years, that sort of thing. Let them make a market for it that way. Put a carbon tax that Canadian producers can live with, and a user fee that American agriculture can live with, and you've paid for a viable water aqueduct."

Graham stands and moves toward the door, saying, "I'm in need of fresh air. In a couple of hours, I'm on a red-eye back to Tokyo."

June says, "Look, I went out on a limb at a press conference to announce the Wishbone water project. What am I supposed to do now?"

Dimitrikov says, "Ms. Elgar, that press conference was what I'd call misguided in its timing and lack of coordination with the real parties in interest. I suggest you engage a public relations firm to work with the people in our communications shop to figure out how to best set the record straight from your point of view."

June gathers her handbag and coat and stalks out of the room.

Knight says, "Brad, if you're finished here, let's you and I go downstairs with Rod Graham."

Brad nods and pulls on his crinkled travel raincoat.

Dimitrikov says, "Well, is that it, then? Here are the deal

points: firm deal to build Wishbone and the loop; water to be priced based on bids; carbon tax; prima facie presumed to be a good economic deal for Canada unless rebutted by a one-year study proving 'clearly' otherwise. I think that's everything, Ambassador McMillian."

McMillian keeps his head still, saying nothing, not making eye contact with anyone. He continues to hang back as everyone else leaves.

Dimitrikov says, "Was there something else you wanted to bring up?"

McMillian shrugs and says, "Um, well, one thing. I didn't want to prolong the conversation with all the others in the room. Better to keep it between the government negotiators."

Dimitrikov sits down again, and gestures for McMillian to do the same. McMillian simply leans on the table next to Dimitrikov and says calmly, "I'm informed that the pipe mill industry of Canada has strong views on the economics of the project."

Dimitrikov leans back and says, "Right. Can you be more specific?"

"They feel their industry would be injured unless there was a set-aside in pipe procurement for Canadian-sourced pipe."

"Really. Should I get the Trans-Rocky and Elgar people back in here?"

"Um, no. That could lead to unseemly grasping for commercial advantage by interested parties."

"Aren't you confident that your pipe industry will be competitive when it comes time for Trans-Rocky to solicit bids?"

"Yes, of course. Um, I think you and I can cut through a tremendous amount of resistance from the standpoint of our economic proviso, with a certain set-aside for Canadian product."

"To be clear, you are talking about setting aside a portion of the steel pipe contract that only Canadian pipe mills can bid on, right? As in, like, fifteen percent?"

McMillian stands again, shrugs into his topcoat, and starts for the door.

Dimitrikov stops him with, "At least give me a counter."

McMillian turns and says, "Our industry is adamant at fifty percent."

"Ian, you are talking about a pipeline that runs over a thousand miles in the United States. That is a deal breaker. Have a nice day."

"Forty percent."

"Not going to happen."

"What is going to happen?"

"Twenty-five percent."

"Nothing less than thirty, Mr. Dimitrikov."

"If it's thirty percent, does that go in the heads of agreement as not subject to change?"

"Agreed."

"I really should run that by Trans-Rocky, at least."

"No, Mr. Dimitrikov, you really shouldn't."

"Very well, thirty percent."

"You'll have a draft heads of agreement out to us when?"

"Monday latest, I should think."

"Good day, Mr. Dimitrikov," says McMillian before heading out the door.

Dimitrikov, alone in the room, stares out the window into the gathering gloom of a cloudy night in Washington. He looks at his watch.

Rod Graham, Alden Knight, and Brad Oaks stand under a

streetlight on Virginia Avenue as a light rain begins to fall. They make no move toward a car or shelter. One looks at his watch.

Dimitrikov pours a glass of water and dials a number.

"This is Alden."

"You were right. He insisted on a set-aside."

"And?"

"He wanted the moon. I agreed to thirty percent."

Knight covers his cell phone and looks at Rod Graham and Brad Oaks. "It's thirty percent."

Graham says to Brad, "Hell, you guys can't handle seventy percent of the new project. I'll be awarding more than thirty to Canadian mills anyway."

Knight turns back to the phone. "I need to talk to you about that."

"Nope, it's a done deal at thirty percent. It goes into the heads of agreement at thirty. Nonnegotiable."

"They'll have to live with it then." Alden clicks the call off.

Graham grins and says, "Come on, guys, I'll buy you dinner."

Brad dials Sarah Jane's cell phone. "Sarah Jane, it looks like we have a deal, but with some soft spots. Canada is holding out for a set-aside, and State gave them thirty percent. They also have the proviso on exporting water in the second pipeline, but they have to fish or cut bait on that in a year's time. So, basically, we have one hell of a project to bid."

Sarah Jane is quiet, then says, "Well, Mr. Brad Oaks, you have done yourself proud. I just wish Daddy were here. By the way, June was supposed to be at that meeting. Did she show up?"

"Yeah, and got chewed out pretty good about her presser."

"OK. How'd she seem to you, Brad?"

"Hard to describe, Sarah. Distant maybe? She left early. I mean, I'd have to say wiggy," says Brad.

"Wiggy."

"Ya know?"

"Uh-huh."

CHAPTER NINETEEN

Sunday, December 1, 2019; Napa, Elgar estate

Brad puffs from his day-after-Thanksgiving-dinner run, noting with alarm that he needs to devote some serious time to roadwork if he's ever going to get back to the shape he was in the day the Iranians shot at him next to the United States trade representative at the State Department. The very same Alden Knight heads him off from going upstairs to change and tugs him into the living room, where Sarah Jane is pacing. Knight says,

"The heads of agreement came in over the fax."

Sarah Jane puts a glass of mineral water back down on a coaster while holding in her other hand a faxed scan of a three-page document with the State Department logo. She says,

"Read this piece of dog shit," and thrusts the fax in his hands.

Brad takes it, saying, "This is where I came in. Somebody else die?"

Sarah Jane stabs the fax with her fingernail and says, "Shut up and read."

Brad carries the fax to the window for more light and begins to read. He stands motionless and then turns the first page. After a long moment, he turns the second page. He then flips back to the first page and glances through the whole fax again.

He looks up at Alden and Sarah Jane, now standing at his side, and says, "OH. BAD. WORD."

The phone rings. No one moves. Finally, Sarah Jane goes to the kitchen and answers.

"Oh, hello, Rod. Happy Thanksgiving to you, too. Are you still in Japan? How's Rita?"

"We're still here. The Palace Hotel has put up their version of the Pilgrim dinner with the Indians in the lobby. I'll send you a photo. It's a hoot. Hey, there's a rumor that the heads of agreement is out. Do you know anything about it?"

"It must be the middle of the night for you. We just got our copy. Still picking ourselves up. I'll fax it right away to the Palace."

"What does it say?"

"You've got to see this for yourself. Call us back when you've recovered. Best to Helen, I'm headed to the fax to send it out now. So, you never said how Rita is . . . Well that's encouraging, don't you think? Yeah? OK, then, more to be thankful for. 'Bye for now."

She levels her intense eyes at Alden, then at Brad. "You boys don't say a word till I get back from the fax machine to hear it. Not. One. Word."

Knight shrugs and zips his lips with an index finger. Brad shakes his head and imitates the same gesture.

Sarah Jane returns with a cup of coffee for Brad. The two men eye her as she settles herself with stocking feet under her on a leather armchair. Alden gets up to poke new flames in the fireplace. After he returns to his chair, Sarah Jane says,

"All right. You can talk. You two powerhouse lawyers, dissect this thing for me."

Alden and Brad look at one another. Brad says, "You're the

ambassador. You start."

Knight swallows a sip of sparkling water and says, "First of all, it's unprecedented . . ."

"What else is new? That's every day with this administration," she scoffs.

"We thought you wanted to listen," says Brad.

"Specifically, it's unprecedented for our State Department to carve up pieces of the pie on their own, without so much as a how-do-you-do to the commercial parties. It's the weirdest scramble of international eggs I've seen in my lifetime when it comes to the set-aside.

"But it's also unprecedented as a trade agreement with Canada. This compact validates the vision of your father and this man here," he says, nodding to Brad. "And it's the green light for the Wishbone pipelines, plural, just as you've hoped for."

"Yes, but . . .? There's got to be a 'but,'" she says.

"It's in the set-aside. You go over that, Brad."

"OK, here's the breakdown. Thirty percent pipe fabrication sourced in Canada. Forty-five percent pipe fabrication sourced in America. Twenty-five percent pipe fabrication sourced from any country of origin other than predominantly Muslim countries. Pipe shall be made from steel plate as follows: seventy-five percent steel plate from countries other than predominantly Muslim countries, twenty-five percent steel plate from Russia as country of origin."

Sarah Jane says, "Alden, did you know about Russia?"

"Nope. It must be another instance of cozy-up with Russia," says Knight.

"Another instance of 'wheel and deal,' you mean," says Sarah Jane.

"Other than that, it's as it was when we were in

Washington," says Brad. "Two pipelines approved in the same right of way. Oil in one. Water in the other, provided that Canada makes a finding of 'no significant economic detriment' to Canada exporting its water. They've got one year for their economic study. And 'compensation for the water shall be determined by Canada in a competitive environment.'"

Amaya descends the stairs and sits unnoticed on the bottom step, peering into the living room.

Sarah Jane says, "OK, let's take it from just our perspective. Elgar Steel definitely has a job to bid on. We have to be competitive. There is no set-aside just for Elgar. And we can bid on how much of it?"

Brad says, "As I read it, we could bid on up to seventy percent. There is the forty-five percent American set-aside for pipe fabrication, plus another twenty-five percent that's up for grabs provided it has steel plate from Russia."

Sarah Jane says, "That's pretty interesting. I'm thinking Russia doesn't much care who makes the pipe—they just want to sell the steel. So, how much Japanese steel could go into the job?"

Brad says, "Theoretically, seventy-five percent under the heads of agreement, but of course, they'd have to compete against steel from Canada, the US, and all over the world."

"The non-Muslim world," says Knight.

Sarah Jane says, "What's up with that?"

Knight says, "The new politics. Here we had an Iranian plot to install defective pipes in a major oil pipeline in America, intended to cause catastrophic damage when they burst. The policy hawks of the new politics came up with a pretext for what they now are calling 'preemptive sanctions.' It's a ban on goods instead of the ban on people that they promised but then found they couldn't implement."

Brad says, "But politics aside, the Japanese have an open shot at this job, and how much they get depends on price. Not all mills can make plate to these specifications, and not all pipe mills can handle those sizes and steel hardness. The Japanese steel mills are in a good position from the standpoint of quality and availability."

Knight says, "And China can bid, and no doubt will be aggressive."

Sarah Jane says, "China could make all the steel not set aside for Russia, yes. But we're in bed with Shin."

Brad says, "You bet. We have a letter of intent with Shin, and to the Japanese, that's as firm as it can possibly get. No wiggle room there even if we wanted it, which we don't."

"OK," says Sarah Jane, "so we're in the same position as always, and we can go for seventy percent of the job."

Knight turns to Brad and says, "Does your deal with Shin preclude you from using Russian steel?"

Brad says, "Well, sure, assuming Shin could supply it. Not in so many words, but that's the intent. I suppose there may be some room to open up the letter of intent and let Elgar bid with Russian steel for the twenty-five percent Russian set-aside. That's an interesting twist."

Knight says, "The reason I bring it up is that I also got a fax from State, saying that they want meetings in Moscow with their new consulting engineer and prospective pipe bidders."

Brad says, "Could we even produce that much, Sarah?"

Sarah Jane says, "Hmm. Don't count us out exactly. With a big-enough Wishbone order, we might go to the banks to finance an expansion."

A voice from the stairwell says, "Sunrise Trading has good

relations with one Japanese bank."

The other three look at each other, then around the room, then notice Amaya.

"Sister, have you been listening to all this?" asks Sarah Jane.

"I listen to everything."

"Well, come on in by the fire. Don't just hover over there in the shadows," says Sarah Jane. "After all, you have a stake in Elgar Steel and its future as much as I do. I didn't know you were downstairs, or I would have brought you in sooner."

"Thank you." Amaya turns to Brad and says, "Don't neglect to shave."

Sarah Jane glances at Brad, who looks away, stifling a smile.

Knight says, "Well, I can get you in on the first Moscow meetings if that's something you're interested in."

Sarah Jane says, "It might well be. I need to talk to Sandoval and a couple of other people. Will it wait a day?"

Knight says, "I'll make a phone call to check," and steps out on the patio.

Sarah Jane moves to Brad's side and says, "Can you check the horse barn with me this morning?"

"Yeah. If you want to talk there."

"I'm thinking there, Brad."

"Gotcha."

She winks at Brad and scratches her chin to remind him to shave. She says, "Come on back downstairs, and we'll get into this with Alden." She turns to Amaya and says, "There's fresh coffee in the kitchen if you want to come with me."

Amaya says, "I can't believe your kitchen was exploded. It looks like it was born here. It is fresh and new. Bigger than any kitchen I have seen."

"It was a mess. But they did a wonderful job of restoration.

It's just the same as it was except the gas pipes have some extra thingies in them, and we have security cameras in there now."

The kitchen wall phone rings.

Sarah Jane says, "Excuse me. That'll be Rod."

Sarah Jane takes a long time with Rod Graham on the phone. Amaya carries a cup of coffee out to the patio and sits in the mid-morning sun. She has finished it by the time Brad, shaven and in shorts, sandals, and faded Giants jersey, sits beside her, grinning with contentment.

Sarah Jane and Knight emerge to the deck through the new kitchen French doors. Brad asks, "What's up with the Grahams?"

"Rita's gone from stable to slightly improved. Given what she went through, any improvement is too good to call slight. Rod's as baffled as we are about the heads of agreement. Yes, he's overjoyed he has his pipeline deal, but he's real old-school about the Russians. He thinks he'll have to keep a closer eye on their steel than he would have with Iranian pipe. He's wrong about that, but, like I said, he's old-school."

Knight asks, "Has he heard about meetings in Moscow?"

Sarah Jane draws chairs together for herself and Knight and slips her hand in his. "He didn't say, and I didn't say. Time enough for that later, I guess. He's starting to talk to me more like project owner to pipe vendor. That's a good sign, too."

Brad says, "It sure is. He looked like a broken man last time I saw him in Tokyo."

"What do you know about those meetings, Alden?"

"They're on a fast track, Sarah Jane. The Booth Engineering folks want to establish their authority. That's why the meetings are in their Moscow offices. They want people there week after next."

"Sheesh. Brad, what do you think? I think you ought to go because I want Sandoval to stay here and run the damned plant like normal for a while."

Amaya touches the corner of her eye. Then she applies a napkin to stop another tear. She clears her throat, stands, and says, "I think I shall go upstairs to lie down. Please forgive me."

Brad and Sarah Jane exchange brief glances. "Of course, Sister."

"Excuse if I am impolite," Amaya says. She turns and walks up the stairs to her room, her shoulders shaking and her napkin dabbing her eyes.

"Should I leave?" asks Knight. "I'm kind of a fifth wheel, I think."

"Hell no, Alden. You're actually the fourth wheel, and we need you for stability. Right, Brad?"

Brad doesn't answer right away. Then he nods silently and sits down. Sarah Jane squeezes Knight's hand, and says, "Walk with me, Brad. Meet me where we meet."

Brad nods. "Give me a sec." He mounts the stairs two at a time and taps on Amaya's door. "Come in," he hears.

"Look, I'm going for a walk with Sarah for a few minutes in the barn, in case you want to come looking for me."

"It is a nice place to walk and talk. She took me there yesterday. She showed me the stall where she kissed you. We both laughed. So now you are going to Russia?"

"Not until sometime next week. This week, Sarah and I are taking split vacations to have more time with you. She'll be here through Wednesday while I go to the plant. Then we switch, and we're all here next weekend."

"Brad, I am smothered in kindness and hospitality. It is a little rich for my blood, as the English say. What happens when you go to Russia and my sister goes to her steel mill next week?"

"We'll see, and we'll figure that out as we go along. The main thing is that you can rest and recuperate right here at the Elgar estate in the lap of luxury, which you so richly deserve."

"Brad, I have simple tastes and needs. As you say, we'll see. Have a nice walk and talk in your barn."

Brad and Sarah Jane walk arm in arm in the streaky sunlight that seeps between boards to illuminate dust motes kicked up by the animals. Sarah Jane says,

"I like my half sister way more than I ever thought I would. I won't say more than I like June because June's essence is my own blood, and because she and I have lived decades beside one another. Daddy may have been randy, and his Tokyo behavior was a betrayal to Mother, but I have to say I really do like your Amaya."

"All of what you say is true, Sarah. Amaya is struggling between feeling alone where she is at home and feeling not alone in a strange place."

Sarah grips Brad's strong arm and says, "I walked with her out here. I won't say I put in a good word for you—I didn't need to. She's utterly for you. What I did talk about is life here in Northern California. In the West, generally. Diversity and freedom to explore. Our art scene. She could have as many gallery annexes as she could handle between Napa and Los Angeles. Four or five that I could name immediately. She didn't push back. She acknowledged everything I said."

Brad says, "Yeah, well, that could mean anything. The Japanese way is not to dispute or argue. She could easily have been saying that she understands and appreciates all of the advantages of this place, but secretly hold reservations based on her own unspoken sense of place.

"We have a very strong sense of place, Sarah, every one of us. Well, some people may not feel that as much as others, but I do know the powerful feelings that can attach to place. If you're somewhere you don't want to be, you never stop thinking about being somewhere else. Especially if you know exactly where that other place is. And if you're in a place you like to be in, you never think about it much or at all. Amaya's thinking about two places at once. Ultimately, she'll decide. No one can help her out of the in-between."

Sarah Jane nods her head vigorously and stretches her legs into a forward stride. "That's what I was going to say. No, that's not true. You said it better than I ever could. But I get it. Mother and June and I would have packed up to traipse around the world with Daddy. His work might have made that necessary, but he managed to keep it all together here and in Stockton.

"He decided not to move to South America when they wanted him to build a pipe mill down there. He didn't go, so we didn't go. I've always wondered if I could have gone. I tell myself that I would have so the family wouldn't split up. I tell myself that, but I never faced the experience, really. I don't think about this being 'my place,' since, as you say, I am happy where I am. But if I were forced to be somewhere else, or went somewhere else because my life got complicated, or I went somewhere for some special reason, I'm sure that I would miss this place. Not just miss it: I would crave it. Craving this place might even ruin what I went somewhere else for. I've run all this through my mind before."

Brad says, "What I know is that I don't want to be alone anymore. I don't want to squander a chance not to be alone. That's more important to me than place, I think."

"I get that you have a chance not to be alone. But watch it when you think your great thoughts about place. Is Tokyo a place for you? Is anywhere in Japan? I guess the Palace Hotel is a place. But, hell, that's a luxury hotel, which my company pays you to stay in. I'm happy to do it, but all I'm saying is, you have a pretty limited and privileged exposure to Japan as a place."

"I know."

"And you really don't know what the effect of place, or a different place, might have on you. You lost what was 'place' for you fourteen years ago. Napa became the new place. You are happy—well, somewhat happier anyway—in the new place. You haven't faced having to choose a different place. Not Washington and not Tokyo."

"Sarah, I may be one of those who don't attach so much importance to place as I do to people and work."

"OK, but that presents the same problem, doesn't it? It's not our plant but the people there you identify with. And not the farm but me, and other people here."

"So what do I do, Sarah?"

"You do your damn job, Brad. Or you simply drop out like the hippies did. That hasn't worked out very well for them, I can assure you. I've seen them. I know some of them, and they would love to have the kind of job and responsibility you have now."

"Because there's purpose in the job, right?"

"Yes, that's a good way to put it."

"Amaya's shrink is always talking purpose to her, purpose with a small 'p' and more like a daily task list."

"She told me about that. But her shrink is treating a traumatized individual who's smart and sensitive. Thank God, you missed trauma by the skin of your teeth. I don't think it's exactly the same thing."

"No, you're right. I'll never get over wanting the chance to not be alone anymore until I actually have that chance. Amaya might get over her trauma. Probably will. At least get over constant turmoil. So I'm now thinking I have a long, long wait ahead of me."

"Yeah, that's about where I come out on this thing, Brad. I'm thinking if you up and move to Tokyo right now, you're going to start to feel magnetized to this place, not Tokyo. That would be hell on earth."

Brad stops walking and is quiet before he replies. "I have to think about that. I sometimes do my best thinking on an airplane. I've got a long flight to Moscow, for starters."

"Brad, you do your best thinking anytime. On a plane or on your feet or on the phone. You have a synthesizing mind, just like Alden said. You've already made the best decision, to just let Amaya go where she needs to go. She won't discard you. She and I talked a long time. As your Japanese friend said, she's what you need. She's deep.

"Here's our stall, Brad. Want a kiss?"

"Actually, I was thinking more of a turkey sandwich."

She laughs and kisses him anyway. "There, and don't think I won't do it again next time I have you in the barn by myself. As for the sandwich, go ask Alden to make it for you. He's feeling a bit vestigial around here this weekend."

"I'm glad you two are an item, Sarah. So this seems serious, right?"

"There's no doubt in my mind, Brad. You know me, and you know very well that it's hard to turn my head. But this is the real deal for me."

"Does that mean you'll move to Washington? To find your

place there?"

"Touché, Brad. You know, I think I would. But I'll whisper something to you here in the barn that you cannot ever say or even think out loud."

Brad nods and looks at her.

"Alden is thinking to make a graceful exit at some point."

Brad nods again. "That edge in his voice, talking about new politics and preemptive sanctions?"

"I'm not going to say anything more. See if something comes out over turkey sandwiches."

They reach the same door where they entered the barn. Brad opens it, and they both wince as the sun hits them full in the eyes. They stand looking at the Elgar estate, the family home, and the patio.

Brad says, "This is a powerful place, and I mean 'place' in every way we were talking about."

Sarah Jane and Brad reenter the house. Sarah Jane waggles her fingers at Knight and says, "I'm going upstairs for a few, Alden."

Brad calls out, "And I'm foraging for game in the kitchen. Want to join me?"

Knight grins and comes into the kitchen. He rinses out wineglasses from the night before and puts them in the dishwasher. Brad opens the double doors of the refrigerator and starts off-loading foodstuffs to Knight, who arranges them on the counter. They shuffle turkey leftovers, lettuce, cranberry sauce, and a breadboard with a rustic wheat loaf in an assembly line and set about to manufacture sandwiches for four.

"I like your boss," Knight says.

"Yup."

"I guess she likes me," Knight says, glancing over at Brad

like an expectant teenager fishing for encouragement.

"Yeah, I guess. Want cheese on yours?"

"I'll pass on cheese. This is sure a great place here."

"Uh-huh. Did you sell your place in Orange County?"

"Hell no. No way."

"So USTR is a temporary gig?"

"It was always indefinite. It's an itch I'm glad to have the chance to scratch. But it's sure no reason to sell the homestead."

"Mayo?"

"Sure. I'm out of my doctor's jurisdiction."

"Speaking of that, how do you like your boss?"

"Um. Well, I can't say I'm in love. Like I am with yours."

"No doubt. What do you think about the new politics?"

"You want yours with cranberry?"

"On the side. Amaya never tasted cranberry in her life before yesterday."

Knight chuckles. Then he says, "What's new about the politics is that for the first time in my life, I'm working for people who don't value critical analysis. You can be left, you can be right, you can be upside down, but in my book, you have to take governance seriously enough to have an inquiring mind. And you have to believe in the scientific method, and value that sort of analysis, and base your actions on analysis of pertinent data. Shall I put extra cranberry on hers?"

"Go ahead and put it in a side dish for her."

"I don't really mind that the State Department is picking up Wishbone. It's a relief, frankly. I had a conversation with the ethics lawyer in our shop, and she about threw up. Of course, most of her colleagues in town are downright seasick these days. But I don't want Wishbone to interfere with me and Sarah Jane, and vice versa."

"Alden, 'preemptive sanctions'?"

"Yeah. It's bullshit, of course. But it's exactly what I'm saying; it doesn't require a lot of pesky critical thinking. You pick out a threat and boycott everything that comes out of whatever part of the world it comes from. Unless, of course, it has anything to do with petroleum. I'm fed up. And I don't mean the corn bread stuffing."

"I can understand that. And I understand about the false promise of always taking the easy way. The bumper-slogan way. The wheel-and-deal way."

"Over in the USTR shop, we call it 'Hashtag wheelandealRus.'"

"Brad, I don't mind telling you, I'm so fed up, I think I'll be back in California before the end of next year. Where exactly depends on a lot of things. Her place or mine, so to speak."

"Interesting. I'm going through something similar."

"About Elgar Steel?"

Brad says, "No, no. The other thing. Her place or mine."

"Gotcha. Well, women have a way of getting you to think you'll follow them anywhere, don't they? Evolutionary trait, I think."

"Hmm. Have you given that scientific analysis, or is it just your intuition?"

"Pure bullshit, bumper-sticker, easy-way intuition. Call the girls."

Wednesday, December 4, 2019; Napa, Elgar estate

Sarah Jane ducks out of the kitchen to answer the doorbell rung by an express deliveryman. She signs for the cardboard box, about the size of a bread box, smiles at the deliveryman, and closes the door behind her as she studies the carefully handwritten address. It is from the Tokyo Metropolitan Police Department with the name Tanaka printed beside the return address. She raises her voice, but not her eyes from the package.

"Amaya, can you come give me a hand with something? I'll be in the living room."

Sarah Jane retrieves kitchen scissors and starts to cut the layers and layers of tape.

"I am here, older Sister. How can I help you?" Amaya stands in the hallway in new sandals, a denim wraparound skirt, and a cornflower-blue cotton turtleneck.

"Hi, thanks. This just came to me from the Tokyo police. Help me figure out what it is." Sarah Jane moves to one end of the sofa with the package on the middle cushion. Amaya seats herself next to the package. Together, they fish through newspaper and Bubble Wrap until they unveil the black lacquered box in which Ernie had saved papers and remembrances of Amaya.

"Oh, my. I thought this had been lost forever," says Sarah Jane.

Amaya reads a one-page enclosure on top of the lacquered box:

Dear Ms. Elgar, herewith is returned the enclosed box of personal possessions of Mr. Ernie Elgar, which had been unlawfully stolen from your home by alleged suspect Iranian who illegally entered the goods into Japan. Please excuse inconvenience for taking so long to recover this property. Thank you for trusting Tokyo Metropolitan Police. It is signed by Mr. Tanaka and Ms. Hiradi.

Sarah Jane carefully opens the box and notes the contents,

255

the first being the letter to June and her, handwritten by Ernie two weeks before he had died. She had read the letter hastily when it was first discovered, but now intends to reread it with greater understanding and care. Amaya sits quietly.

Sarah Jane says, "I'll put this box back in the upstairs office. You're free to look through it whenever you want, Amaya."

Amaya bows her head and expresses her thanks. After a pause, Sarah Jane says,

"So much has happened since we found this box that it seems like years ago. Now I look on it with nostalgia, even though it's been less than three months."

"I am sure that I shall feel nostalgia when I look at the letters that I wrote to Father so many years ago," says Amaya.

"Yes, no doubt. Perhaps it'll make you homesick."

"Sarah Jane, I have to tell you that I am already homesick. This box can only intensify my feelings."

"Really? I hope you've felt welcome in our home. Personally, I'm delighted to be getting to know you."

"Oh, do not take my comment as ungrateful. In fact, I have felt overwhelmed with your attentions. I love this magnificent home and the farm, as you call it. And also the art and music and restaurants you have introduced to me. It is almost like taking too rich a meal after years of simple Japanese food.

"Still, I am homesick for my modest life in Tokyo, and whatever business my stores might have had. I will soon return to that life, Sister."

Sarah Jane stands and pats Amaya's shoulder as she transfers the lacquered box to a hunt board at the foot of the stairs. On her return, she says,

"You're welcome to stay, and will be missed if you leave. But have you spoken to Brad about going away?"

"No, I have not."

"He won't be happy about this, Amaya."

"I am not leaving his life, or yours. That's not it."

"You have to make him understand that, Amaya. Your future together isn't really my business, but I don't want him hurt."

"I could neither hurt nor permanently leave Brad Oaks. He has been the shining knight of childhood dreams. I am sure he will understand, though."

"Amaya, don't be so sure about that. Men are possessive and impulsive. He more than most. He has had little experience with a serious relationship, and that ended tragically. I'd even say it deeply affected his ability to deal with any relationship with a woman after that. But he's taken to you. His sincerity shows. Just be careful—that's all I ask."

"What should I do? What should I say?"

"I won't try to coach you on this. None of us is young and naïve anymore. Give thought to how and when you say this to him."

"I have no experience in such conversations either, Sarah Jane. Perhaps I will make a mistake. I will think about it, though."

"He's coming here tomorrow and stays through the weekend. He wants to take you out in the canoe at some point. You might also consider a Dramamine an hour before." Sarah Jane smiles brightly at her own joke.

"I shall consider everything you have said, older Sister," says Amaya, unsmiling, with furrowed brow.

CHAPTER TWENTY

Sunday, December 8, 2019; San Francisco Bay, near Black Point

A bittern, its breast streaked with rufous-brown and creamy-white feathers, lifts from the mud bank's short stubble, the same color as the bird, and beats its pointed wings in a slow swim through damp air to a better fishing spot upwind from the green aluminum canoe, which had flushed it. Windblown ripples of the backwaters of San Francisco Bay make metallic slaps against the bottom of the drifting canoe's hull. Brad, kneeling on the bottom in front of the rear seat, knees braced in the curves that shape its sides, brings up his binoculars to watch the bittern float to its landing and walk into the camouflaging oblivion. Amaya turns slightly toward him from her front seat and says,

"I think I'd like to go back, Brad."

"Sure. It'll be half past ten by the time we get back to the farm. There's some chop coming up, and it's a good time to turn around before the breeze freshens."

"I didn't mean that. I love it here more than words can say. If it is time to turn around, then you must do as you think best."

Brad back-paddles on the shore side of the stern, then, as the canoe rotates, front-paddles on the outboard side, bringing the canoe completely about. He applies strong, slow J-strokes, and the canoe picks up momentum along the shore they just passed.

"Then what did you mean?"

"I want to go back to Tokyo."

Brad pauses his strokes. The canoe drifts to a stop. Amaya does not move. He dips his paddle into the water again, and the canoe moves forward.

"I'm not unhappy, Brad. I am very happy. I have never seen shorebirds the way you have shown me. I love San Francisco and Napa and the people of Elgar farm. But . . ." Her voice trails off.

Dip. Stroke. Handle-twist so the blade turns nearly vertical as a rudder, for guidance. Glide. Lift. Dip. Stroke.

"My sister has been welcoming and loving. She has introduced me to gallery owners and artists, and my days have been blissful here."

Dip. Stroke.

"The San Francisco Bay and hills and bridges have magical beauty."

Twist. Glide.

"I have never seen such expanse of land as the Elgar vineyards."

Lift. Dip.

"The autumn colors of the grapevines are like the finest woven kimonos."

Dip. Stroke.

She twists around again, as far around as her bright orange flotation vest will allow, to look at his face. She sees blue eyes intent on a faded pickup truck with a canoe rack ahead of them. She waits for him to speak.

Twist. Glide. Lift.

"I love you, Brad."

Dip.

"I cannot bear to think of being alone again."

Stroke. Brad's rhythm picks up; the canoe moves slightly faster.

"The Wishbone will keep you from me."

Stroke. Dip-stroke. Dip-stroke. The bow of the canoe lifts slightly, and water slaps underneath it.

"Please slow down a little, Brad. Talk to me."

Glide.

"You know that Wishbone will crowd everything out," she says.

"Not you. Not the flower of you in my mind from the seed you planted."

"No. But the time, Brad. It will crowd out the time. I do not make wine. I do not make steel pipes. I collect and sell art from my culture. In another city."

"You're leaving my life?"

Stab-dip. Stroke.

"Do not use words to hurt me."

Dip-stroke.

"You hurt me by leaving."

Glide. The canoe rocks, rises, settles, and rocks again.

"We are mature adults, Brad. It is time for me to go."

"And then what? Wait for me to fly to Tokyo on business? Like an Ernie Elgar?"

"You know I will wait."

"So we just drift like this canoe, waiting for my work to bring us together?"

"Brad, if I do not go to my work, what happens to me here when you are away on yours?"

"That's modern life, Amaya."

Drift.

"My life is modern. I have made my life against obstacles . . ."

"I know . . ."

". . . which have made purpose in my life, like the purpose that you have. That Sarah Jane and June and everyone else here have."

Sweep-stroke back, turning the bow again toward shore. J-stroke.

"Will you never come here again?"

Dip. Stroke.

"A time may come."

Glide. Twist. Lift.

"God, Amaya, that sounds like a Zen mantra. Be modern now, when something modern is called for. Say it simply and plainly."

"I will say what you said to me one time. 'Until I return.'"

Brad and Amaya take off their soggy shoes at the front door after stowing the canoe and life jackets in the barn.

"Ahoy the mariners! How 'bout a drink?" says Sarah Jane as she opens the door. What she sees are two glum faces. She steps back and suppresses the urge to ask what is wrong. She has eyes. She doesn't need to ask. Amaya blushes, nods her head in a slight bow, and walks on dampish feet to the stairway and up to her room.

Brad watches her ascend the stairs, turns to Sarah Jane, and says,

"A beer would be good."

His eyes meet Sarah Jane's under frowning brows, and he says simply, "Don't ask. She's going to Tokyo. It's not good. But it's not as bad as it could be. It's a mess." Sarah Jane says, "You should pass on that beer and have a word with her."

Brad goes upstairs, peels off his canoeing khakis and jersey, and takes a long shower and shave. Amaya waits for him to finish and then helps towel him off. She has changed into the Mexican top Sarah Jane gave her, light-brown cotton with sunshine-colored bands on a diagonal, white cotton slacks, and new huaraches. "I did not mean to make you unhappy, Brad."

"Well, I am. But at least you were honest. It's better than being unhappy and not knowing why. When do you want to go to the airport?"

"Not today, Brad. I cannot stand to walk out before spending tonight with you. A flight tomorrow, I think. But you see now, don't you? Your business life changes like spring lightning. I see it now up close. I am not as pliable as you suspect I am."

"Stop talking in the negative, please. I said I understand, and I do. I don't like it a bit. But please don't speak long judgments about barriers between us. I always knew you had to return to Tokyo; I just didn't know when. You didn't walk away from your life to have a turkey dinner in Napa with me. I only worry about what it means for the long term."

"We will always have time together, Brad."

"Amaya, you and I talked alone after your ordeal. We were in your suite. I had just poured out my heart to you about our chance to be together, made miraculous by all the external assaults on it. We agreed on one simple truth—that the most important thing is to be together for the long term, not just times together on the fly."

"I know, Brad, but we also said that there is another big consideration: where. Even if it is less important, this consideration is very much in front of us and cannot be avoided."

Brad stands and holds his arms in front of him, palms up. He says, "What's wrong with where we are? Why can't we establish base—a home—here in the Bay Area? You can go back and forth to Tokyo anytime you want."

"But Brad, I cannot be uprooted so quickly. Let me return to my homeland and prepare myself for the rest of our lives. And you should not dismiss making Japan a possibility for us."

"Amaya!" His voice rises. "I'm a forty-five-year-old man licensed to practice law in America. I can't just walk away from that to start a new life in Japan," says Brad, with an incredulous wave of his hand.

Amaya stands a little straighter and says firmly, "Brad, my love, I am a forty-five-year-old woman who has experienced life-shaking events in just ninety days. I am still adjusting to those events. Father dies, leaving me an enormous inheritance. You suddenly come into my life, and then I promise to return my inheritance if your business dreams do actually come true. I fall in love with you. I know my love is reciprocated. I venture into opening a second store. I am abducted and drugged, and think I lose everything in my life. You rescue me and restore what I think I lost. Now you bring me to your life in California, America. I am showered with gifts, with new stimulations, with meeting my American sister and seeing her fiefdom in the Napa Valley. I eat cranberry and turkey and potatoes with an ambassador as you talk about pipelines thousands of miles long. I attend music and art events in San Francisco."

Amaya steps to the suitcase resting on the antique blanket chest at the foot of her bed, closes the open top, and zips it furiously. Her voice rises slightly as she says,

"I am being acted upon in so many directions by so many

new people in my life. I am accustomed to solitude and my own resourcefulness. My head spins. I am overwhelmed. I have to assimilate at my own pace, Brad, or not at all."

The suitcase zipped closed, Amaya takes a deep breath. She wills her heartbeat to slow. She is in love but making war. She turns to Brad and says,

"Promise me to consider the other aspects of my life, Brad. I said I was going home tomorrow. I've changed my mind. I believe that another day and evening here would be consumed with debate and ill will. I do not want that between us. The most practical solution is for me to return today. That allows me to arrive late Sunday and attend to my two stores on Monday."

Brad takes a swift step closer, but Amaya holds him away with her hand on his chest. She lowers her voice to say,

"We are not breaking up, just breaking a stalemate."

She looks at him with wide eyes that search his. She pleads,

"Please come to Tokyo just as soon as possible. Maybe even straight from Moscow. My head is swirling. I can't say anything more about this now."

Brad moves to the door. After a beat, he turns and says, "We can't run away from stalemates all the time, Amaya. However, I won't try to stop you from going home today if you're set on that. Sure, I'll be returning to Tokyo pretty soon, and again and again pretty soon after that, for as long as I can foresee. But we can't keep pushing off this decision.

"I'll get on the phone and try to change your reservation. If you've packed, I'll take you to the airport. I hate airport goodbyes, Amaya."

"It won't be goodbye, Brad."

"I wonder. But I won't debate it any longer."

An hour later, Sarah Jane goes upstairs and taps on Amaya's

door. She enters quietly when Amaya invites her. Amaya stands quickly and dabs her eyes. She says softly,

"Honored Sister, please do not think less of me for needing to return, I . . ."

Sarah shakes her head and smiles. "You have much to do and even more to think about. Brad's bringing his car around. But before you leave, I have to tell you something, privately, to add to the things for you to think about."

Amaya lifts her eyebrows and asks, "Privately means what?"

"I mean that I would ask you not to tell Brad what I'm about to tell you. I'm jumping the gun just talking to you about this, but in view of your sudden decision to return to Japan, I feel I must."

Amaya's gaze drifts away and down. She bows her head and says, "As you wish, honored Sister."

Sarah Jane says, "Amaya, Elgar Steel is about to bid on the largest, most significant project in the company's history."

Amaya nods and says, "Wishbone, yes. I wish you great success—"

Sarah Jane holds up her index finger and shakes her head. She says,

"Thank you, but let me finish. I want you to consider exactly how that success will affect Brad. And how that will affect the decision you're occupied with. When you assume that Elgar Steel will succeed in gaining Wishbone contracts, you must also understand that the actual manufacture of the pipes will change things for everyone employed there. New responsibilities are inevitable, and in Brad's case, that may mean an abrupt change in his ability to make travels in the same way as before."

Amaya steps back and frowns. "Please explain."

Sarah Jane says, "Amaya, I can't explain because an

265

explanation would require well thought-out details. I simply don't have such details. Those will occupy my thoughts for the next month or so. But I have to tell you as a sister and a friend who knows that you're weighing options. Keep in mind that some changes may follow that upset some of your planning."

Amaya looks away, her hand on her suitcase. "But how can I not tell Brad what you've said?"

"Because I've asked you not to. It's way too soon to raise uncertainties of that nature. I implore you to honor your commitment to me and not speak of it to him until the changes materialize, and he reveals them to you himself."

Amaya thinks, *Is she trying to prevent me from leaving? By putting pressure on me, to make me uncertain of Brad's return to Tokyo? No. That is not her character. If Brad cannot come to me, then I shall come to him. I shall decide when and where to travel. That is better than her deciding whether or when Brad travels. She is not my boss. I shall decide it.*

She calls on her reserves of stoic tranquility. She straightens herself and turns slightly to face Sarah Jane, her knees locked, her face impassive, and her eyes lowered. She bows to Sarah Jane and holds the bow for five slow beats. When she stands straight again, she says firmly,

"It shall be as you have requested. You may count on my word. I shall only ever speak of it with Brad if and when he speaks of it to me."

Monday, December 23, 2019; Elgar Steel Plant, Stockton, California

Brad hesitates in front of Sarah Jane's closed office door, his jaw tight. It's unusual that she has called a meeting in this way, an e-mail written before dawn, setting 8:15 a.m. as the time for him to come to her office. Something about that simple departure from her normal casual approach between them has set him on edge. He exhales, and taps on the wooden door frame.

"Come." Even that one muffled word vibrates with a certain tension on her part. At least he hears it that way. He opens the door.

"Had your coffee, Brad?" she asks from behind her desk, previously Ernie's desk. On it stand framed, faded photos of the twins in their twenties with Ernie and Deidre, taken on the patio of the farm. This morning, she is in a starched-collared white top and muted-gray pantsuit. Half-rim reading glasses attached to the loops of a narrow black band perch on her nose.

Mounted on the wall behind her is the first steel sculpture she ever made on the floor of the Elgar shop, a stainless steel abstraction of a great blue heron gliding for a landing on marsh grass. She does not automatically pour him a cup of coffee as she usually does, nor does she look up from the morning report from security (no injuries that night).

"Yeah, thanks, no more for me, Sarah," Brad says, throat still tight. He stands rather than simply drop into a chair, as is his custom.

"OK, then. Come take a seat. This'll be an easy meeting, Brad." With that said, she looks in his eyes and smiles a stiff smile. "Have you recovered from Moscow?"

Brad chuckles, nods, and says, "Yeah, I'm fit as a fiddle again. It kind of took a toll, I must say."

Brad is more than a little puzzled. He and Sarah Jane have already discussed the trip a number of times since his return, including the effects of Russian hospitality, the harsh winter, and the sleepless flights there and back.

"You know, Brad, these international trips are not only hard on *your* system. We're beginning to feel a pinch around here with you away so much." Sarah Jane is not smiling. Brad feels uncomfortable and says nothing. After a beat, she stands and walks to the window overlooking the Stockton ship channel. Without looking at him, she says to the window glass,

"2020 is only a week away. We get our first shipment of Shin steel toward the end of March. Everyone is going to be busier in this place than at any other time in corporate history. Ernie isn't here. I'm going to need all hands on deck when Wishbone production gets under way. There's a board meeting coming up in a month. I want to make some management changes."

She stops, and says nothing for a quarter minute. Then, "Wishbone is a game changer. When things change that much, for the better or for the worse, there's usually a change at the top."

Brad is now sitting straight in his chair, leaning forward, his ears feeling a heat he can't explain. Since she has not asked him a question, he decides to remain quiet.

She turns from the window, folds her arms in front of her, and says, "Brad, we don't have much time to do the succession planning we've both put off for too long. Well, it starts today. I'm going to ask the board to give you my old job. Actually, the title will be executive vice president and chief operating officer."

"Sarah Jane, what about Eddie Sandoval?" Brad blurts out.

"He's a great chief engineer, and you'll promote him to works manager. He'll help you do your job the way he's helped me, and Daddy before me. That's exactly what he's ready for now." Sarah Jane crosses from the window to the corner of the desk, where she half sits on the corner nearest Brad. She continues,

"And Brad, you're going to find a chief counsel to build the legal team we need when production gets hot and heavy. I assume you'll be able to on-board that person before April?"

Brad stares at her. This has hit him out of a clear blue sky. But he has given some thought to it on his own. He says, "That cup of coffee sounds pretty good to me right now, if you don't mind."

Sarah Jane does not budge. Instead, she gestures to the gleaming thermos and tea service on her credenza. Brad closes his eyes briefly, then rises to fill a coffee cup. When he returns to his seat in front of her, he has thought of his reply, and thought of other consequences. He says,

"April will be plenty of time for me to take care of that. Hell, around these parts, Sacramento and the Bay Area, you can open any door, and three lawyers will fall out."

Sarah Jane throws back her head and gives a spontaneous laugh that relieves the tension in her neck and upper back. "You're a tough act to follow, Brad Oaks. Can't just be anyone."

Brad notices her relax but does not permit himself to laugh. He says,

"I'll have three suggestions on your desk by the middle of January. I get unsolicited resumes nearly every day. I know the folks around here with some experience, and I won't disappoint you."

Sarah Jane stands and returns to her post at the window. She says, "Brad, that's not all. Your job is at the plant now. Full time, all the time. I also have to have someone who can take over what you do in Washington and in Tokyo."

Brad had not been anticipating this. He blinks, and feels

heat rise along his neck. He says, "You're grounding me?"

She turns and says levelly, "Brad, I'm promoting you if you hadn't noticed. Is there a problem with that?"

"No problem at all. I'm honored and grateful. I never thought I'd have such an opportunity. I should have said so right off the bat."

Sarah nods gravely. Her eyebrows lift slightly. In a calmer voice, she says,

"I know why you didn't. It's perfectly understandable. But this is what the business needs, and what your career needs, and those things don't always coincide like this." Sarah Jane moves from the edge of her desk and walks behind Brad's chair. She reaches one hand to touch his shoulder, and then withdraws it as he turns to face her.

Brad says, "Sarah Jane, I think we should start sending Eddie Sandoval to Japan to liaise with Shin Steel and Sunshine Trading. He did an excellent job in Tokyo last fall on the business, social, and diplomatic fronts, as well as his customary good engineering work."

Sarah Jane breaks into a broad smile and does a pirouette with outstretched hands. She says,

"Thank you, Bradford Alan Oaks. That's exactly what I had in mind. But I can't tell you how much I appreciate your own insight and judgment to come up with the same solution."

Brad stands, nods, and says with a smile, "OK, boss. Anything else?"

She looks at him a moment. "There sure is, but it's personal. Look, Brad, I know what's foremost in your mind, and it's your Amaya. We need to talk about that, too. You're in a difficult spot just grappling with what your future with her will be. I know that. But there's something else entirely coming at us like a freight train."

Brad walks to the window this time, and speaks to the western horizon. "Buying back the stock. I know. The deal is that if Wishbone goes through, we can buy her third at a fair price. Wishbone's now a reality. I've been thinking about that."

"No, Brad, you can't think about that. Not from Elgar's point of view or mine or June's. You're conflicted. Yes, we have a negotiation ahead of us, but you can't be any part of it. That's off-limits from our standpoint, and I sure won't tolerate you negotiating for her."

He turns and chuckles. He puts up one hand as a Stop sign, and says, "Don't get the wrong idea here. I'm not talking about the buyback negotiation. I'm talking about after we—you—get her stock back."

"What do you mean?"

"How much time do you have, Sarah? I don't want to be rushed when I get into that."

Sarah reseats herself behind her desk, folds her fingers together in front of her, and says, "Take all the time you need. It's almost Christmas Eve, and I want to be able to ponder your great thoughts at the farm. By the way, are you coming to dinner?"

"Of course, Sarah, if I'm still invited."

"Are you accepting the promotion?"

"Absolutely. I have no hesitation about that. As you just said, I have some serious work to do in my private life because of it."

"Then come over tomorrow in the afternoon, and stay through the twenty-sixth. Boxing Day, as June calls it."

"Will she be there?"

"As near as I can tell, she will. With her, you never know till

271

she actually walks in. So, go on about the stock."

Brad brings his chair closer to the end of the desk so she can turn slightly to talk to him without such a barrier between them. He says,

"Sarah, one of the things I thought about on the flight home from Moscow, since I wasn't sleeping, is opening up some of the Elgar stock to the employees."

"Whoa," says Sarah Jane.

Brad holds up one hand again and says, "Just hear me out. I'm thinking about an employee stock ownership plan in some form or another. Maybe it's not as large as a third. Maybe it's a new, nonvoting class of stock. But it gives our people some equity in the rebirth of Elgar Steel. We'd have to figure out how broad to make it, but I'm thinking that it's based on years of service, not necessarily job title. Maybe some of it could be used as a continuity bonus to hold onto really key personnel, like Sandoval, but mostly, it's a way of getting the people who make our products a little more money out of the growth and earnings of the company."

Sarah Jane says, "I'm blown away. Now you're thinking like a real executive. Thinking in a way that I should have thought. And you sure have my attention. This way, if we ever do merge with Shin Steel, our workforce will have a stake in that as well. By the time that happens, I'm hoping you'll be in this office. But that's getting way ahead of myself."

Brad stands and says, "That's as far as I've gotten. But if you like it, and I get the idea you do, I'll get the wheels turning to come up with an outline of the plan for the board to consider next month." He puts his half-empty coffee cup and saucer on the tray on the credenza, turns, and takes three steps toward the door.

"That's it? You're walking out of the meeting?" Sarah's eyes twinkle as she needles him.

"My brain has nearly run out of gas," says Brad, "and I still have a day's work ahead of me. We can kick it around at the farm. Hey, Sarah?"

"Yes?"

"Thank you for the promotion. Thanks for getting me out of the weeds on the legal side. You're right: this is the right thing for all of us at this time. Now, I have some real spadework to do with my Amaya."

Sarah Jane stands, walks around the corner of the desk to take his arm, and says as they stroll to the door, "Brad, she's a smart woman, and I think she's the real deal for you. I expect she'll make this move if you convince her you're right for her future."

"Sarah, I'll want to go over there after the holidays to talk—"

She interrupts, "Brad, that's not going to happen on Elgar time. I absolutely meant it when I said your 'place,' as you like to say, is right here at the plant from now on. If you can grab a couple of personal days sometime, maybe something like that would work. But in terms of Elgar doing business with Shin and Sunshine, that's going to be me as lead and Sandoval as second chair, effective January first."

Brad stops in his tracks. He looks at her for a trace of malice, but sees none. "That makes it real tough, Sarah."

"Well, Brad, good steel pipe is tough, and that's our specialty. I can see how one short trip for the two of us together to introduce the changes and have a brief transition would work, but I emphasize that it would be real brief from your standpoint. It's probably not more than two days and a reception or something along those lines for you. You've got a job to do here that will absolutely not tolerate a longish trip overseas. The more you get into my old job, the more you get stuck at the plant or going to the customers."

"Ernie would be proud of you, Sarah. You kick butt when you have to. I'm to be your new executive vice president and chief operating officer, Sarah, and that's effective when? January first, right? Well, I've got a week of personal time coming to me before then, and I know where I have to be. This will be my last trip to Japan for the foreseeable future, and I have to make the most of it. For me and me alone. No introductions, no receptions, no transition, no steel, and no expense account."

Sarah Jane turns to him with a worried look, and says, "But you will come back?"

Brad says calmly, "The offices are closed on the first. I'll be at my new desk the start of business on the second. Let me have a rain check on Christmas, Sarah."

"Sure, Brad, you got it. I hope you get what you're looking for."

Amaya Mori is just closing her Ginza shop when she hears her desk computer chime. She replaces the satsuma matte-black flower vase she is dusting back in its glass-fronted case, locks the door of the case, and walks to her desk. She opens her e-mail and sees at the top of the day's long list an e-mail from Brad. Her chime has been set to sound only with the arrival of one of those. She reads:

Last minute again, I'm afraid. Look, if you don't have other Christmas plans, what do you say to a week in Kyoto? We could take long walks along the Kama River and in the Imperial Palace gardens. The hotels are pretty booked, but I'm working on it. I'm leaving today and arrive at the KIX Osaka airport around 4 p.m. on the 24th. I can be in Kyoto forty-five minutes later. Any chance at all? This is important, Amaya. Xoxo Your Flower.

Her eyes light up as she lets out a pent-up breath. "*Bakka-san* gaijin," she mutters: crazy foreign man. Then she picks up her phone immediately and calls the executive assistant of the chairman of Sunrise Trading. When she comes on the line, Amaya puts a smile in her voice and pleads for compassionate understanding of a last-minute request to use the Sunrise Trading *ryokan*, a private residence in Kyoto for use as an inn exclusively by Sunrise executives, located just north of the ancient palace grounds. In it, there will be a balcony leading through a private garden to the path along the slow-flowing Kama River, a private Japanese hot bath, and specially prepared meals served in their personal suite of tatami-matted rooms. She listens patiently to her friend's explanation that such a thing would be "very difficult" on such short notice during the Christmas holidays. The Japanese phrase "very difficult" is most accurately translated into English as "impossible."

Amaya then explains in very frank terms exactly why she has made such an urgent request. The voice on the other end of the call softens as she switches from panic to conspiratorial mode. Of course, the *ryokan* has been reserved for weeks in advance. But it is for the chief of the overseas steel section, the man who is handling the Wishbone account. Protocol in Sunrise Trading's use of such things as the *ryokan,* or cars, or the jet, always takes into account business priorities and rank, and since Amaya is a director of Sunrise, and the guest is, well, who the guest is, what was at first very difficult becomes a confirmed booking, with exchanges of Christmas felicitations, and a blunt demand that Amaya end the week with a ring on her finger.

Amaya hangs up the phone and types a reply to Brad's e-mail:

Of course I will cancel my long-standing holiday plans in order to spend Christmas with you, and of course Kyoto will be perfect. Do not trouble yourself further searching for hotel accommodations; I have located a chilly garret for our stay. The four-story flight of stairs will invigorate us every day. Give me your travel details. I will meet your flight with car and driver. While you are here, you should see my shrink!

CHAPTER TWENTY-ONE

Tuesday, December 24, 2019; Osaka, Japan,
Kansai International Airport

Brad emerges from the baggage claim and customs clearance area of the KIX terminal to face a crowd of expectant relatives of incoming travelers, jumping up and down for a better view, and silent drivers holding handwritten signs for prearranged fares. To his left is an incessant sound of sleigh bells that catches his attention. He squints. He moves in that direction, carrying an overnight case and pulling a roller bag. Closer to the sound, he sees a large poster being pumped up and down on a wooden handle, with the annoying sleigh bells attached to the perimeter of the poster and dangling a few inches on each side. The poster is in English. He squints again and reads:

"Jingle Brad

Jingle Brad

Jingle over here!"

Oh no, he thinks. *That Girl!*

Just then, he hears a high-pitched shriek, and That Girl comes into view behind the poster, which now rotates as that girl hops in tight circles, laughing. She is in black ski pants and a red-and-white woolen sweater. Atop her bobbing head is a bobbing Santa Claus floppy cap edged in white cotton, with another annoying bell at the tip of the cap. She is a picture of glee, folly, and conspicuous rebellion against her usual sophistication.

Suddenly, Brad is engulfed in an embrace, with sleigh bells jangling overhead and giggles poured out on his cheek. When the giggles subside, she seductively mutters something truly unsophisticated in his ear.

More giggles. Even more stares from strangers caught up in the spectacle. Before he can utter a word, or even a kiss, she takes his small bag in her hand and thrusts the poster handle into his, pulling him and the bells and the bags toward the exit. There is nothing else for Brad to do but pump the poster handle up and down and follow That Girl to a waiting Sunrise Trading car.

Tuesday, December 24, 2019; Napa, Elgar estate

Sarah Jane reads the caller ID, "evil twin," on the kitchen cordless. She allows it to ring three more times as she pours mineral water into two ice-filled tumblers, then punches the "on" button. She brings a smile to her voice,

"Come in, Canada."

June's voice is remarkably clear and relaxed as she says,

"Sarah, the Wiggy is no more."

"Say not so, June. Are you ill?"

"You might think so; in the head. I know how you think. But no, my machinery and programming are functioning. But I had to release the wig maker."

"Your former intern? The Muscle with Cosmic Smile? That's harsh, June. What did he do to deserve that?"

Sarah sinks into a living-room chair, the phone in one hand

and the water glass in the other.

June says, "S. J., I'm rethinking my purpose. The ACEA purpose."

"And what does he think?"

"Nothing. You put your finger on it, S. J. He doesn't think. Never has."

Sarah smiles into her reflection on the glass top of the coffee table, sips slowly, and says,

"June, that can't be a surprise to you, right? That was never in the, um, job description."

Marooned in luxury, June stands and walks to the full-length window of her condominium, and stares into the setting sun on Lake Ontario's western horizon. She says,

"I may be deserving of some cynicism, but please give me a light dose of it so that we can talk seriously."

Sarah Jane stands and says earnestly,

"June, how's this for a plan? I'm up for some serious talk myself. Flight loads should be light tomorrow, the actual Christmas Day, so why don't you come to the farm and plan to stay the week, or as long as you'd like? We can make evening mass together and settle in for a long-overdue heart-to-heart."

June catches her breath in a thrill of pleasure, calms herself instantly, and says,

"Where are your menfolk, S. J.?"

"Alden's in Orange County with kin. Brad's in Kyoto with our half kin. You're welcome to come home, June."

"Thanks, S. J. I'll get on it."

June arrives at the farm in a car rented at the San Francisco airport, too late for evening mass. Before very long, she and Sarah Jane have rationalized passing up the next and the next on Christmas Day. Now wearing Hollywood golden-era slacks and blouses from their mother's wardrobe, the twins are in deep conversation in the living room, decorated mostly in wineglasses, mineral water stations, and fond childhood ornaments they have just placed on a fragrant Scotch pine, which Sarah had ransomed from the Boy Scout lot the day before.

They have drawn two armchairs closer together, facing embers and spiffs of flame in the fireplace. Sarah is quiet as she has been throughout the evening, except when needed to get supper on the table and make encouraging sounds responsive to June's complaints over her current dilemma of career and conscience.

The ACEA mission to defeat pipelines seems to have run its course in June's secret heart. The internal wave of this riptide is amplified by the realization that her fling with the young Canadian had also run its course, and that the gentleman really didn't have any deeper appeal than had been exhausted. With a warmth Sarah had not witnessed for years, June has suggested that she feels the urge to return to Northern California, where her roots run as deep as the old vines of the estate.

"I mean, I should be at your side, S. J., in the steel plant as your vice president. It's the natural plan of succession. I hear Daddy's voice telling me this."

Sarah Jane blinks, reaches for a tumbler of mineral water, and suppresses the urge to throw something across the room. After a beat, she says, "Go on."

June's eyes sparkle as she spreads her arms in a cinematic shrug. "That's about as far as I've gone with it. It's so clear to me, S. J., and so right. So Elgar. So deeply *twin*."

Sarah Jane nods and, as if recalling a summer of fishing,

recounts her years in the steel mill before Ernie had made her vice president. In those years, he had never made reference to bloodline or family. There were family discussions, there were vineyard and farming discussions, and then, during the week, there were periodic meetings on production, safety, and bids. There were never steel-business-and-family-succession discussions. She says,

"June, that all started when you and I were twenty-eight. I didn't have a business meeting with Daddy at the steel mill until I was thirty-three, and then I was on the hot seat, reporting on why the spiral-weld mill was off-line again. I wasn't alone with Daddy in that meeting. I was, let's say, under observation by a big crowd.

"June, do you want to start out again? In an hourly job on the floor of the mill you've never even walked through? Do you want to learn what each mill does? What every worker does? The safety and union rules everywhere? What the electrician union workers do, the iron workers, the carpenters? The other crafts? We don't have superfluous vice-president titles or jobs. This would be like exile for you, and you may never make supervisor, never mind vice president, and never mind executive vice president. Sweet June, this is a nonstarter."

June is quiet as she clears wineglasses and tumblers and puts them in the dishwasher. She returns with plates of cheese and slices of baguette.

"Sarah, you're right. I'm not going to spend the rest of my life learning steel mill operations from the bottom up. If that's how you intend to run the company, what are you going to do about your old job as vice president?"

"I intend to fill it, June."

The room is quiet for a long time, after which June says,

"Have someone in mind?"

"Yes, I do."

Again the room is quiet. June says,

"S. J., I understand about business-confidential information, but I'm an owner, and I'm your sister."

Sarah sips mineral water and places the tumbler carefully on a coaster. She says,

"OK, June, it's going to be announced on January second, and will go to the board a few days after that. Brad Oaks will be Elgar Steel's next executive vice president."

June stands and walks to the kitchen patio French doors. The patio is strung with red-and-green lights. Her first reaction is to explain to Sarah Jane all the reasons that a lawyer, and particularly this one, would be the worst possible choice for that position. Wheels turn in her head, though, and she packs away all thoughts of trying to talk her sister out of this decision. Here is opportunity, not something to argue against. When she turns and returns to her armchair, she asks,

"Then who will be our Washington vice president? That's the sort of thing I'm a master of. You want experience in the job; I've had experience in spades. You wouldn't have your water pipeline without me, or at least any Canadian water to put in it. I'm tailor-made for this job. I can hit the ground running in Washington, and have even more clout in Ottawa and provincial capitals." June beams at her sister like one Napa High cheerleader to another. Again.

Sarah Jane stares at June as she gathers her thoughts. She says,

"My one and only sister, twin, Elgar family survivor, what I have to say to you about that is not unloving. Just keep that foremost in your mind. Whoever is in Washington representing

Elgar is there out of my total trust and confidence. That's why Brad was there and why he did such a good job. That, and he was always grounded, and never lost sight of the Elgar Steel home office, even when he had a brilliant idea and was perfectly capable of just running with it in Washington, or Tokyo for that matter.

"On the other hand, you've spent the last too-many years opposing the very project that will contribute to the recovery of Elgar Steel from the doldrums. You've been poisoning the well in Canada and the United States against our principal product, pipes for oil and gas transportation. You not only lack knowledge about our operations, our products, our people, and our work ethic, you've been in opposition to the company on the public stage.

"I now have to remind you that when Daddy died, and we were in an uproar over a stranger in our lives who owned a third of the business, as a bequest of our father, you chose to run around my end and attempt to deal directly with her. And then lied to me about what you were doing. Brad was right. He called it devious. Then he called it sabotage. Either will do. But June, you will not do for my Washington, D.C., advocate. Not even close. Again, you're a great sister, but you're poison to my steel mill."

"*Our* steel mill."

"Wrong. The Elgar name is our name. The Elgar farm is our property. The Elgar wine is our wine. The profits of the Elgar steel business produce our dividends. But the steel mill, its surging business plans and its high-quality products, those are not ours. Those belong to my other family, the Elgar workforce, and you aren't one of them."

June blinks. Her chin is shaky. She looks away from Sarah

Jane. "You disown me, Sarah?"

"I hope your question doesn't mean you didn't hear what I said, especially about you personally. But I'll say it again slowly if you want me to, and sound out the big words. We have all night, and I have nothing better to do than to make this abundantly clear to you."

"Sarah, I'm running out of options here. I suppose you'll tell me next you don't want me in the wine business—that you think I'll turn it into vinegar."

Sarah stands and smiles. She collects the empty water glasses and takes them to the kitchen sink. She opens an Elgar Pinot Noir, pours two glasses, and returns to the armchairs, handing one glass to June.

"Look, June, I'm sure you could do very well in a management job at the winery. I'll tell you what you need to do if you're interested. The first thing is to enroll at classes at UC Davis to study winemaking. Come to think of it, maybe a course at the Culinary Institute up the road would suffice, and add depth to our business from the standpoint of fine food and pairing. But you need preparation in the granular details of some aspect of the business. Actually, you need it in every aspect. It's been my observation that your environmental tirades lack technical foundation. You're good at the slogans, and skimming and skating over the hard parts. Maybe that's good enough for your donor base, but it's not good enough for running a wine business.

"Don't forget, we're farmers here, first and foremost. We're stewards of the fruit, the grapes, above all. The winemaking comes after that. Well over eighty percent of my involvement at the winery is with vines in the ground, or to be planted in new ground as we expand."

June is sullen. She looks at Sarah. "Look, I don't want to go back to school, especially under your direction. You'd be another Deidre. I'm about tapped out, S. J. I need to do something good. What do you think?"

Sarah thinks, then says in a gentle voice,

"Hey, June, look what you did in Canada just now. Not the environmental tirades, the environmental solution. Look at the water project. That breaks the ice. Daddy was always talking about getting Canadian mountain water down here to California. Why don't you get involved in something like that? It's a connection you would have with him. You could pick up from the last project without missing a beat."

"Sarah, would Elgar sponsor work like that? Hire me as a consultant?"

"June, this shouldn't be an Elgar Steel mission. That commercializes it from the get-go. If there are more water-export opportunities from Canada, we'll be there to bid on the pipe and other steel jobs. But you won't get far if you're like a sales rep for Elgar. Maybe you ought to get some educational grounding in that stuff. It's bound to help. But I wouldn't be any part of that. You'd have no Deidre, at least not out of me. You're good at fundraising. Sure, you could make a pitch to Elgar Steel, and we might throw in some modest contribution if it's a good pitch. But, this would be *yours* alone. Doesn't that sound better than working for me?"

"S. J., that's pretty good. I think I'll sleep on it."

Monday, December 30, 2019; Kyoto, Sunshine Trading ryokan

Mrs. Yosani, head of the household staff at the *ryokan* for thirteen years, has heard the quarrels and rows of her guests countless times before. She always listens, not out of salacious curiosity, of course, but rather to gauge the tone and depth of fury, and thus to prepare herself for impending disaster, much as does a farm animal at the onset of earthquakes. She measures this one very low on her Richter scale, but troubling nevertheless, since its theme has reverberated in the inn's customary tranquility for three straight nights. This one is not like those most familiar to her ears, with middle-aged married couples, after plentiful sake, in pitched martial battle over (usually in some combination): infidelity, indifference, lost ardor, too little money, alcoholism, late hours, long absences, too much money, office jealousies, discourtesies to the other's relatives, inheritance planning, or spending patterns. She has developed techniques of intervention, if necessary, for each category and combination.

With this pair, however, the issues are different. She has never before been confronted with the core contention of their dispute. It is not whether to marry but where; not how to live together but in what country. Shall it be a privileged life of comfort in the State of California near the San Francisco Bay, where it never snows, or in Japan as members of the elite in the modern aristocracy of the art and international business worlds? But a privileged life is always the unspoken premise. Since the subject of money never arises, she presumes that they presume that money is not and will never be in short supply. This couple never row over real or suspected indiscretions; to the contrary, they repeatedly declare intentions of lifetime fidelity. Most bewilderingly, neither of them takes sake during or after meals. Their exchanges are sober, articulate, and respectful.

At least up to now, an hour before midnight. Tonight, the

man has been raising his voice. Mrs. Yosani has decided upon the need to intervene, and now is ready to present what she hopes will be soothing and conciliatory lidded Imari bowls of clear miso broth of her own preparation. She kneels at the edge of the wood-and-parchment *soji* sliding door and, in a pause in the heated discussion, says brightly, *"Sumimasen"* ("Excuse me"). The voices fall quiet. She hears rustling of *yukata* and bedclothes, then a high, thin voice: *"Hai?"* ("Yes?")

Mrs. Yosani slides the *soji* open just enough to enter and place the tray holding the bowls of broth on a small table near the door. She says, in Japanese, to Amaya,

"Excuse me for intruding, but I just finished making tomorrow's miso and had exactly two bowls left over, so I thought I would bring them to you since you will be leaving tomorrow."

Amaya says, in Japanese,

"You are very kind. It must be that our voices carried and possibly alarmed you. I assure you that we are both well, and that we appreciate your thoughtfulness."

Mrs. Yosani waves her hand from side to side in front of her nose in denial of the implication and says,

"No, your voices have not carried and have caused no disturbance. I do not understand spoken English very well, so have no way of knowing what you have been talking about. You have been ideal guests. I shall leave you. May I say, however, if it is not presumptuous of me, I have a cousin who lives in Japantown of San Francisco and is very happy there, and feels right at home as though she never left Kobe."

Amaya stifles a giggle and puts the back of her hand over her mouth. After a moment, she says,

"I am glad for the information and hope that your cousin

287

remains happy in her new home."

Mrs. Yosani blushes, bows, and closes the *soji* behind her.

"What was that all about?" says Brad.

"She wants us to enjoy the hot broth in hopes we will stop arguing, or at least not at the top of your lungs," Amaya says with a smile.

Brad sips half the warm broth, replaces the lid on the bowl, and slumps back onto the futon bed. Shaking his head, he says, "Amaya, we absolutely must stop arguing and take the next step in our lives. I'm sorry I raised my voice, but not sorry for what I've been saying all along. Look, what would happen to me if I leave Elgar and move to Japan to be with you?"

Amaya puts the bowls back on the table and joins Brad, her hand on his chest. She says,

"There is much potential here with your special knowledge. Sunrise Trading sees a great future in pipeline projects now that they have the Wishbone to build upon. You could easily enter Sunrise at a high level and help build that future. There is no doubt that if you did, you would soon be on the board of directors, and help guide the entire new direction for our trading company."

"You sound like an executive recruiter," says Brad. "What about my life here? I'll always be a gaijin, a foreigner, and not completely accepted. You've told me many times that even you are not completely accepted because of the circumstances of your birth. That's something you should want to get away from, not pull me into. Besides, if you had a Japanese man as a husband, in an arranged marriage, let's say, or even if not, the husband's wishes would always prevail, and you wouldn't even have this discussion."

Amaya rests her cheek on his chest and nods her head

quietly. She says,

"I know. You are right. It's worse now. I didn't want to tell you. My doctors warned me. My abduction is a new stigma, it seems. Some—many—consider my experience to shame me, to soil me."

"God! Don't you see? You have to get away from here."

"Shhh. Do not let anger take you over, my man of reason and steel," she says. "It's all right. I do not allow myself to be influenced by people with such an attitude. I live in my small groups, Brad, in a vessel of repaired shards. The man and woman whose home I lived in before the earthquake took them from me, they were not my real parents but my mother's foster parents. Mr. Ernie Elgar was the last shard of my own blood. I am proud of my groups. Every person I am close to has spent time and effort to achieve something of value to herself and others. Some are teachers. Many are art dealers, some in London and New York. I have recognized fine people and attached to them.

"So it is with you, Brad. With Sunshine, you could surround yourself with the more enlightened of our businessmen, and you would be the best person there to open up global markets."

Brad fans his fingers through the length of her hair. He says,

"Amaya, you're describing a job that might or might not be there. If it is there, and it's as you describe, it has me getting on airplanes and marketing pipeline and other global business outside Japan. That's precisely what you hated about my old job at Elgar. I have a new job now. It's not a supposition. It's a reality.

"And part of the new reality is that I will stay put and do only a fraction of the business traveling required by my old job, and a smaller fraction of what Sunshine Trading might have me do."

Amaya says politely, "Your new job will be very difficult. Since our time together in Napa, I have thought a great deal about such responsibilities and what they will mean to you. Of course, less travel is to be expected with such responsibilities. You cannot make steel pipes in office buildings and hotels. So, I hope that you consider the possibility I have suggested, where you continue with the talented work that has brought you so far—the work of international negotiations. Sunrise could be such a place."

Brad stares at her, wondering, *How could she have known?* He keeps his thoughts to himself. He says simply,

"Amaya, you once said to me that you would feel more courtesies and acceptance if you were a visitor to Japan than you do living here. Well, you can become an actual visitor here. You could travel from San Francisco to Japan anytime you want."

Brad lifts himself to rest on one elbow. He grips her small, bare shoulder and says,

"But more importantly, I don't want to be recruited by another company. I'm invested in Elgar Steel more than I can describe. They're part of my foster world I told you of. The centuries-old culture of Japanese men is loyalty to clan and master. Well, I don't have a clan or master, but I do have loyalty to the Elgar family and their business. I have no desire to consider Elgar as simply a stepping stone to another, more flashy company. How could I leave them?"

Amaya is quiet. She sits up, takes his hand, and kisses it. "Brad, Sunrise is *my* foster world. My mother's childhood was devastated when she went to live with foster parents. All I have of her memory are her childhood impressions of when the bomb fell on Hiroshima, her fright, and her final separation from her very own mother. The Sunrise Trading company became a bedrock foundation for her, like a castle, with her foster parents as the lord and lady. I felt my world had collapsed when they were killed. But the Sunrise organization became my next foster world. They are my sanctuary. How could I leave them?"

Brad is silent and very sad. Amaya says,

"Let us sleep, Brad. The solution does not lie in argument. It lies in our hearts and will emerge when our hearts are ready."

"Amaya, how often does the Sunrise board meet?"

"There are three board meetings each year."

"So, three airplane trips. Which could be extended for whatever other meetings, or reunions, or art acquisition time you might need or want."

Amaya says nothing.

Brad says, "I've tried to address all the complications orbiting around the single truth that we both want to live our lives together. It seems to come down to a choice one of us has to make. If I leave Elgar behind for a life in Tokyo, I can't go back. I'm not indispensable to Elgar. Oh, I could jump on an airplane and return physically at any time. But I couldn't jump in and out of my career. You, on the other hand, would not have to abandon your art, or Tokyo associations, or involvement in Sunrise if we lived together in the San Francisco Bay Area. In fact, you might find that new experiences in America would enhance opportunities in your business and your contributions to the expanding business of Sunrise."

Her silence does not lift his sadness.

The next afternoon, at the departures terminal of Kansai International Airport, Amaya, in a gray pinstripe jumper over a mustard-colored, long-sleeved turtleneck top, keeps up a cheery banter about future visits she intends to make to California, and future returns she is sure that Brad will make, notwithstanding the restrictions Sarah Jane has attached to his new position.

When it is time for him to enter security and board, he says to her,

"Nothing is resolved."

"No, but it will be when it is time."

"I came to Kyoto this week to deliver an ultimatum," he confesses.

"I know. You are wise not to have done so."

"I'm not so sure. This was the time to resolve it, Amaya."

She straightens the lapel of his navy-blue blazer and kisses his lips. "Since we did not resolve it, now was actually not the time. You cannot impose a deadline on this the way you do in the building of steel things, my Man of Steel."

He tilts her chin with his right hand and kisses her. He says,

"Amaya, I need you in my life, my entire life, every day. I need you beside me in my world, in my job and my home. In my canoe. I need you beside me in the next job that they seem to be grooming me for. I'm better when you're with me all the time. When I most need your spirit and strength to get over a sudden rough patch, it's immediate. I can't go packing that in my travel bag to then bring out on some indefinite, future trip to be with you. I need you as a constant, not a variable."

He smiles. He says slowly,

"When you can come to my world gladly, two sisters of your blood are waiting for you. I'm waiting for you. And there's a ring waiting for you."

Amaya lets out a low moan. "Be in lighter spirit at this parting, Brad," she says with trembling chin.

"Have I said anything to you that's unloving?"

"No."

He says, "I've just said to you the kindest, most loving thing that I can possibly say, Amaya. I've said everything there is for me to say. I submit the case to you to judge. We've reached the threshold of our highest mortal happiness."

He turns and walks quickly into the security area without looking back.

Friday, January 3, 2020; Tokyo, the Law Offices of Wright and Haseo

Amaya looks across the desk of Parker Wright as he makes notes on a yellow legal pad. Behind him, she sees the spines of law books on the shelves of a wall-to-wall bookcase made of bleached cryptomeria, the simple, elegant Japanese cedar. The bookshelves surround a center space with no shelves, holding a hanging scroll. Her eyes linger on the nineteenth-century painting of a courtesan holding a mirror and wearing a gray silk robe with cinnabar-colored collar and sash. Delicate willow branches with tiny, sage-colored leaves droop above her head, her black hair loosened and spilling past each cheek to below her shoulders. Below the scroll rests a seventeenth-century white porcelain bowl with a scalloped edge. The bowl's exterior is decorated with persimmon-colored chrysanthemum blossoms and pale-blue diminutive clusters of leaves and vines.

Her shoulders release tension, and she sits back comfortably, watching Parker finish writing and look away at a middle distance out the window of his office, where tiny snowflakes swirl before melting in gray air. She smiles when she sees him blink and turn his attention back to her to say,

"It's not a legal question."

"No."

"I am outside my element."

"I didn't come here for legal advice."

"Then I can't bill you for this meeting," he says, with a mock pout.

Amaya thinks for a beat, then releases a burst of laughter. He laughs. She says,

"You see? That's exactly why I came to you. You are able to dispel the heaviness."

"The thing is, Amaya, I lack the expertise."

"Think less of what you lack and more of how you feel about what I have said. I seek inspiration more than advice."

Parker looks again at his yellow pad, where he has drawn a straight line down the center of the page, and a horizontal line across the upper part. "Pros" and "Cons" stand as headings above meticulous notes of her recitations over the past forty minutes. She catches his eye as he lifts that page and rolls it over the top of the tablet, seemingly to keep its minutiae from distracting him. He says finally,

"The first thing you said to me is that you love him."

"Of course I do."

"And you are convinced he loves you?"

"There is no doubt."

He tilts his chair back, fingers laced behind his head, and says,

"Do you believe you deserve happiness with him?"

She hesitates.

"That hesitation may be significant. I don't know enough to explore it with you, but do please keep it in mind for future reference and examination."

Caught off guard, she lowers her eyes and says, "That's interesting. I shall."

"For the record, I truly believe you do deserve it. It's vital that you do too. Now to your question. I take inspiration from Olivia."

Amaya smiles and looks back at Parker. "She is an exquisite person."

"She is that. You know, I have made offices in London, Dubai, Los Angeles, and now Tokyo. She has made our home in every city where work has taken me."

"So many places," she says vaguely.

"Yes. Always one home."

"She is a loving person."

"She is that. Amaya, the inspiration I take from her is commitment. She thrives in a life of hospitality, warmth, and adventure. Olivia is living her commitment to us. The center of our home is not me, not her, but us."

She turns her head to examine the transient snow.

"Amaya, Mr. Oaks did not hesitate to put himself in the hands of a man with murderous intent. I was as close to him then as I am to you right now. He did not waver. I would do the same if it were Olivia."

"I know his bravery," she answers tensely.

"I expect you do. I remind you of his commitment."

She waits a beat to regenerate a drop of poise. "Where does Olivia gain inspiration?"

"In general or in this particular area?"

"This, please."

"As it happens, I do know that. Somewhere along the line, in one of those moves, I asked her directly. What she said was, Ruth."

Amaya turns to face him, brows drawn together quizzically. She tilts her head slightly.

"No, there is no one named Ruth in her family or circle of friends. This is an ancient Ruth, the same of the eponymous eighth book of the Old Testament."

"So, a religious belief? A commandment?"

"No, neither. I am not a biblical scholar, but I do know that the story is of two lonely people beset with troubles who commit to one another."

"A man and wife?"

"No. Two widows."

"They are bound by a duty?"

"No, no, absolutely not a duty. A choice. A risk. A life commitment uttered freely and without hesitation."

Amaya senses the onset of religious dogma and makes to leave. She smiles and says,

"Perhaps I have overstayed my imposition on your billable hours. I should leave. I'll read this Scripture lesson when I get home."

"Wait."

Amaya resettles herself, her eyes fixed on him. She watches him move to the bookcase and draw from a nearby shelf a black, soft leather-bound book. She waits.

Parker reseats himself and methodically moves his fingers through the thin pages. Her eyes join his for a beat.

"Don't worry, I'm not going to read the Book of Ruth or even Chapter One. The story details are not germane to this discussion." He winks. "And you needn't fidget. I won't preach, and I don't mean to suggest any religious overtones. Those matters occupy scholars of bygone times and would only distract us.

"What I want to make sure you hear is the single most enduring declaration of commitment I know of in literature. And I'm going to read it to you before you go.

"The widows are Ruth and her mother-in-law, Naomi, whose paths have reached a defining juncture. Naomi urges Ruth to return to safer, familiar territory, to turn back rather than venture to a new life, to a new place, and to a new culture. The two stand alone on an empty road. There is no demanding voice from the clouds or flaming bush. They are two individuals whose relationship with one another is on the verge of change. Ruth declares to Naomi, and to all of us at such a crossroads." He reads:

Entreat me not to leave you,
Or to turn back from following after you;
For wherever you go, I will go;
And wherever you
Lodge, I will lodge; your people shall be my people,
And your God, my God. Where you die, I will die,
And there will I be buried.

With a gasp Amaya brings the back of her hand to her mouth in reaction to the sensation in her mind of the words wedging securely into a tight space. That had been the empty space of being alone she once told Brad of, the unnamed empty space she had resisted filling up.

It had been empty of commitment.

That night in her apartment, Amaya prints out the text from her desktop computer. She copies the words in slow, careful cursive. She makes her own translation into Japanese hiragana characters. She brings out an ink stone, mixes black ink, and selects long brushes and writing paper. She writes her translation of the discovery over and over in gracious calligraphy,

297

tears flowing down her cheeks, her heart filled with commitment.

ABOUT THE AUTHOR

John W. Feist is the author of the novel *Diamond Mornings* (eLectio Publishing, 2015). His second novel, *Night Rain, Tokyo,* reflects memories and imaginings from trips to Japan as a lawyer for steel, coal, and shipping companies. That was when he lived and canoed in Northern California. He's also lived in Washington, D.C., and lobbied for Western steel and pipe manufacturers. Back in the day, he tested water wells for salinity in Western Kansas oil-country farms. Now he lives in Falls Church, Virginia, where he is close enough to Washington to enjoy its music, theater, and museums, and watch the other madness there at a safe distance. John has appeared on Washington-area stages, and has provided live audio descriptions of theater and opera performances for The John F. Kennedy Center for the Performing Arts.

ACKNOWLEDGMENTS

I acknowledge the insights provided by my former colleague Joe Powers, living in Napa, into the engineering of oil and water transmission pipelines and the manufacture of pipe-making equipment. *Ogallala Blue*, William Ashworth (2006), and *Ogallala, Water for a Dry Land*, John Opie (2nd ed., 2000), inform the aquifer aspect of this book, and both works are eye-openers on the topic. Grateful thanks go to Marcia Trahan, my editor, who always notices what isn't there and coaxes for more.

Made in the USA
Coppell, TX
26 July 2020